WEST ON
66

Also by James H. Cobb

Sea Strike
Choosers of the Slain

WEST ON
66

JAMES H. COBB

THOMAS DUNNE BOOKS
ST. MARTIN'S MINOTAUR
NEW YORK

THOMAS DUNNE BOOKS.
An imprint of St. Martin's Press.

www.minotaurbooks.com

Map illustrations by Jackie Aher

Library of Congress Cataloging-in-Publication Data

Cobb, James H.
    West on 66 : a novel / James H. Cobb.
        p. cm.
    "Thomas Dunne books."
    ISBN 0-312-20621-6 (hc)
    ISBN 0-312-27130-1 (pbk)
    I. Title
  PS3553.0178W47 1999
  813'.54—dc21   99-27251
                                                                            CIP

First St. Martin's Minotaur Paperback Edition: April 2001

10 9 8 7 6 5 4 3 2 1

To the truckers, patrolmen, and tourists.
To the keepers of motels and the keepers of faiths.
To the tellers of truths and the tellers of tales.
To all of the Road Warriors everywhere
who know the magic of Route 66.

Also

to James Dean and Natalie Wood.
Like the Mother Road, legends go on forever.

ILLINOIS

*In leaving Chicago on US 66, you will find the route
plainly marked through city streets, running southwest
from the Loop district . . .*

On the radio, the Platters sang "The Great Pretender" to a
lightning static backbeat. It was September in the Year of Our
Lord 1957, and a storm was rolling in from Lake Michigan.
The heavy overcast had turned the city gray—gray buildings,
a gray lakefront, a gray beach with gray waves sullenly nuzzling
against it. Only the traffic signal on Lake Shore Drive hadn't
been infected yet, and its red didn't look too healthy as the '57
and I rolled up to it.

A porthole-fendered Buick sedan sat in the outside lane. As
I waited out the light, I glanced over and noted its business-
suited driver gingerly giving us the eye.

I knew what he was seeing. The car, a sleek and souped-up
black-and-white Chevrolet hardtop, riding high-tailed and bel-
ligerent with an ominous rumble in her twin pipes. The driver,

lean and leather-jacketed, with too-long brown hair combed back, a young punk like the writer had warned about in that "This Generation Is Going to Hell" article in *Collier's* last week.

And was this the reality? Close enough, I guess. I blipped the gas pedal, and the '57 snarled, scaring the eyes of the Buick driver forward again.

Slouching behind the wheel, I wondered again just what I'd hoped to find back here in Chicago. Whatever it was, I hadn't found it. There had been a tract house I'd never seen before and a young sister-in-law who had struggled heroically to be a good hostess to a total stranger. There had been a niece in the toddler stage who didn't have a clue about who this new guy was supposed to be. And finally, there had been an older brother I really didn't recognize anymore.

It was my fault, I guess. Maybe if I'd come to visit a couple of years ago, things could have been different. Maybe if I'd even been able to get back when our folks had died. But that hadn't been in the books, either. I'd been inhabiting a frozen mud bunker just short of the thirty-ninth parallel when Dad had been killed in that yarding accident. And when pneumonia had gotten Mom, I'd been working deep cover in a high school out around Glendora, trying to get a lead on a marijuana dealer who was recruiting part-time sales help from the local student body.

Frank had followed Dad into railroading. Me, I'd enlisted in the army straight out of high school. Frank had settled down, making Chicago his home. I'd volunteered for Airborne, doing a tour on the line in Korea and then another as an MP in Japan. Frank got married and started a family. I'd taken a liking to police work and had signed on with the Los Angeles County Sheriff's Department after getting my service discharge.

Somewhere along the line, Frank and I had stopped living in the same world. Now he had the house and the wife and the kid, while I had the stories about making a combat jump out of a C-119, walking a midnight beat in the Ginza, and being one of Marilyn Monroe's bodyguards at her latest movie premiere.

Which one of us had it the best? Hell, I don't know. We just didn't have it the same anymore. I'd taken three weeks off to come back and get reacquainted, but it hadn't worked out so well. Things went fine for the first three days. But by day four, we'd run out of old times to reminisce about.

It's not good to only live in the past with a brother. You need some here and now to balance things out.

This morning, on day five, I'd packed my gear and headed for the door. A big break on an important case out on the coast, I'd said, lying politely. I had to get back. Frank and his wife politely said they were sorry to see me go and promised that next year it was their turn to come out to Los Angeles.

It could happen, I guess.

Before I left town, there were a couple of last things I'd had to take care of. For one, I drove out to Graceland Cemetery and said a private good-bye to Mom and Dad. I owed them an apology for not being there when it was time for them to move on. Dad understood. He was always very big on a man doing his duty. And Mom, she'd forgive you anything. I also promised that Frank and I would somehow find something in common again one of these days. They seemed to be satisfied with that.

Afterward, I'd driven around town for a couple of hours, just to see if I could pick up the feel of the place again. I couldn't. Chicago had never really been a hometown to me. Dad's job with the GM&O had kept us moving from one whistle-stop along the Alton route to another for just about all of my life. Chicago meant only a senior year in high school and a recruiter's station. Then, too, Los Angeles has spoiled me for living in a stacked-up city. The narrow urban canyons along the Loop give me claustrophobia now.

The stoplight went green. For a second I considered re-spooking the guy in the Buick by breaking traction and burning a little rubber as I pulled away from the intersection. I relented, though, satisfying myself with the '57's clean surge of acceleration.

My gas tank was full. My bags (one B-4, one sleeping) were in the backseat, and there was nothing else in this town that I needed except for a way out.

I found one at the head of Adams Boulevard, a block beyond the entrance to Grant Park. Once it had been called the Old Joliet Road. At another time, it had been the Pontiac Trail. Now it was marked in a flash of black on a white shield.

Illinois

US

Route 66

Appropriately enough, Bill Haley and the Comets took over from the Platters with "See You Later, Alligator." A good road omen. It was time to head for home, my real one. I hung a right and aimed us down Adams. The baritone purr of the '57's engine seemed to grow more contented as we followed the shields west through the grimy shade of the city's streets.

We cleared Al Capone's old stomping ground in Cicero just ahead of the cresting rush hour traffic, then on around the Joliet bypass, riding the four-lane through Wilmington and past the rail yards and the workingmen's neighborhoods. Out beyond Joliet, the pastures and cornfields began to outnumber the junkyards and the factories along the roadway, and the big-town sprawl became a dissipating smear across the bottom of my rearview mirrors. I edged the speedometer needle five miles over the limit, and the '57 and I began to seriously kill some road.

The '57 is the only major vice I can afford on a deputy's salary. We've been together for close to a year now, ever since I found her sitting forlornly in the county impound yard with a smashed grill and a crumpled front fender. Some doting daddy out Sepulvida way had bought her fresh off the train from Detroit as a birthday present for his teenage son. Three weeks later, carrying a cargo of empty beer bottles, sonny boy had put his new wheels into a palm tree and himself into the hospital. Daddy was going to be tied up with medical expenses and lawyer's fees for a while, so he was more than pleased to let me take over the payments. After I'd gotten the papers signed, I'd had her towed out to Don Blair's legendary speed shop in Pomona. There we started having fun.

Sonny boy might have been a drunk-driving dork, but he'd known something about fast cars. He'd asked Daddy for a One-Fifty Series, two-door centerpost sedan. Most of the stock car teams running Chevys use this model because it's both the lightest and the strongest chassis Chevrolet makes. Then he'd gone down the options list and had checked off the entire Corvette performance package for the new 283-cubic-inch Turbofire V-8: 9.51 compression ratio, mechanical lifters, a Duntov cam and valve set, duel exhausts with tuned ramshead headers, and twin Carter four-barreled carburetors on an aluminum competition manifold. The whole nine yards.

But no matter how good something is, you can always make it better. While the bodywork was being straightened out, Dollar-a-Deal Don's guys and I pulled the engine and knocked it down to the nuts and bolts.

We gave her a full porting and polishing job, smoothing the valve seats and widening and buffing the intake and exhaust ports in the heads so she could breathe easier. Junking the factory mufflers, we replaced them with a set of Porter steel packs and installed a crossover pipe. Then we dropped in an aluminum flywheel and added one of Dean Moon's custom dual-point distributor and ignition systems.

We blueprinted the entire mill from the pan up, minutely examining every component for possible flaws and Magnaflux-testing the critical ones. Then we put it all back together, deburring, balancing, and polishing as we went, trueing it far beyond its factory specifications. When we finished closing that engine up again, it was more totally right then anything ever conceived on an assembly line

I went underneath next and did a few things to help keep the rubber on the road. The shifter assembly for the close-ratio three-speed transmission went from the steering column to a Corvette-style floor stick, and the battery was moved to a battery box in the trunk to help centralize the weight distribution. I shod her with Goodyear Blue Streak racing tires mounted on NASCAR-rated six-lug competition wheels, and then I beefed up the suspension—stabilizer bars fore and aft, extra extended-length leaves in the outrigger springs in back, heavier coil springs in front, and stiffer Gabriel shocks all the way around.

Some of these latter items required a little handshaking around the LA County motor pool. They were lifted out of a Chevrolet "Police Interceptor" parts package and were intended for use on official police vehicles only.

Well, hell, I'm officially police.

I'd lived on cornflakes and macaroni and cheese all last winter. It was worth it, though. Car and I have put together something of a reputation out at the drag strips at Pomona and Paradise Mesa. And on other less formal occasions back up in the Hollywood Hills, we've left the owner of more than one Coupe DeVille and SK-model Jag wondering just why in the hell he'd wasted all that money.

More seriously, the '57 has served me well as part of the young badass cover I've built for myself doing plainclothes work for LA County Metro. It doesn't look like a cop car, and most of the time I don't look like a cop. We match.

Pontiac, then Bloomington, the tires thudding rhythmically on the expansion ridges between the concrete road slabs. Flatlands and farms, the fall's harvest being lifted out of the chocolate cake soil. The pretty good Chicago rock 'n' roll station I'd been listening to faded on me, and I made do with some pretty poor country out of Springfield. Funk's Grove and miles of maple forest flamed dully in the dying light of a fall day, the sunset buried behind a wall of clouds.

As I was rolling through McLean, the storm I'd been trying to outrun finally caught up with me, and I turned on my windshield wipers and headlights at the same time. My stomach also reminded me that lunch had been a long time back.

A café on the little town's main street had a sign promising "genuine home cooking" in its rain-spotted front window. And who knows? Maybe they could've actually delivered. However, I preferred the sure thing south of town to the gamble.

Ahead, alongside the big road, there was a low, sprawling clapboard building, a drowsing herd of parked truck and trailer rigs, and a scarlet banner of neon advertising the Dixie Trucker's Home.

The Dixie is an icon on 66. It just might have been the first true truck stop in the United States. A lot of its regular patrons say that it's still one of the best. God knows it's sure one of the busiest. On a good Saturday, a thousand people a night might pass through here. This was a rainy evening in mid week, though, and the stop's broad parking lots were two-thirds empty.

I topped off the '57's tank with ethyl at the car pumps. Then I found a parking place well away from the clustered vehicles around the restaurant. There was no sense in running the risk of having some road-dopey PIE driver back his rig into my wheels. Breathing in the rain-freshened air, I crossed to the restaurant, my old jump boots crunching on the wet gravel.

As I pushed through the door, a blast of warmth hit me along with that unique combination of sights, scents, and sounds that mark a real trucker's "choke & puke": Monel metal and raw diesel, scarred Naugahyde and cigarette smoke, hot bacon grease, and Patsy Cline on the jukebox.

There was also an invisible line drawn down the linoleum of the big, brightly lit dining room. On one side were the mere mortals, the tourist families, the traveling salesmen, and the locals out for a supper away from the home table. On the other were the elite, the long-haul drivers, big, weary men who leaned in over their coffee cups, seeking a break from the kidney-hammering vibration of the highway.

Once, so they say, the Dixie's management had set aside an entirely separate dining area just for truck drivers. The truckers hadn't liked that much. They'd felt as if they were being dis-criminated against. So the one big room had been restored and the truckers had contentedly gone back to segregating them-selves once more, assured of their proper place in the world.

I seated myself on the mortal side of the room, and a comfortable-looking middle-aged waitress brought me a cup of coffee as if there weren't any other beverage worth considering on a stormy night on the big road. The hamburger steak looked good, and I said so, with fries.

The waitress hustled away and I took my first contented sip of a hot black brew strong enough to idle a Kenworth on. I was starting to get my vacation back. Being on the move again had erased the dissatisfaction of Chicago.

I'd blitzed Route 66 on the way out from Los Angeles, push-ing the '57 and covering the twenty-four hundred odd miles in only five days. I had twice as much time to get back in. What to do with it?

The steak showed up, and the first forkful jump-started my enthusiasm. The old traveler's tale about always stopping to eat where the truckers do might not be valid elsewhere, but it definitely applies to the food at the Dixie.

OK, I had some free days on my hands. Why not wander around some? Why not drink a little beer and listen to a little rockabilly in a few roadhouses? Why not hang around a few speed shops and talk a little car? Why not run a little back road "five dollars a gear" with some of the local talent?

Why not find a girl?

Maybe like the one who just came in through the door.

She was only average height, but she carried herself tall. She had that pale, creamy brunette's skin, and when she flipped back the hood of her car coat I could see that her glossy hair was the color of well-polished saddle leather. Her eyes were dark as well, with an onyx glint to them you could note clear across the room, dominating a face that was both delicate and strong.

She was maybe five years younger than me. Twenty-one to my twenty-six, balanced right on that knife-edge between girl and woman. Youthful enough so that a ponytail still suited her, yet old enough to know how to walk in heels.

She was alone and beautiful, and you could bet safe money that every male eye in that restaurant, including mine, tracked her as she crossed to the counter. But that's all we did, for she radiated an air of cool self-possession that went a long way beyond anything you might expect from someone her age. It was as though she entered that room knowing that there wasn't a damn thing there that was going to impress her. She took the end stool, the one that would let her keep her back to the wall, and slammed down an invisible barrier between herself and the rest of us.

Caging a light for a cigarette from the appreciative counter-man, she sat very still for a little while, her eyes lowered and half-closed as if she was marshaling her strength. Then she drew herself up once more, giving her cloak of regal invulnerability a tug back into place. She glanced around the room and took what looked like a stenographer's notebook or sketch pad out of her shoulder bag. Slipping a pencil from the wire coil across the top of the pad, she flipped it open, focusing on it.

Writing? No, not with the way her hand swept across the page. Drawing.

I returned my attention to my hamburger steak, my overt attention anyway. But ignore her? Uh-uh, Jack. Even as I got my glands back under control, my "cop's eyes" began to notice the subtleties.

She'd walked in. Her coat was almost soaked through, and there was mud caked on her expensive pumps, shoes that weren't meant for a hike on a stormy night. Her pleated plaid skirt and matching wine red sweater were new and of high quality. But they had that slightly rumpled and stale look of clothing that's been worn for too long at a single stretch. The girl also carried that slightly self-conscious air of someone who likes to look good but who knows that she's not at her best.

Then there were the shadows under her eyes. Short of sleep. And the careful way she counted the change in her purse before ordering. Short of money.

Most of all, though, I noted the air of wariness about her. When she had entered, she had paused for a moment and carefully "read the room," verifying that there was no one here except for a crowd of harmless strangers. And now, whenever the door opened her head came up, alert for whoever might be coming through.

I'd seen that look before, plenty of times. All lawmen have.

Slum kids and runaways have it. And battered wives. And streetwise prostitutes. It's an ingrained, instinctive kind of wariness that doesn't just come from being afraid. It comes from living a life where the blows can come at you from any direction at any time. It's born out of an existence where dodging and running and fighting isn't anything special; it's just how you stay alive.

It didn't match up with the rest of her. Not at all.

As she quietly ate her sandwich, I found myself accepting a fourth cup of coffee and ordering a piece of cherry pie that I didn't particularly want, just to study her for a little longer.

People are your stock-in-trade when you're a police officer. You constantly find yourself trying to figure how they get to be the way they are, what makes them and what moves them. Something else was going on here, something beyond a pretty girl in a rain-wet car coat. Who was she? What combination of experiences and events had put her together? And what would happen with her next?

The problem is, even a cop can't go crashing into someone's private life for no good reason. And you can take an across-the-room fascination just so far. The waitress brought my tab, and I paid it there at the table. Tossing a quarter down beside my plate, I stood up to leave.

And she was standing beside me as I turned, studying me levelly out of those dark, expressive eyes. "Excuse me," she said quietly, "but are you headed south? I could really use a lift to Saint Louis if you are."

To Saint Louis? To Miami? To Tierra del Fuego? Oh yeah, I think so.

"Sure. Why not."

Every other guy in that room hated my guts as I led her back out into the night. If they'd known what was waiting for me out there, they might not have been so envious.

Her wariness returned as we left the pool of light around the truck stop buildings and headed out across the parking lot. She walked fast, her head turning as she scanned the darkness, acting as though she expected hostility out of the night. The feeling was infectious. I found myself cranking up my own alertness level, suddenly wishing that the '57 wasn't so far back in the shadows.

She had reason to be wary. They were waiting for us. Three of them. Three men moving fast out of the chasm of total blackness between a couple of parked big rigs. A massive form in a dark raincoat loomed in front of me, and a vicious sucker punch drove into my guts.

If he'd taken me totally by surprise, he would have laid me out with a couple of broken ribs. As it was, it felt as if I'd been swiped across the stomach with a two-by-four.

But I'd caught sight of his arm cocking back and I was just barely able to ride with the punch. I think I could have stayed on my feet if I'd really wanted to. However, I didn't. I dropped hard to the sodden gravel, curling into a semifetal position.

I wanted them to think I was out of it. I wanted them to shift their attention elsewhere for a second. But most of all, I wanted the gun under my jacket. Maybe Robert Mitchum or

Troy Donahue could duke it out with three guys in a dark alley and win, but I just work around Hollywood, not in it.

My move paid off. Their focus was all on the girl now. While the biggest of the trio had been taking me out, the number two man had been clamping his hand across the girl's mouth, not even giving her a second for a decent scream. Now, despite her frenzied efforts to resist, they were hustling her swiftly back into the shadows.

It was as sweet a snatch as you could have asked for. They'd just gotten a little overconfident.

I rolled to my feet. Drawing the Colt Commander from my belt, I executed a fast MP cock, snagging the front sight on the pocket of my jeans and pumping the automatic's action to lift a shell into the chamber.

All three of the gentlemen recognized the dulcet clang of a .45's slide going into train. They spun to face me, two of them starting moves that looked like they might have guns at the end of them.

But by then, the Colt was leveled.

"Okay, that's it! Let her go!"

The girl didn't wait. She tore loose on her own. Snatching up her fallen shoulder bag, she started to back toward me.

"Lisette." Just one quiet word, almost a whisper, from the big man who had slugged me.

"No!" The girl packed more raw hate into that single-syllable scream than I ever could have thought possible.

What in the hell was going on out here? Obviously a whole lot more than I'd ever conceived in my café fantasizing. OK, Saint George, you were hot to rescue the fair damsel in distress. Well, the dragon's just shown up and he's brought along a couple of buddies. Get with the rescuing.

There was a coiled-spring tension in all three men. My gun was just barely holding them. They were waiting for me to make that one little mistake that would let them regain the initiative. Trying to pat them down out here without backup would be a real bad idea. In fact, some instinct told me that even announcing that I was a cop might trigger an explosion of blood, guts, and feathers all over this parking lot.

The girl and I had to disengage. We had to get out of here before one of these guys got the nerve to try for a weapon, or a passerby mistook me for a stickup artist, or any one of a thousand other little dumb-ass things happened that could get us killed.

"You know how to drive?" I asked quietly.

"Yes," she replied, raking her dark hair back. She sounded like one cool kitten for somebody who had just barely ducked a kidnapping.

"My keys are in my right front pocket. It's the black-and-white Chevy down at the end of the line. Go get it and bring it down here."

She didn't reply, but she passed around behind me, carefully not blocking my line of fire. A moment later, a small, warm hand slid into my pocket, retrieving the keys. A moment more and her light footsteps ran away across the gravel.

I realized there was a very real possibility that she could just steal the '57 and leave me standing here with these goons. But just then I had to trust somebody and my list of available prospects was god-awful short.

"Boy." It was the big man speaking again, the one who had tried to deck me and the one I was beginning to sense was the leader of this show. "You don't know how much trouble you're making for yourself." It was a voice as cold and gray and gritty as wet concrete.

"Yeah? Well, in case you haven't noticed, you're the one standing at the wrong end of the gun at the moment." I'd been slowly panning the automatic across all three of the kidnappers, but gradually my sight picture had come to rest in the center of the big man's chest. That same instinct that had told me to keep my mouth shut about being a cop was whispering another message now. It said that if it came to a fight, I'd have to kill this guy with my first bullet to have any chance at all of getting out alive.

"This is a family affair," he continued. "My family. It's no business of yours."

"You made it my business, man, when you took that swing at me. And if this is a family affair, you'd better tell Uncle Fred over there to quit edging sideways. If he gets out of my line of sight, I'll pull this trigger and then look to see where he's got to."

Oh, I was way ahead on the witty repartee, but I was running short on time. Where in the hell was the girl?

A flash of headlights and a familiar rumbling roar answered me. Tires spun and gravel rattled in the '57's wheel wells as the girl fought with the stiff racing clutch; then she had the car lurching down the parking lane toward us.

She was smart. She didn't pull in behind me. She turned and pulled up alongside, putting the headlights on the men and giving me my first good look at them.

They were like the three bears. Three sizes. Baby Bear, Mama Bear, and Papa Bear.

Baby Bear was my age or maybe a little younger: thin, acne-scarred, and wearing a beat-up army field jacket. He had enough grease in his DA to make the rainwater bead on it. Among the three, he was the only one who looked uneasy staring down the barrel of the Commander.

Mama Bear wasn't all that motherly. Medium height, dark eyes, lean and wiry, hawkish, almost Indian-like features. An Apache warrior in a snap-brim fedora and a trench coat. The only regret he displayed was likely born out of the fact that he couldn't reach that ominous-looking bulge in his side pocket.

Papa Bear was the big man.

He beat my own five-ten by a good four inches, and he probably outweighed me by at least a hundred pounds, damn little of which I suspect was anything but bone and muscle. A gray-black fringe of hair showed beneath the brim of his hat, and his large, angular head sat square on his massive shoulders, like a cinder block balanced on top of a refrigerator. His skin seemed to fit loosely over his skull, as if the cinder block was being carried in a sack of flesh, and his mouth was a lipless slot across the bottom of his face.

The eyes, though, they were what got you. Like some last lingering memory out of a nightmare. Colorless, cold, and without a whole lot of what you would consider human behind them. Those eyes were fixed on me now, promising that next time he wouldn't make the mistake of leaving me alive.

I risked a sideways glance. The girl had the driver's side door open and had slid across to the passenger seat. She watched me for the next move, her face underlit by the dashboard lights. I sidled across to stand behind the open door.

This was going to be the tricky part. We were about thirty feet back from the three men, and I wasn't going to be able to keep them solidly covered and get into the car at the same time.

And they knew it.

I was going to have to be inventive. "Reach over and kick on the high beams," I whispered.

She obeyed and the headlights flared. The three men winced back for an instant in the brightness, and in that instant I dived behind the wheel. I jammed the gun into the crack in the seat back, hit the clutch, and slammed the floor shift into low almost within the same second.

The '57 screamed and lunged forward as I firewalled the gas pedal, her rear tires scrabbling for traction like the claws of a startled cat. The acceleration slammed my door shut, and the three men were barely able to fling themselves out of our way.

Shucks.

I aimed for the dark passage between a parked grain truck and a Texaco tanker, praying there was room enough for us to fit. There was, by about three inches. My radio aerial thwacked loudly against a sideview mirror, and then we were out and clear of the parking area and turning on to the frontage road that looped around the truck stop.

"Are they going to come after us?" I demanded.

"You can count on it," the girl replied grimly.

"What kind of car?"

"A 1957 Chrysler. A black coupe. One of the fast kind."

Fan-damn-tastic. There were maybe three production automobiles built in the United States that the '57 couldn't just walk away from. And the 300-C Chrysler was at the head of the list.

"Any of those three guys know how to really drive?"

"Randy, the youngest one, is a first-class wheelman."

We were batting a thousand tonight, folks.

"There's a seat belt over on that side," I snarled. "Put it on and pull it tight. You might need it."

There was a gap in the traffic on 66, and I blew past the access stop sign and onto the highway. Fishtailing a little, we accelerated hard out onto the four-lane, our tires slashing through the water sheet on the concrete. After an entire evening of drizzle, the sky had to pick right now to really start unloading. Rain roared against the windshield like a pattern of buckshot, and the wipers overloaded in seconds, leaving nothing to be seen but sodden blackness and glare-starred car lights.

The '57 didn't like it. She started riding dangerously loose as we passed through eighty. With more water under her tires than pavement, she was hydroplaning like Miss Thriftway. It would be almighty easy to break loose on this road tonight and take a real short drive to hell.

Under these conditions, the guys chasing us had all the edges. I couldn't identify car makes or gauge distances in my mirrors, while they could catch and hold me in their headlights. My first warning of their presence would be when that big 392 Hemi engine came pulling them up alongside. In any kind of a shoving contest, the Chrysler would have the edge as well. It outweighed the '57 by a good half a ton. Well-handled, it could bounce us into the ditch like a Ping-Pong ball.

Most of all, though, the guys behind us would know just how bad they wanted to win this race and how crazy they'd have to drive to do it. I'd have to guess.

The girl sat straight and slim on the bench seat, not looking out into that berserk night but watching me, waiting for me to pull another miracle out of my back pocket.

Ho-kay, the safest place you can be when you are being tailed is behind the guy who's tailing you. The trick was how to get us there. I had to get off the highway and disappear.

A bridge exploded at us out of the night, and we thundered through it like a bullet through the barrel of a rifle. Lights ahead. Town lights. A sign. ATLANTA 1 MILE.

Right! Here we go!

The white numbers on my odometer dial clicked off a countdown like the army missile men use out at White Sands. Nine-tenths of a mile, eight-tenths, seven-tenths . . . The tailgate reflectors of a lumbering Campbell 66 Transport tractor-trailer blazed in my headlights.

"Hang on!" There was no time for more words than that.

We snaked around the truck. Gaining a little clearance on the big rig, I cut back in front of it. One-tenth of a mile to the Atlanta turnoff. I stood on the brakes, praying that whoever had been putting up these signs had gauged his distances right.

For a long sickening second, absolutely nothing happened. Finally, as I savagely pumped the brake pedal, we caught pavement and the '57's tires sobbed and grabbed. Behind me, air horns blared as the trucker protested my committing suicide across his front bumper. Then the turnoff materialized on my right and I swerved for it.

We came off 66 hot, way too·hot to make a ninety-degree turn on rain-slick pavement with any kind of safety. But then, "safe" wasn't really a consideration at the moment, was it? We were waltzing like a pig on ice, and I pulled us down a gear and leaned on the gas, praying we'd dig through the water and find some traction. For once, I didn't get a celestial busy signal.

I'd used up every inch of both lanes and was hanging on the edge of the ditch when the '57 got her feet back under her again. The Chevy's wicked acceleration canceled out our lateral slide, and we hurled down the narrow frontage road.

The girl sat half-twisted in her seat, looking back. "One set of lights followed us off the highway," she reported calmly. "They're coming fast. I think it's them."

Son of a bitch! I hoped that the rain had cleared the streets of Atlanta, Illinois, because they are about to receive visitors.

We thundered across the T intersection where the frontage road met the main street of the little farm town, the roar of the '57's engine penned up and echoing between the buildings. I had an impression of a set of grain elevators and a stone-sided courthouse outlined in the watery glow of a few weak street lamps. Then we were out the other side and tearing back into the night.

The frontage road started a wide left-handed turn, angling back toward 66. Then a couple of things happened at about the same instant. For one, that malignant quad set of glowing car eyes in my rearview mirror disappeared as we broke line of sight in the curve. For the other, my own lights caught a flash of another sign at the side of the road. Somebody-or-other's FARM FRESH PRODUCE. JUST AHEAD.

This time around, I didn't even have a second to yell a warning before I went for the turnout. We slithered through the produce stand's parking lot with the brakes locked up, shoving a wave of mud and gravel ahead of us. The side of an unpainted plank building loomed ahead, and I got off the binders long enough to aim for a patch of darkness behind it, sincerely hoping it was a driveway or lane or something and not somebody's duck pond.

We lucked out again. A driveway circled the produce shed. We tore around it, broadsiding to a stop just beyond the building and in the shelter of its shadow. Instantly I killed the lights and engine and we lay doggo like a U-boat on the bottom of the ocean.

For about ten fast heartbeats we sat there and the tapping of the rain on the car top was the only sound in the universe. Then a pair of headlights streaked past out on the frontage road, going like a bat out of hell and not slowing at all as they dwindled away into the night.

I recovered the .45 from where I had hastily stowed it. Moving by rote, I ran the pistol through its unloading drill. Clip out of the butt. Shell out of the chamber. Shell back in the clip. Clip back in the gun. Gun back in my belt. Secured. Finally, I glanced up at the girl.

A barn lot arc light down the road cast enough illumination to silhouette her, and I caught the faint pale flash of a smile. "Lisette Kingman," she said with a touch of ironic humor in her voice.

"Kevin Pulaski. Pleased to meet you. Cigarette?"

"Thanks," she replied. "I have my own."

Fatima extra-lengths, no less. I guess I couldn't have expected her to smoke anything as plebian as a Lucky Strike.

We shared a light off the glowing car lighter, and I cracked my window, admitting a cool draft of air flavored with cow and wet clover. "Okay, Lisette Kingman," I said. "May I ask who those guys were and why I ended up doing this?"

There was a pause over at the other side of the '57's front seat and a silence except for that inaudible sound of mental wheels turning. By the time she spoke, I knew that I wouldn't be getting the full story, or necessarily the straight one.

"Those men are business partners of my late father. There's a problem concerning an inheritance. They've become kind of pushy about reaching a settlement."

"I guess that's one way to put it."

"That's why I'm going to Saint Louis, to see about part of that settlement. And I still need to get there."

She studied me again, those wheels still turning.

"You might want to consider going by way of the state police barracks in Springfield," I said. "They have ways of taking care of pushy business partners."

She shook her head emphatically. "No. Maybe later, when I have some things worked out. But no police for now, for a lot of reasons."

Well, that answered the question about whether or not to flash the tin on her. Miss Kingman didn't want the cops in on this. Okay, so I'd oblige her and not be a cop for a while. I slouched down behind the wheel and took a drag on my Lucky, pretending to think.

"Okay? Will these guys know that you're heading for Saint Louis?"

"He will."

"The big man?"

"Yes. He's called Mace Spanno."

The girl hesitated as she spoke his name, as if invoking it too often might summon him up like the devil. Lisette Kingman didn't frighten easy. She hadn't even blinked at doing ninety down a storm-wracked road in the middle of the night. But Mace Spanno scared her. I had a hunch he might be the only thing in the world that could.

"What do I call his friends?"

"The other man in a raincoat was Nathan Temple. The one in the army jacket was Randy Bannerman. He's pretty much just a driver. Temple, though, is . . . bad."

"As bad as Spanno?"

"Close."

I nodded, matching faces and names in my mind, recalling and burning in the details of heights, weights, postures, and attitudes for later reference.

"Okay, Princess," I said. "Saint Louie it is."

She straightened a little. "You'll still take me?" Then she paused for a moment. "Why?"

She was a girl who could get a lot of mileage out of one syllable. Just now, she was asking me to justify my putting my neck on the line for a total stranger I'd just met along the road.

It was a pretty good question, too.

"Because I said I would. And when I say something, I generally mean it."

I shifted my weight in the seat and got my feet slotted in halfway comfortably between the floor pedals. "It may take us some time, though. We're going to stay put awhile and give your friends a chance to get way the hell out ahead of us."

"When they realize we're not on the highway anymore, won't they come back looking?" she asked.

"I'd doubt it. By the time they figure we've ducked out on them, it'll be too late. We could have cut down any one of a hundred different side roads or town streets around here. Granted these guys know where you're headed, their smart-money move will probably be to try and pick us up there. Do they have any idea about exactly where you're going in Saint Louis?"

There was another flash of that wry smile. "At the moment, I don't even know exactly where I'm going in Saint Louis. That's another of those things I have to work out."

"Okay, Princess. It's your show."

I wasn't going to push any points yet. We'd let this deal solidify a little more first. Reaching over, I turned the ignition key to auxiliary and switched on the radio. The night wave skip was coming in, and a little fiddling with the tuner brought in some blues from downriver. Faint but clear, it was good music to stare out into the night by.

A couple of pieces played through before I glanced at the girl again. Lisette was curled up against the passenger door in her coat, already asleep. A car seat shared with a stranger was apparently the safest haven she'd known for some time.

A lawman, at least any kind of a one that's worth a damn, is always on duty. The mere fact that I was on vacation two thousand miles away from my home beat was irrelevant. I'd just had a hot case dumped in my lap. Why was she being hunted? The real reason, not this crap about an inheritance. I only had fragments to work with yet, but one in particular stuck in my mind. Back at the Dixie, Lisette had said that one of her pursuers was a good wheelman.

Wheelman is the underworld slang name for a fast getaway driver. A very handy guy to have around if your profession happens to involve bank jobs, smash and grabs, and rubouts.

"Car," I asked quietly, "what in the hell have I gotten us into?"

The '57 didn't have any more of an answer than I did.

I lit a second Lucky and sent a stream of smoke out of the half-opened window. Over the radio, the soft cry of Miles Davis's trumpet echoed bleak and bittersweet in the night.

MISSOURI

Saint Louis (Pop. 816,048; alt. 445', radio stations: KMOX-1120kc., KSD-550kc., KXOX-630 kc., KWK-1380 kc.; several auto courts on western approach over US 66 . . .

I drove south to Saint Louis the same way I'd have walked a combat patrol north of Seoul, nervous and not taking anything for granted. I'd said that Spanno's smart-money move would have been to go on ahead once he'd lost us, but that didn't necessarily have to be the case. He and his boys could have staked out 66 somewhere down the line, waiting for us to hedgehop past again. Accordingly, every set of headlights in my rearview mirror felt like a gun barrel aimed at the back of my skull.

Once in Springfield and again in Litchfield, I bailed off the highway, driving figure eights through the rain-washed back streets to see if we were being followed. And at a picnic ground at Mount Olive we lay doggo again, waiting to see what might come crawling in out of the night. Nothing did.

We moved on, the eternal cornfields a flickering, shadowy fringe along the edge of our headlight fan, an occasional window glowing golden in a gaunt American Gothic farmhouse.

At about one o'clock in the morning, we crossed into Missouri. Driving through the brick fortress entrance of Chain of Rocks Bridge, we followed the odd curve of the spidery span as it arced across the black waters of the Mississippi. Beyond the bridge and the big deserted amusement park that shared its name, we picked up the Saint Louis beltway that circles the city to the west.

Lisette slept for most of the drive, and after she awoke she didn't have much to say, not even about our destination for the night. Somewhere along the line, I'd started handling the detail work. Fortunately, I had a pretty good idea about where we could fort up.

The Coral Court is over on the southwest side of town on Route 66. Set back in a grove of pin oaks, the motel is a low, sprawling art deco affair, all glass brick and coral tile. It has all the conveniences, too, including a separate, fully enclosed garage with an inside entrance for each room.

This feature probably makes the Court an ideal rendezvous for couples who want to sample a few hours of unobtrusive paradise together. It also makes the Court a good place to disappear into if you have somebody on your tail. I'd noted that point when I'd stayed there on my run to Chicago.

When I went in to sign the register, the sleep-soggy night clerk resolved my concerns about how I was going to set up the accommodations.

"We only got one left and it has a couple of twins," he said, squinting at me in the dim office night-light.

I made a show of thinking about it. "Ah, it's late. I'll take it anyhow. You got a pay phone around here anywhere?"

"Yep, by the ice machine. But we got phones in all the rooms, too. Pay here at the desk for long-distance."

He didn't ask if I was alone, and I didn't say. And when I filled out the registration card I listed my '57 two-door as a '56 coupe and transposed a couple of digits in the license number. They were the kind of mistakes a tired man might naturally make. They also might be enough to throw off anyone who might come around with a ten spot and a hankering to check out the guest list.

Unloading was easy enough. I had one suitcase and Lisette had what she stood in. As I pulled down the door of the parking bay, I took one final look out into the night, just to see if anyone was looking back.

The unit was clean and well maintained, but with the same slightly old-fashioned futuristic look as the motel's exterior. It also had the slightly frayed around the edges feel a motel room gets between redecorating. There was a load of tension in the atmosphere as well. There always is when a man and a woman share the intimacy of a living space for the first time. The girl still hadn't said a word about how I'd set us up for the night, drawing her air of cool detachment more tightly around her even as she tossed her coat on one of the beds. You'd have to look pretty deep to see the trace of scared little kid in her eyes.

"This will be all right," she commented offhandedly.

"It'll do for now," I replied, swinging my B-4 bag up onto the luggage stand. "I hope you don't mind having a roomie, but with your friends cruising around out there I don't think your being alone is such a hot idea."

"They aren't my friends and, no, I don't want to be alone."

"Okay then," I nodded toward the suitcase. "If there's anything in there you can use, be my guest. I'm going out for a few minutes to check around and see how secure we are here. Keep the doors locked until I get back."

Lisette nodded, and again that calculating expression flitted across her face. "You seem to know a lot about this kind of business."

"I do. Hands-on experience in a little place called Korea."

* * *

I gave the knob an extra tug to ensure the lock had caught before turning away from the door. To tell the truth, I was already pretty sure no one had tailed us here, but no sense in taking any chances. The line about checking things out gave me a good excuse to get away for a few minutes, though. It also gave Lisette an opportunity to snoop through my stuff to her heart's content.

Not that she'd find anything out of the ordinary beyond a gun-cleaning kit and a spare box of shells in a side compartment of my bag. My only tie-ins with the law were my badge and identity card, both of which were in my hip pocket right now. During the next day or so I'd have to smuggle them into their usual hiding place under the '57's spare tire.

I noticed rents torn in the cloud cover as I walked toward the front of the motel, and a few wet-looking stars glinted in the sky. The last droplets of rain were being wrung out of the dying storm, and there was a softness to the air. Somewhere along our night's run we'd caught up with the retreating edge of summer, and I tugged the zipper of my jacket open.

The phone was where the clerk had said it would be, beside a humming Coke cooler and under an arc light that drew a few tentative moths. I stuck in a dime, and a few minutes later another telephone rang out on the coast.

Let's see, two o'clock here. Midnight on the coast. Give him two rings for his wife to poke him awake and tell him to answer the phone. One more for him to swear. Two more to stagger down the hall and ricochet around the corner. One more to knock the phone off the hall table and swear again and . . . now.

Seven states away, someone snarled incoherently into the mouthpiece. The long-distance operator tentatively inquired if anyone there would accept a collect call from Kevin Pulaski. She acknowledged the second snarl as an affirmative and fled.

"Hello from beautiful Saint Louis, Jack."

"Pulaski, you baby-faced little Polack bastard! What in *thee* hell is the idea!"

"Yeah, man. Nice talking to you, too."

Few people have ever been named better than Jack Le Baer, aka Jack "the Bear." He looks like one, he sounds like one, and after a long, hot day in the LA basin he frequently even smells like one. He can also identify on sight 90 percent of the habitual criminals in the greater Los Angeles area and probably tell you where they're hanging out, who they're hanging out with, and what they're planning to do next. He's also never taken a dime of graft in his career (at least on any felony counts), and for sure he's never taken an ounce of shit off anyone, at any time, for any reason.

This latter point probably explains why, after fifteen years of working the streets of Los Angeles as a city cop, Jack had still been carrying a silver badge. It's also why LA County was damn glad to get him when he decided to swap his police shield for a deputy's star.

You see, the Los Angeles County Sheriff's Department is the glue that holds together the patchwork of small, not so small, and pretty damn big police jurisdictions that make up the greater LA area. We provide backup for the big guy and little guy alike, and we fill in all the cracks between. We go where we're needed, when we're needed. We don't wear white hats, and we don't ride horses. We do wade hip-deep through all of the same kinds of crime, crud, and corruption encountered by any major police force in the world. And considering that that this is California we're talking about, we even have a few depravities unique unto ourselves.

Three years ago, when I was only about halfway through my Sheriff's Academy training, Jack had come lumbering down the line one morning at roll call, sourly eyeing the front rank of gray-clad cadet deputies. When he came to me, he stopped, aimed a banana-sized finger in my face, and said, "This one. He looks like a punk." A week later and I was infiltrating a gang of car strippers under his direction, working as part of the intelligence detail attached to the county's Metropolitan Division. We've been partners ever since.

"Do you have any idea what time it is here, Pulaski?"

"Whatever it is, it's two hours earlier than it is here. Look, Jack, I'm onto something and I need you to run some people through Records and Identification for me."

"Okay, kid. Just a second and let me get a pencil. . . . What do you mean, 'I'm onto something'! You're supposed to be on vacation, you knothead!"

I would have to be patient. The Bear doesn't function too well when aroused rapidly from hibernation. "I am, Jack. I just sort of stumbled into something out here."

"Well, stumble out of it again! Where the hell are you? Saint Louis? Saint Louis has cops; let them handle it and let me get back to sleep!"

"It's not that simple, Jack. I'm not sure just what I've got going here. I need this dope and I need to give somebody a fix on me."

That brought him awake real fast. Jack had been doing police undercover work back when I'd still been in second grade. He knew that in effect I was saying, "Here's where you start looking for the body if I disappear."

He was suddenly all business. "Okay, kid. Let me have what you got."

I gave him the word: the Dixie, the girl, the men, the descriptions, and the story of how we got here and where we were. All boiled down to as few words as I could manage.

"That's the package, Jack. I've got no real idea yet on just what the hell is going on, but I seem to have a chance to get inside of the deal. I'm going to play along until I can get a fix on the setup; then maybe we can call it in to the locals."

"Right. These hoods look like the real product, huh?"

"Yeah, about as badass as they come. Beyond Los Angeles R and I and Intelligence, see if you can get any kickbacks out of Chicago PD, the Illinois attorney general, and the FBI. These guys have got to have some kind of a mob connection."

"How about the skirt?"

"The biggest 'I don't know' in the deck."

"She's a looker?"

"She'd knock you dead, Jack."

"Ah, Christ. I should have known. Watch your ass, kid. You're right; you're into something really screwball back there. And I'm two goddamn thousand miles away, so I won't be around to bail you out if you mess up."

"I'm not planning on messing up. Just get me those kick-backs. I'll be making another touch with you within the next twenty-four hours."

"You'll have it. And, Pulaski, one other thing." A faint plaintive tone crept into my partner's voice. "Couldn't you have called this shit into me at the office tomorrow?"

"Are you kidding, man! Do you know what time it is here? When you get into the office in the morning, I'm probably still going to be asleep."

A nun-stunning blast of profanity issued from the phone, followed by the sound of what might be the demolition of a small piece of furniture. I grinned and replaced the receiver in its cradle.

The second I opened the door of the motel unit, I knew that I was going to be in for a real interesting time. The room lights had been turned off, all but the small shaded reading lamp between the beds. Lisette was lying on the inside bed, apparently having taken advantage of my absence to use the shower. On emerging, however, she hadn't bothered with the clothes she'd been wearing.

Somewhere during her two decades plus, Lisette Kingman had learned that a man's shirt is one of the three sexiest things a woman can wear. That old white cotton of mine had never looked better. Its tails barely concealed the upper curves of her thighs and did nothing at all to hide the long satin-skinned legs below. The upper two buttons had been left undone as well, artfully drawing attention to the firm high-riding mounds of her breasts.

Her hair had been brushed into a sheening brown plume

that trailed over her shoulder. A touch of fresh lipstick had been added, and I could catch a spicy hint of perfume in the room's atmosphere. Wild rose. She'd been watching the door like a Siamese cat curled up in front of a mouse hole.

I was being set up for something soooo bad here.

"Everything all right?" she asked casually.

"Yeah, no sign of anybody. I think we're okay for now."

I checked the door lock again and set the chain, tossing my jacket on the unoccupied bed. Matching her, casual for casual, I crossed over to my suitcase and dug out the Colt's cleaning kit. Settling down in the room's single easy chair in the far corner from the beds, I began to conduct a ritual.

I carry my gun tucked inside my waistband, using what's called a Maqui holster. That is, just a circular rawhide thong looped around my belt and back through itself to hold the pistol in position. It's good for concealment, and again, it doesn't look "cop," both of which make points for me. But it does expose the weapon to a lot of perspiration, and perspiration is murder on a gun.

I've seen veteran plainclothes officers walk up to the firing line to qualify, only to find that sometime during the past month their service piece had sweat-rusted solid from a lack of attention. Of such men it may be said that they died because they were too damn stupid to stay alive. I don't intend to be buried in their corner of the graveyard.

Lisette watched as I popped the clip out of the Commander and jacked the action a couple of times to verify that it was clear. "Do you always carry a gun?" she asked.

"I got into the habit in the army and never got out of it."

"Are you still in the army now?"

"Nope. Got out awhile back. Looking around now for something new."

"Headed out to the coast?"

"I live out there. I was just back visiting my brother in Chicago."

That's how the old cons tell you to do it. Keep your story

simple and as close to the truth as you can keep it. Just don't tell them what you don't want them to know.

I began buffing the past night's oil and the day's accumulation of grime off the automatic's frame using a dab of alcohol and a square of rag, studiously not paying attention to the girl. This wasn't the easiest thing in the world to do as she pulled herself up straighter in the bed, her shirttails playing a shadowy game of peekaboo.

"Would you be interested in making some money on the way back out?"

I could feel her gaze fixed intently on me.

"I generally don't object to making money," I replied. "But then, a lot would depend on what I'd be doing and for how much."

"I'd guess you could say you'd be acting as a bodyguard and chauffeur," she said quietly. "Your job would be to get me to a certain place and to get me away again. As for how much, I can't give you an exact figure, but your share should amount to somewhere around a hundred thousand dollars."

The six figures just sort of hung in the air of the motel room like a smoke ring, and I stopped wiping down the Colt's slide. "A hundred grand is way too much for a simple bank job, Princess. You must be figuring on knocking off a federal mint."

"You won't be involved in committing any crime. This money will be free and clear."

"Hey, excuse me, but a chunk of change that size is never 'free and clear.'"

She shrugged. "Then you can call it loose money. It isn't stolen, not in the way you might be thinking anyway. The police won't be looking for it. If you're careful about how you spend it and don't pull the tax people down on you, no one will ever ask where it came from."

I swabbed out the barrel with a patch on the end of a short ramrod. "I'm asking."

The girl nodded. "All right. Here's the story. The essentials, anyway."

She sat up, bracing herself on one arm and tucking her legs under her.

"Back on the road I told you that I was after an inheritance, and, in a way, I am. The money we're talking about was my father's, partially anyway. And just now I think that I have about as much right to it as anyone else."

"But some other people disagree, like maybe these old business partners of your dad's?"

She nodded again. "That's right. You see, my father wasn't a very nice man, except to my mother and me. Putting it bluntly, he was a criminal, a gangster, like those men who are after me now."

I gave a low whistle. "Let me guess. He screwed over his partners. He ripped off his own gang."

"He wanted out," she said defensively. "He wanted a different kind of life for himself and for his family. But once you're in with the mob, getting out again isn't easy."

It was okay to look straight at her now and to watch the far aways and long agos play in those midnight eyes.

"Ten years ago, he tried to make the break," she continued. "He had a chance at a lot of money. Their money. He stole it and he ran with it. But he didn't make it. They hunted him down. They found him, and they killed him."

All of a sudden, I knew where some of the hate in that scream had come from.

"Spanno?"

"Yes. I think he was the one who found Dad." One of the girl's elegant eyebrows lifted. "But he never found the money."

"And Spanno is after you now because he thinks you know where it is."

"That's right."

"Do you?"

Lisette hesitated, then shook her head, "No. Not yet. But with help I think I can find it."

She went on swiftly. "Look; I've been working on this for a couple of years now. Talking to my mother. Talking to some of my father's friends from the old days. Going through news-paper files. Most important, there's something else, something that my father left me. Something that no one else knows about. I think it's the key to finding this money.

"Here's the deal. You have a car, a gun, and some nerve. Right now, I need all three. I'm offering you a partnership, half-shares in everything we recover. Just help me get to where I need to go."

Son . . . of . . . a . . . bitch!

It was a wild story, but the girl made it sound convincing. Lisette Kingman either was feeding me a straight line, or at least part of it anyway, or was a great liar. Unfortunately, work-ing as a deputy has taught me that there are a whole lot of really great liars in the world. I'd given up on being a good judge of character a long time ago.

"That is one kooky yarn, Princess."

The girl didn't flare up or look wounded at being doubted. She simply nodded. "It is. But it's the truth. I can't afford to lie to you."

Maybe not. But I had to push. I couldn't seem like too easy a mark. I took the oilcan out of the cleaning kit and soaked down another cleaning patch. Offhand again, I started applying a new film of protection to the alloy of the snub-barreled au-tomatic.

"I don't suppose you can back any of this up?"

"You saw how Mace . . . how my father's partners were after me back at the truck stop. That should prove something."

"Maybe. If they are the hoods you say they are."

"Who else could they be?" The girl nestled back against the pillows, her sleek legs unfolding out ahead of her again, a small, negligent hand caressing the shirt back into place.

"Maybe three private dicks trying to bring back the runaway spoiled brat of some millionaire. *It Happened One Night* for real. Or a jealous boyfriend and a couple of buddies out to spoil the good time of his cheating girlfriend. Or maybe even a trio of psycho-ward commandos trying to throw a butterfly net over their prize pistachio. Hell, I can think of all sorts of stories just as good as yours.''

Again Lisette just nodded, refusing to get angry. "That's right," she said soberly. "I can't prove a word of it. You'll have to accept my story entirely on speculation. You're going to have to gamble that I'm telling you the truth. You're going to have to gamble again that we can actually find the money. And you're going to have to gamble that we can do it without Mace Spanno killing you. Because I'm definitely not making that up. If you get involved, he's going to try. I've already seen him destroy everything and everyone else in the world close to me. If you help me, he'll try and do the same thing to you."

"You've got an interesting way of selling a proposal, Princess."

"I have to tell you the truth. If I lead you into this deal without letting you know where you really stand, I'd as good as be murdering you myself."

She settled back deeper, regarding me levelly. One hand went up to the top closed button of the shirt she wore. "You have all the choices here," she said. "You can walk away from this right now. I can't. I have two dollars and twenty-seven cents in my purse, that pile of clothes on the chair over there, and this one chance. I have no place to go and nothing else I can do.

"I can't show you any proofs, I can't make any guarantees, and I can't give you any promises. I don't have any front money to give you in return for your help, and I don't have any collateral to offer in exchange . . . except for myself."

Her fingers moved, opening the button and deepening the shadowy rift down the front of her solitary garment. "And if you want that as part of the deal, I'll agree."

Beyond the release of that single button, she made no attempt to play the sultry seduction scene. She didn't need to. We both were very aware of the quality of the goods she was putting on the table. Lisette Kingman might be down to her last chip, but it was a blue one in any man's game.

I found myself wondering what answer I would give if it were just me sitting here without a badge in my pocket.

I socked the clip back into the Commander, giving the magazine base an extra tap to make sure it was fully seated. I stood and crossed between the beds, setting the cleaned automatic down on the lamp table. The girl lay back, letting the shirt gap open. She watched me somberly, waiting.

Sinking down on the outside bed, I reached over and switched off the reading light, leaving only the faint outside glow that filtered in through the room's curtains. After a few seconds, I spoke to the pale outline in the darkness.

"Awhile back, I learned never to make any big commitments when you're either drunk or tired. That's how I ended up throwing myself out of perfectly good airplanes in the army. Let's sleep on it, Princess. We'll talk about it some more in the morning. Okay?"

"Okay"

I tugged open the Hollywood zips on my jump boots. Kicking them off, I stretched out on the outside bed. A few feet away, I heard a slithering rustle as Lisette slipped under the covers.

God, being noble can be a pain in the ass sometimes.

"Hey, Princess."

"Yes?"

"Mind answering me one thing now, though?"

"What?

"Back at the Dixie, why was I the guy you hit on first for a lift?"

A soft chuckle came back. "Simple. Because you were the guy I most hoped would say yes."

I swore under my breath again, turned over, and concentrated very hard on getting to sleep.

I opened my eyes. Something was wrong. The angle of the bright morning light slatting through the window blinds indicated that it was still way too early for any sane human being to be awake and functional. My ribs ached dully, the sucker punch of the night before having finally caught up with me. My beard rasped on the percale pillowcase, and I suffered from that chafed and sweaty sensation unique to a man who has slept in his pants. This felt way too close to a hangover when you consider that I hadn't taken a drink the night before.

Lisette sat at the writing desk, half-turned toward me and sipping a cup of coffee from the room's little complimentary hot plate. She'd redonned her air of cool regality along with her clothes, and she was trying to hide just a little bit of a smile.

Another cup of coffee sat on the lamp table beside my head. Sitting up, I reached for it. It was that instant powdered crap that always reminds me of K rations, but it was hot and there had to be some caffeine in there somewhere.

"You meant it all last night, right?" I croaked. "It's real? The whole thing? Your dad, the hoods, the money?"

"Cross my heart and hope to die . . . literally."

Great, she had a sense of humor on top of everything else. I pretended to think for one more gulp of coffee. "Then you've got a deal. Let's go hunt for your buried treasure."

I retired to the bathroom and dealt with the three S's, restoring myself into something that resembled a human being. When I came out, I found Lisette brooding over an open Saint Louis telephone book.

"Okay, Princess, what do we have?"

"What we have is this," she replied, handing a second, smaller book back over her shoulder.

It was a palm-sized paperback, battered and broken-spined. A sketchy desert scene featuring an old-time western stagecoach shared the tan buckram cover with the book's title:

A Guide Book to Highway 66
By Jack D. Rittenhouse

"That's our treasure map," she said. "It came out in 1946, and my father used it on the road trips he made out to the coast, including the last one."

I suddenly recognized it. A revised edition had been for sale in gas stations and restaurants all the way out from the coast along Route 66. It was a tourist guide, listing the eating and sleeping places, gas stations, and historical sites all along the old highway from Chicago to Los Angeles.

This one had seen a lot of use. Its pages were grimy, age-darkened, and scribbled-on. Mileage numbers written in pen and pencil, check marks, underlinings, cryptic words, and notations in a man's hasty handwriting.

"He had this with him when he was killed?"

"Yes."

"How'd you get it?"

"That's a long story," she replied, turning away from the desk to face me. "During that last year, when he was home between trips, my father and I would sometimes play what we called the road game. We'd sit together and he'd show me this little guidebook and we'd pretend to take the trip out to California. You see, he promised me that one day soon our family would be doing it for real. We'd go through the pages, and he'd tell me what the country was like and what we'd see . . ."

"And?"

"And we never did get to make the trip. A couple of months after my father was killed, the Los Angeles coroner's office returned some of his personal belongings to us. That book was with his things."

"And nobody thought that this might have been important," I asked, propping one hip against the writing desk, "especially with a couple of hundred grand drifting around loose?"

Lisette shrugged her slim shoulders. "Apparently no one did. I have a hunch that somebody made a mistake and that the book was sent back to us by accident. I remember that when Mother told Mace about Dad's things arriving he came over and tore everything apart, even ripping out the suit linings and splitting the seams. But by then it was too late."

"It was?"

"Yes," she said defiantly. "I'd already sneaked the guidebook out of the box and hidden it away. It was mine! It had belonged to Dad and me. It was my part of him.

"Mace never even knew the book existed. I never let him know about it. It wasn't until years later that I began to realize just what it could mean."

I ruffled through the pages again, not seeing a damn thing that said $200,000.

"Okay, boss, where do we start?"

"Here." She reclaimed the book and flipped it to page 20 and the Saint Louis heading.

Something had been scribbled along the page margin in blue ink: a set of initials, C. R., and a street address.

"I don't recall seeing that notation before Dad made his last run to the coast," Lisette explained. "I made a few inquiries in certain places, and I learned that Dad had dealings with a man called Calvin Reece here in Saint Louis. For some reason, Dad must have looked this Reece up on that last trip. Maybe Dad told him something about his plans. He and Reese were supposed to have been friends."

"Your dad could also have just been paying back an old pinochle debt."

"Maybe, but it's still a start."

I guess it was.

It looked like a hot day, so I swapped my leather jacket for a red nylon windcheater that would do for concealing the Commander. I also supplemented the Colt with both of my spare clips and a little something left over from my days in the Airborne. The U.S. Army and I refer to it as a paratrooper's knife. The uninitiated and the sensationally minded would call it a switchblade, a four-inch fang of folding steel with two spring-loaded buttons. One deployed the fighting edge; the second snapped out a hook-shaped shroud line cutter.

I zipped the little knife inside my right-hand boot, adjusting the laces so it would ride comfortably in concealment. It's gotten me out of serious jams twice already, once when I had a bad water landing in a swamp near Fort Bragg and then again when . . . Well, never mind. The Yokohama police never reported finding a body, so I guess that one doesn't officially count.

Most cities have a wrong side of the tracks. Saint Louis has a wrong side of the river: East Saint Louis, the tougher town back over on the Illinois bank. That's where we were headed. We cut through the heart of the Missouri side, past Checkerboard Square, and on toward the Old McKinley Bridge. Up to that point, you were driving through classic Middle America, solid, middle-class, and just starting to crumble a little around the edges as the city began to come down from its World War II boom. But get across the bridge, beyond the big river port and the bigger rail yard, and you started picking up the hard places.

Soon we were bouncing along a pothole-studded residential street lined with houses one evolutionary step above shack. The '57's gleaming chrome and glossy paint were out of place here. The cars usually found in such neighborhoods either just barely ran or were listed on a police hot sheet.

It took awhile. Street signs had a poor survival rate over here, and a lot of people didn't bother with house numbers. However, eventually we found the address listed in the guidebook.

Unfortunately, the listing was a little out-of-date, like since about the start of Truman's second term. Once it had been some kind of two-story rooming house. Now it was just an abandoned building, partially burned and boarded up. No one had been living here for a long time.

We'd hit a dry hole first shot out of the box.

"I don't suppose it would do any good to ask around?" Lisette asked glumly over the rumble of the engine.

"No. No, it probably wouldn't. We've already got enough people out there with a valid reason to kill us. There's no sense in getting ourselves murdered incidentally."

A group of Faulkner novel rejects were already eyeing us from a porch across the street. I popped the '57 back into gear and headed back toward civilization.

"It was an outside shot at best, Princess," I went on. "It's been ten years. A guy in the rackets wouldn't likely have stayed put for that long."

"I know. I've already checked the phone book and Saint Louis information. There isn't a Calvin Reece listed anywhere. I just . . . hoped."

"A better bet would be to check the state pen or the county coroner. This guy Reece might have run out of luck a long time ago."

She slouched low on her side of the seat and stared out at the gray-faced building fronts we passed.

We returned to the more prosperous corridor along St. Clair Avenue and were en route back to the Mississippi bridges when suddenly I whipped the '57 around in a U-turn in mid street.

Lisette pulled herself upright. "What's wrong?"

"Nothing. I just thought of something," I replied, sliding the car into a curbside parking slot. "Stay put. I'll be back in a second."

Getting out of the car, I strode down the block toward a corner café.

It wasn't so much what I'd thought of as it was what I'd seen when we'd passed the last cross street. A pair of East Saint Louis Police cruisers were drawn up close to the far side entrance to the greasy spoon.

I'd hit the jackpot on this one. Not only were there a trio of street cops coffeeing up in one of the booths, but one of them was a gray-haired patrol sergeant.

The three looked up with suspicion as a Levi's-clad civilian approached their table. But then I flashed my star and ID and suddenly I was a member of the family.

"Pulaski, Los Angeles County Sheriff's Department. Okay if I sit down?"

"Sure. I'm Kinney. That's Thomson and Beltrain over there." The sergeant indicated the two patrolmen on the far side of the booth and then gestured me down beside him. "Jesus, LA; you're a long way from home."

"Tell me about it. I was wondering if you local guys could give me a hand on something."

"Depends. What's the pitch?"

In the police, just like in the army, if you ever really need to know something, ask a sergeant.

"I'm in town trying to locate somebody, a man by the name of Calvin Reece. He was involved in some of the mob action back around '47 and before. All I have on the guy is a ten-year-old East Saint Louis address. I checked it out and there's nothing there now. I was wondering if there might still be any word on the street about this guy?"

"Calvin Reece . . ." The three Saint Louie blue suits swapped glances. "Reece . . ."

Kinney suddenly bobbed his head. "Yeah, sure! Desperate Jesus, but I haven't heard that name in a while. I remember him. A shine. A real badass back during the war."

"Is he still around?" I asked. "Do you know where I can get ahold of him?"

The sergeant's expression turned cautious. "That depends, LA. Have you been downtown about this yet?"

"No, I haven't. I'm not holding papers on anyone, and I'm sure as hell not planning on making any arrests." I crossed my arms and slouched in the booth, looking disgusted. "In fact, I'm supposed to be on my goddamn vacation just now."

Remember, keep it as close to the truth as you can manage. . . .

"Here's the deal. Out in Los Angeles, we've been having trouble with some of the mobs moving into our territory. That includes some of the old Chicago boys. We're putting together files on some of them, including a couple of guys that this Reece may have known.

"Anyhow, I made the mistake of mentioning in front of my captain that I was passing through Saint Louis on the way to visit my brother. And he gets this bug up his ass about saving the county some money by just casually having me drop in on this Reece to ask some questions."

I leaned forward again and lowered my voice. "Gimme a break, Sarge. This is a chickenshit detail, and I'm on my own time here. If I go through channels downtown, the friggin' suits'll have me filling out friggin' paperwork for the rest of the week."

The friggin' suits downtown and their friggin' paperwork are something that street cops everywhere agree on. I had a sympathetic audience.

Kinney shrugged. "What the hell. Yeah, as far as I know, Reece is still in town. But I don't know how much you're going to get out of him. Like I said, he was a real badass. He ran stolen liquor and he stole most of what he ran. After the war, though, 'bout '48, he knocked off a bank and did some hard time. That must have knocked some of the sass out of him, because I haven't heard much about him since. Last word I had was that he was running a place off Tenth Street. That would be over on your beat, wouldn't it, Thomson?"

The older of the cruiser crew nodded. "Yep. I know who you mean now, and I know the place. A little hole-in-the-wall barbecue joint, the Three Star Grill. We've never had any trouble out of him."

"Yeah," the younger squad man added. "Good food and never even a drunk and disorderly. He seems to be a pretty good guy for a colored."

"Thing is," Thomson continued, "I don't think the pen softened Reece up all that much. You'd better watch yourself if you plan on talking to him, Pulaski. He still doesn't take shit off anybody."

We found the Three Star Grill on a backwater business street, wedged in between a pawnshop and a hardware store. This neighborhood was in better shape than the residential district where we'd found the rooming house, but it had a long way to go before it could be called uptown.

"How did you find out about this place?" Lisette inquired, glancing at me curiously.

"I know a guy who owns a good Ouija board. Relax, Princess, it's all just part of the deluxe service."

I parked the '57 in front of the place, where I'd be able to keep an eye on her. Three tough-looking Negro teenagers lounged on a set of steps a couple of doors down. Their attention focused on Lisette and me as we got out of the car.

I caught the eye of the trio's leader, and for a long moment we swapped stares. Over on the hard side, it's real important to establish your position in the pecking order. I sent the kid a message. *No, man. Not us and not today.*

The gang leader's gaze moved on. We understood each other.

An old-time embossed tin ceiling set low over the half-dozen dark wood booths that ran down one side of the little restaurant. A couple of colored workmen who'd been talking quietly in one of the booths got a lot quieter as Lisette and I entered. A row of stools faced a counter on the other side, a single open doorway leading into the kitchen behind it.

All of the room's furniture and fixtures were old and battered by a lot of hard use, but there was also a well-scrubbed cleanliness and sense of order to the place. It had the feel of an army mess hall maintained by a tough, no-nonsense company cook. An incredible spicy aroma flowed out of the kitchen door, a tantalizing scent that made the saliva gush and provided a pointed reminder that one cup of coffee three hours ago didn't make for much of a breakfast. As a smoke hound from way back, I realized that I was in the presence of genius.

That presence stood behind the counter just now, coldly eyeing us. By what I'd been told about him, this had to be Calvin Reece, and yeah, he looked like he didn't accept a whole lot of shit off of anybody. He was a human fireplug. Not tall, but burly and solid. So much so that he looked like dynamite would be needed to take him off his feet. He wore jeans and a checked shirt with the sleeves rolled up, a sauce-stained white cloth tucked under his belt serving as an apron. Balding, he had a fudge of a beard on his chin and a mean-looking mass of scar tissue over his left eye.

"What do you want?" He didn't have to actually say the "the hell" to add it in as part of the sentence.

I made a show of thinking about it for a couple of seconds, then said, "Well, it's like this. This lady and I were in the mood for some really good barbecue. And I don't know about you, but I've never known a white man that could throw a decent rack of ribs."

I'd found the key to the lock. Reece chuckled shortly, a sound like a couple of cinder blocks mating. "That's because such a thing ain't never been borned, boy," he said. "Sit down; I'll set you up."

Behind us, the other customers went back to their conversation.

The Three Star was the kind of place where you didn't look at a menu; you just ate what the cook damn well felt like fixing that day. Not that I was complaining. The baby back ribs had a sauce that would make your mouth burn for an hour after you finished eating and leave you enjoying every second of the experience. The baked beans were baked and not just boiled and camouflaged under a little brown sugar, and the steaming golden corn bread had had extensive congress with butter and honey well before we ever became involved with it. A couple of bottles of Miller Highlife, chilled to about two degrees short of freezing, washed things down. Lisette got a glass with hers.

"How'd that sit?" Reece inquired, emerging from the kitchen. The other two customers had left, leaving Lisette and me alone with him in what I'd bet was a lull before a major lunchtime rush.

"I'd call that barbecue," I replied sagely, swirling the last half-inch of my beer around in the bottom of the bottle. "Now, Mr. Reece, can we talk with you for a second?"

He got suspicious again real fast. "You some kind of cop?" he demanded.

I wonder sometimes if they can smell us the way some cons

claim. I shook my head. "No, I'm just the hired help. The lady here is the one with the questions."

Lisette was ready to pick up on my opening. She had her purse open, and she took a photograph from it, a picture of a dark-haired smiling man in an out-of-date suit. "Mr. Reece, do you know this person?" she asked, passing the photo across the bar.

Reece did. You could read it in his face. But he was a long way from letting down his guard. "Maybe. How come you want to know?"

"This man's my father."

Reece almost dropped the picture. "Sweet Jesus," he almost whispered. "You're Johnny 32's little girl?"

Lisette nodded.

"I will be forever damned," Reece went on musingly. "I can see the look of him in you. Johnny was a handsome sumbitch for a white man."

"So you did know my father!"

"Yeah, darlin'." Reece nodded. "I knew your daddy. And I expect you know about him, too, else you wouldn't be here."

Lisette nodded her own reply. "I know what he was, and I know that you were his friend in those days."

"We did work together some." Reece smiled reminiscently, a quick flash of white teeth against dark skin. "Back during the war, your daddy was runnin' some big old clubs up in Chi Town, and decent drinking liquor was hard to come by. Me and some of the boys down here had ways of . . . acquirin' decent drinking liquor. We did good business."

The restaurant owner leaned back against the rear counter, lost for a moment in thoughts of his own past. "I'll tell you something, gal. Your daddy may have been way the hell outside the law, but he was still a good man. He always offered a fair price for a load, and he never tried to skim nothin' on the payoff. If the feds or the troopers nailed one of the boys, he was always right there to throw their bail and to pay the juice to the judge. And when another gang took to trying to highjack our trucks, he'd ride along to give us another gun. There was some other stuff, too.''

"Please, what?'' Lisette asked with quiet urgency. She was hearing words about a man who had been lost to her for a long time, and she didn't want them to end.

"Oh, like his looking you right in the eye when he talked to you. Like his not hesitating when he reached out to shake your hand. Things like his always callin' me Mr. Reece whenever other folks were around. Things that don't really amount to too much, I guess.''

"Yes, they do.''

As for me, I kept my trap shut throughout the entire exchange. A spark had jumped between these two people, and for a whole lot of reasons I didn't want to interrupt anything.

"Mr. Reece, when my father made his last trip west back in 1947, did he come to see you?''

The colored man hesitated. "You mean the run where he got killed?''

"Yes.''

Reece nodded. "Yeah, I saw him. He looked me up that evening he passed through Saint Louis.''

Reese's brows came together shrewdly. "You goin' after it, aren't you? You goin' after that money?''

"You know about it?'' I blurted out, silently swearing at myself a split second after it was too late.

Reece shrugged. "Hell, boy, a whole lot of people know about the money Johnny 32 scored off his partners. Just nobody knows where it's at. Unless you do, girl?''

"I might, Mr. Reece,'' Lisette replied.

Reece studied her for a long moment before speaking again. "Well, I guess that's the way it should be. That money was supposed to be for you and your momma anyhow.''

"It was?''

"That's what Johnny said. On some of them runs up to Chicago, him and me, we talked. In the cab of a truck at night, you sort of forget what color your skin is and you can just talk like people. Me and Johnny, we talked about what kind of lives we were livin' and about what was wrong with them. He showed me a picture of your momma and you lots of times. And I showed him a picture of this gal who seemed set on making me an honest man.

"We both talked some about getting' out of the gangs and going straight, but we both agreed that you'd need one last big score to do it right. I guess Johnny was trying for that big score on that last run west of his."

"Did you get out, Mr. Reece?" Lisette asked.

"Yeah, I did. Sort of the hard way, though. I knocked over a bank and got sent up the river for it." He reached up and rubbed the ridge of scar tissue over his eye. "I did five real hard years for that. But they never found my money, neither. And when I got out, I found I had me a whole lot better woman than even I knew. She'd took the roll and bought this here place for us. Ever since then, she been keepin' me too busy runnin' it for me to get into trouble anymore." He gave that cinder block chuckle again.

"What did my father want that last time you saw him?"

Reece went grim again. "He asked me for a name, darlin'. The name of a man he might call on farther down the line on 66. Johnny knew I'd done some business out toward Texas and Oklahoma, and he was needin' a contact out that way."

"What kind of a man?" I asked.

"A real good one, or a real bad one, dependin' on how you look at it. I don't know what he needed him for. Johnny wasn't sayin,' an' I wasn't askin'."

"Did you have a name for him?" Lisette prompted.

Reece hesitated, "Yeah, but I don't know if I should be givin' it to you. I may have been no damn good, but this man was *bad,* if you get my meanin'."

Lisette leaned forward on the counter. "I need that name, Mr. Reece," she begged. "It's more important to me than you can know just now."

Reece hesitated a second more. "Claster," he said finally.

"Jubal Claster. He was one of a whole pack of white trash Clasters who used to hang around Galena and Baxter Springs back in the moonshinin' days. All I had on him was an old telephone number where he could be reached, and I can't remember that no more. Don't even know if he's still around there or if he's even still alive or not. Although if he wasn't, this world would likely be a better place."

I watched as Lisette's eyes widened slightly. The name meant something to her.

"Thank you, Mr. Reece," she said. "This has really been a big help to me. But if we're talking about bad men, I think you should know that Mace Spanno is involved in this, too."

"Spanno?" Reece scowled. "You mean no sensible soul's laid that piece of shit out dead in an alley yet?"

"Not yet," the girl replied softly. She straightened on the counter stool. "He may come around asking questions. I thought you should be warned."

Reece just smiled a smile that would scare little children and make grown men thoughtful. "Don't worry none about me. Spanno come around asking questions a little while after your daddy was killed. He didn't like the answers he got then, an' he won't like the answers he'll get now."

He glanced over in my direction. "That a fast car?" he asked, curtly nodding toward the '57 parked outside the front window.

"It'll do till one comes along."

"That's good, boy. Because you are gonna plant this little gal in it and you are going to *drive* that sumbitch! Havin' Mace Spanno chase you is bad. Havin' him catch you is a whole lot worse."

I was willing to take those words to heart. I paused before getting back into the '57, scanning the street for any out-of-place pale faces or a lurking midnight black Chrysler. Inside the car, Lisette was already digging the guidebook out of her purse.

"That make any sense to you?" I asked, dropping onto the sun-heated front seat beside her.

"Yes. It explains another entry my father made."

In the Kansas section of the little book, opposite the underlined town name of Baxter Springs, the name "Claster" had been entered and underlined, along with an old-time three-digit rural phone number.

"This is the next man we have to find, Kevin. He's the next link in the chain."

"You sure that's such a good idea?" I asked. "From the sound of this Claster character, even if we do find him, we might just be finding ourselves more trouble."

She turned quickly in the seat to face me. "I'm sure. Just like with Mr. Reece in there, I have to talk to this man. There are things I need to find out, beyond just the money. I can't explain now, but maybe as we go along . . ." Her voice trailed off.

"Okay, Princess. Say no more." I switched on the ignition. "Next stop Kansas and all points west."

"Uh, Kevin, maybe one or two other stops before then?"

"Such as?"

"Someplace where I can buy a pair of flats. Being in heels all the time is killing me. And I need some fresh clothes and some other things for the road."

"Okay. We'll get on the other side of the river and hunt up a department store."

"That will be great. But I really did mean it last night when I said that I only had two dollars to my name. Could you . . . ?"

How come a girl never looks happier than when she's spending your money on herself?

KANSAS

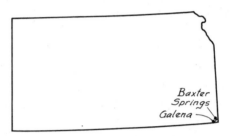

*97 mi. (117 mi.) Baxter Springs. (Pop. 4,921; alt. 842';
Merry Bales hotel; garages: Pruitt Motor Co. and
Tally's; cabin camps include: Baxter, Sunbeam and 66
Camp; small business district with cafés, stores, etc.) A
green and quiet town with an ancient, bloody his-
tory . . .*

We blew out of Saint Louis, cutting diagonally southwest
across the state of Missouri. Eureka, Allentown, Grey Summit
. . . barns in the September heat, red except for the Meramec
cavern advertisements painted on their slab sides.

We lost the four-lane about thirty-five miles out. From there
on, it would be the old eighteen-foot-wide two-lane pretty
much all the way out to the coast. Along this stretch, it even
had those damned concrete lips along the edge of the pavement
that were such a big deal a few years ago. Some congenital idiot
in the highway department came up with the theory that if they
just put curbs along the sides of the highway, a car drifting off
the road would bump against them and be bankshot safely back

into its lane like a pool ball. In reality, however, the curbs only served to trap the heavy Missouri spring rains, turning the highways into rivers. And if a car accidentally did clip one at speed, it generally flipped ass-over-teakettle into the middle of next week. This was one of the reasons this piece of the old road had acquired the nickname Bloody 66.

Saint Clair, Stanton, Cuba . . . we were traveling across the Ozark highlands now, the road curving sinuously through its series of steep-sided ridges and valleys. Except for the occasional vineyard or patch of pasture, the hills were thickly sheathed in brush thickets and hardwood. Occasional pale slashes of limestone could be seen along cliffsides and road cuts, the bony skeleton of the land tearing up through its deep green skin like a compound fracture of the planet.

It was a stealthy and mysterious country, small towns and small houses huddled back into the trees and close to the earth, asking no aid and wanting no intrusion.

Lisette lounged beside me on the front seat, now clad in a scarlet polo shirt and a pair of snug white denim short-shorts. By some unspoken agreement, we stayed away from talk about this thing we were involved in. Instead, we let the radio cue our conversation. She trended more toward the Four Aces while I'm strictly a Jerry Lee Lewis kind of guy. We found mutual ground with Nat King Cole and Les Baxter, though, and we both agreed that this new kid, Buddy Holly, had a lot going for him.

She had a nice laugh when I had a chance to hear it. She also had her own opinions about a wide variety of topics, ranging from Ike sending the troops in down at Little Rock to who was going to come out on top in the World Series.

And there was that drawing pad, the one that I'd noticed back at the Dixie. That afternoon it either sat beside her on the seat or lay cradled open in her lap, the pencil flashing across its pages. The pad itself was of high-quality art paper, and the pencil was an expensive mechanical one—the tools of a professional.

The sketching was either an instinct or a nervous habit with her, something she did almost without thinking. Half a dozen times she'd effortlessly maintained a conversation while drawing. She also had the effortless ability to not let you see what she was working on, and speaking God's honest, I was damn curious.

I finally asked her about it when we stopped for a break at one of the little roadside grape stands outside of Rolla. They had a picnic table out beside the highway under a shade tree, and Lisette was hard at it when I came back with a couple of tall paper cups of iced juice.

"Hey, are you an art student or something?" I asked, casually trying for a look at the pad as I set her cup on the table.

"Not really," she replied, giving the pad an equally casual flip shut. "I've taken some arts and graphics classes, but mostly, I just fool around with it. More like high-class doodling than anything else."

"You seem to get into it pretty deep for doodling, Princess," I commented, straddling the bench across from her.

"Oh, I've thought about fashion design and some other things, but I've never been able to get serious about it."

"Why not, if that's what you want to do?"

I felt the guards click up into place. "Because," she replied carefully, studying the cup in front of her, "what I want hasn't ever really been much of a factor in my life."

I let the subject drop.

Figure her out? Hell no, not even close. However, now and again as we drove, I'd notice her closing her eyes and lifting her face toward the sun, nuzzling into the light and the clean flow of air through the windows. It was kind of a shock when I realized that she was happy.

She was running from danger to danger in a stranger's car, with no money, no future, and only a little hope to her name, but she was still happy. No matter how screwed up a situation this was, it still must be better than what she'd come from.

I found myself wishing to just have the road and the girl out here.

Arlington, the deep cut at the Devil's Elbow, Waynesville, and a sun sinking toward a shadowed ridgeline.

The sky was on fire to the west and the evening air was mellow as bonded bourbon as we came in on Springfield, the Missouri one. Entering the outskirts of the little city, I noticed Lisette had the guidebook out again. With her dark eyes narrowed, she studied one of its pages with that feline intensity of hers, intermittently glancing up at the businesses strung out along the Route 66 miracle mile.

"What's up, Princess?" I inquired as we rolled along at a sedate thirty miles an hour.

"Nothing much," she replied noncommittally. "I'm just checking on something."

"On what?"

"Probably nothing important," she replied, the slight edge in her voice suggesting that I mind my own business.

Her tone changed a couple of minutes and a few blocks farther on. "Oh, hold it! Wait! Pull over here!" she exclaimed, pointing to the curb on her side.

For "nothing important" Lisette was suddenly excited about something. She'd pulled us up in front of the town Lincoln-Mercury dealership. Now the sun gold Premiere Landau that rotated slowly on the big turntable inside the showroom was a good-looking car, and I've heard some interesting things about the new 430-cubic-inch V-8 that Lincoln's just introduced, but I couldn't figure Lisette's sudden automotive angle.

"This place looks like it's been here awhile, doesn't it?" the girl asked thoughtfully, eyeing the place through the passenger-side window.

"It doesn't look like a fly-by-night outfit to me," I replied. And it didn't. The big, brick-faced car agency had a definite air of midwestern solidity to it.

"There're still a couple of salesmen inside. Go in and ask how long they've been here? How long this dealership's been open?"

"What? Why?"

Lisette shot an annoyed look back over her shoulder. "Just do it. Okay?"

"Yezz, bozz."

I got out from behind the wheel and walked around the front of the '57, asking myself, and not for the first time, why I hadn't played it smart and stayed in the army.

I was back out beside the car in only a couple of minutes. "Here's the word," I said, hunkering down at Lisette's window. "The guys inside say that this dealership opened right after the war."

"Nineteen forty-six?"

"Yeah, that'd be when the first new models would have been available."

"Okay." She nodded to herself. "That would have worked out all right then."

"What would have worked out all right?"

"Oh, nothing." The girl looked away and slid the guidebook back into her purse.

It was getting late, so we stopped for the night there in Springfield, choosing a little mom-and-pop motel over on the town's west side. Lisette stayed in the car while I went into the office to conduct negotiations.

"Welcome to the family, Sis," I said, sliding back behind the '57's wheel with the room key. "I got us a two-bedroom unit around in back. And in case anyone asks, you are my beloved kid sister whom I am escorting back to college. Just remember, the last name is Pulaski, with a u."

The girl snubbed out a half-smoked Fatima in the ashtray. "You didn't have to go to all that trouble," she sighed, looking straight ahead. "The conventional 'Mr. and Mrs. Smith' would have been all right."

She'd started to go tense again as soon as we'd started looking for a place to stay. I could guess why, and I decided that it was time for a little clarification in policy.

"No. No, it wouldn't have been all right," I said, half-turning in the seat to face her. "Mostly because I don't happen to buy into rape. Okay?"

Defiantly she looked up. "I'll pay my way on this trip! Last night, I said that was part of the deal. I'm saying yes if you want it. It won't be rape."

"And I'm saying that I don't want it, thank you kindly. Not that way."

We stared each other down for a long second. "Look," I went on finally. "I read in the papers about this nutcase we had out in LA awhile back, a guy who assaulted women. He'd hold a knife to his victim's throat and then make the woman beg to have sex with him. And after that, he'd proceed to screw the living hell out of her. When the cops finally nailed this psycho, he claimed that he couldn't be sent up for rape because, after all, all the women had asked for it."

Actually, I'd helped work on that case and I'd been present at the grinning-ass son of a bitch's interrogation. I'm also pleased to say I was present when his interrogators pointed out the errors in his logic. I even helped pick a few of his teeth up off the floor afterward.

I settled back in my seat. "As far as I'm concerned, it's all the same deal. A knife held at your throat or circumstances held over your head, you're still being forced. Hey, Princess, a guy would have to be either a nut or a homo not to want to get next to a girl like you. Hell, I'll be the first to admit it. But not under those terms. That's not how I do things. I came into this deal on straight speculation—a fifty-fifty cut of the loot, if we find it. Beyond that, you don't owe me a damn thing, especially yourself. Got it?"

I'm not sure if she did. She stared at me as if I'd just stepped off the 8:45 flying saucer from Venus, wary, trying to figure my angle. I guess where she came from, everybody always had an angle and the only loyalty to be found was the kind you could buy. I just sat there and gave her time, not being afraid to meet her eyes. After a second, her fur stopped bristling and there was the start of that wry smile. "Well," she said, "if you insist."

I left Lisette in the room while I took the '57 over to the Phillips station across the highway. Car needed gas, and I needed to make a discreet touch with home base.

"Talk to me, Jack," I said into the pay phone.

"I don't know how you do it, kid," my partner's faint voice came back. "But, as usual, you've managed to stick your foot in a real mess."

"You've got something for me?"

"A three-goddamn-inch-thick file in front of me right now. And that's just our stuff. The kickbacks from back east are just starting to come in."

"Give me the short and sweet, man."

"There's nothing short about it," La Baer replied. "This thing goes all the way back to the midthirties in Chicago, right after the end of prohibition and the bust-up of the old Capone mob."

"Keep talking."

"It seems that one of Capone's lesser money men, a guy named Aaron Leopold, was missed when the feds made their sweep. Leopold was a pretty sharp customer and apparently an ambitious one. When the heat came on, he headed for the storm cellar, taking some of the Capone loot with him, along with a list of the buyable men in the Chicago city administration. Enough of both to put together his own operation."

"And did he?"

"Yep. Leopold lay low for a while and then started pulling in some lieutenants. There were a couple of his old Capone acquaintances, Nick Vallessio and William Bougher, and a couple of new soldiers in off the street, Mason Spanno and John Kingman."

"Kingman wouldn't have happened to go under the alias of Johnny 32, would he?"

"That was his caliber of preference. Kingman and Spanno were a team. Johnny was the rodman, while Spanno specialized in busting ribs and kneecaps. Between the two of them they could put up a very persuasive argument in favor of anything Leopold wanted."

I glanced across the highway at our motel unit. "And what did Leopold want?"

"His own little empire on the Loop. In a couple of years he and his boys had a pretty smooth setup going, too. Prostitution and gambling mostly. They had three or four backroom casinos running and a long string of call girls, along with the usual squeeze and juice rackets on the side. Through the war years they did real well for themselves. Too well, come to find out."

"What happened?"

"They attracted the attention of the Big Boys. The Mob reorganized and started to squeeze out the independent operators. Leopold and his boys didn't have the guns to fight a war or the influence to cut a deal. Instead, they took the advice of both Horace Greeley and Bugsy Siegel. 'Go west, young man!' "

"They shifted their operations out to the coast?"

"You got it, kid. LA was virgin territory back then. We think that in 1947 Leopold made a series of trips out here to scout possibilities and to establish contacts in the local underworld. He knew that LAPD's intelligence people had the train stations and airports under surveillance, so he always came in by car, accompanied by one or more of his lieutenants, usually either Spanno or Kingman. By August they were ready to make their move."

"Did this move involve a load of money?"

"A whole shitpot full. The feds estimated the gang had a war chest in excess of a quarter of a million dollars. Leopold knew how to handle cash. He remembered the way Capone got nailed through tax evasion, so he never used banks to hold the gang's money reserves or to transfer funds. That way, there was no paper trail that could be followed."

"So they ran the loot out to the coast themselves."

"Yeah, Leopold, Vallessio, and Kingman. Spanno and Bougher stayed behind to close out the Chicago operation. The thing is, Leopold and Vallessio never made it out to the coast."

"What happened?"

"Nobody knows for sure, but a couple of days after leaving Chicago, Leopold and Vallessio turned up in a pile of mine tailings, very well ventilated. Whoever buried them misjudged the persistence of the local coyotes."

"Kingman?"

"He was the boy at the head of the list, at least in the opinion of the other two lieutenants. When word reached Chi Town about what had happened, Spanno and Bougher apparently went after Kingman. And they succeeded in tracking him down."

"In LA?"

"Yeah. About a week after Leopold and Vallessio were found, there was a hell of a gunfight in one of those cheap hotels down Long Beach way. Kingman and Bougher were found lying in the hall outside of the room Kingman had been using under an assumed name, both of them shot to pieces. The thing is, a ballistics check indicated that the slugs that put Kingman down didn't come from the heat Bougher was packing."

"Spanno?"

"He was the prime suspect. However, no hard evidence was ever recovered directly linking him to the killing. It never went to trial, and LA Homicide still lists the case as open."

It was getting hot inside the phone booth, and I cracked the door open to admit some road noise and cool air. I needed to get back to the room, but I also needed a little more information.

"What about the war chest?" I asked.

"As far as anyone knows, most of it was never recovered. The key to a bus station locker was found hidden in Kingman's room, along with a steamship ticket. The locker contained fifty thousand dollars in fifties and hundreds, while the ticket was for a slow freighter due to sail the next day around South America to the East Coast.

"Kingman was apparently planning to take a nice, leisurely ocean cruise while the heat was on. The fifty Gs was just his running money. He must have stashed the bulk of the loot away somewhere for recovery after things had cooled down."

"Any chance Spanno could have got it?"

"It doesn't look like it," Jack replied. "According to the Indiana state attorney's office, Spanno surfaced in Gary a couple of months after the LA shootout. And while it didn't take him long to become a pain in the ass to the local law, he didn't seem to be packing the weight a big bankroll would have given him."

I nodded to myself. "Okay, this is all matching up with what I'm hearing out here. So far, so good. Now, what's the current line on Spanno?"

"He's got his own outfit going these days. Loan-sharking, hot cars to Canada, and girls again. He's not one of the Princes of the Loop anymore, but he's not a nickel-and-dime operator, either. Indiana's gone for him twice on racketeering charges. In both cases, key witnesses either refused to testify or kinda disappeared just before the trial. So far, he's only taken one heavy fall. Two years for aggravated assault and battery on one of the prostitutes in his street string."

"What were the particulars?"

"Mr. Spanno is the possessive type. The girl was a good moneymaker, and she made the mistake of trying to leave Spanno's stable and go independent. Spanno personally proceeded to disjoint her like a chicken. She was in the hospital for months. I guess she ended up permanently crippled."

"How the hell did he get let off with just assault and battery?"

"It was a kind of a plea bargain with the Gary district attorney's office. The attempted murder rap would be dropped, and Spanno would be allowed to cop for A and B. And in return, the complaining witness would be allowed to not end up on the bottom of Lake Michigan."

"I can dig it. Now, what do you have on Lisette Kingman?"

"That she was born. Nothing else so far. Nobody seems to be holding a sheet on her and no kickbacks yet from the Michigan or Indiana DMV."

"Okay . . . Okay. One thing more. Where were the bodies of Leopold and that other guy found?"

"Uh, lemme see." I faintly heard papers rustle over the filtering of the phone. "Outside of someplace called Quapaw, Oklahoma."

I nodded to myself again. Baxter Springs is right on the Kansas-Oklahoma border. Throw a rock across the line and it would land in Quapaw.

"Okay, Jack. I have to go. We'll be in Baxter Springs tomorrow. I'll make my next touch within twenty-four hours."

"Right. You want that I should talk to the captain about this?"

"No, hold off. I want to work this deal on my own for a little while longer."

"Okay. Just watch yourself, kid."

"Don't sweat it, Daddy-O."

I heard a snort at the other end of the line and the click of a disconnect.

Driving back across 66, I parked in front of our motel unit. As I entered, I heard the shower hissing in the bath and I discovered Lisette's clothes scattered on the floor of the bedroom she had selected. Her shoulder bag also sat on the edge of the bedside table.

I didn't waste the opportunity. With one ear cocked to the sound of the shower, I went for the purse.

It was plain black leather, with a flap top and gold clasp, good quality and fairly new, showing only a little use wear.

Quickly I ran an inventory. Gold compact, cologne spray, and lipstick. Lisette's colors and scent. A half-pack of her Fatima's. No lighter—ladies like Lisette never have to light their own cigarettes. Comb and brush, handkerchief, wallet—she really did only have two dollars and twenty-seven cents. The guidebook, I'd save that for when I had more time. Photographs, the one of John Kingman and another of an elegant dark-haired woman who must have been Lisette's mother.

Then there were just the odds and ends you always find at the bottom of a woman's purse. Brown bobby pins, an art gum eraser, a broken rubber band, a single golden earring, and the snub end of a roll of chocolate Life Savers. Nothing unusual there.

What was unusual was what wasn't there. No checkbook or check stubs. No address book. No old bills or letters. No driver's license. No charge-a-plates. Not even a library card.

There was nothing in that purse with a name or an address on it. It had been systematically stripped of anything that could provide a hard connection to an identity. The little celluloid envelopes in the wallet showed hazy wear marks where things had been removed. Lisette Kingman had deliberately thrown away her entire past life.

If she was Lisette Kingman.

Her sketch pad had been tucked neatly into an outside pocket of the shoulder bag. The fit was so close I suspected that the bag had been chosen specifically for this feature. I sat down on the edge of the bed and began to flip through it. Now, at long damn last, I could see what she'd been up to.

Over the first few pages there were a number of what looked like fashion designs. Women's clothing, dresses, sports outfits, lingerie, that kind of thing. Intermixed with them, however, were other random drawings. Faces, buildings, what might have been Rainbow Beach back in Chicago. The girl had the knack of shaping a few quick, dynamic lines into a clean and vividly recognizable image.

On the last couple of pages I began to spot things that I

knew. The dining room at the Dixie Trucker's Home. A sketch of one starkly tiled exterior corner of our unit at the Coral Court Motel A third of Calvin Reece, catching and underlining the ingrained toughness and grim humor of the man.

And the start of a drawing of another man, tall, blocky, square-featured, unfinished. A jagged line like a lightning bolt slashed through it.

The shower turned off. Moving fast, I returned the drawing pad to the shoulder bag and repositioned it exactly where I had found it. By the time the bathroom door opened, I was stretched out on my bed in the other room, just staring at the ceiling.

"Hey, where are we going for dinner?" Lisette asked, peering around the door frame. She was relaxed and happy again. Wrapped in a big white bath towel and with her long dark hair shower-damp and flowing down her back, she did look like somebody's kid sister, eyes wide and unconcerned about anything beyond cheeseburgers or Chicken in the Rough.

"Well there, then, now, Princess, I don't know. We'll just have to get out there and explore the epicurean delights of Springfield, Missouri."

"I'm impressed. I didn't know you knew words like *epicurean*."

"Oh, I'm just full of surprises."

"You certainly are, Sir Galahad. Give me five minutes, or maybe a little more."

She whisked back out of sight. A moment later, her discarded towel sailed across the hall and into the bathroom.

So okay, so maybe she didn't really look all that much like somebody's kid sister.

My pack of Luckys lay on the end table, and I lit up, using the motel's book of complimentary matches. Lying back again, I sent a blue plume curling toward the ceiling.

We knocked off the last hundred miles to the Kansas-Missouri line before eleven the next morning. There's not much of 66

in Kansas, just a short hook through the very southeastern corner of the state. You could drive it in a quarter of an hour if
it weren't for the two towns, Galena and Baxter Springs, that
you have to pass through.

This little patch of land was soaked in a lot of history,
though, history and blood, the two being frequently synony-
mous. The Jayhawkers had ridden here before the Civil War,
Quantrill's Raiders during, and the James gang after. And there
had been later incarnations as well.

Galena was the mining town, and at the peak of the lead
and zinc boom its main drag had been called the Red Hot
Street. It had burned bright on Saturday nights as the miners
came roaring in to dump their pay into the pockets of the
pimps, tinhorns, and barkeeps.

Later had come the depression and the strikes. I could remember Dad talking about the bad times in Galena. In a struggle between rival miners' groups, nine CIO organizers had been
gunned down in the streets, and the National Guard had been
brought in to declare things a draw.

As for Baxter Springs, it had been the destination of the first
herds of Texas longhorns to flow up the Chisholm Trail after
the Civil War. Dodge City, Abilene, and all the other hell-
raising Kansas cow towns that came later just followed the ex-
ample that had been set here.

Now the cattle drives were gone, replaced by the big midwestern truck fleets that used Baxter as a home terminal. And
the mines were playing out, leaving nothing behind in Galena
except for grim stories and gritty gray mounds of ore tailing.
Chat heaps, the locals called them. Both communities were
sinking into a peaceful Middle American sleepiness.

Barring the odd corpse that still turned up now and again.

"I tried calling ahead from the motel this morning," Lisette
said over the road wind fluttering in through the '57's windows.
Route 66 had just crossed a one-lane rainbow arc bridge and
now almost tunneled through a thick and humid grove of black-
jack and ground cherry. "The number in the guidebook isn't

good anymore. They've changed over to a whole new directory system. And directory assistance doesn't list a Claster anywhere in either Baxter Springs or Galena.''

"That doesn't mean all that much, Princess," I replied. "Reece wasn't listed in the phone book, either. Claster might not have a phone, or he might be living in a rooming house or an apartment. Even if this Jubal guy's moved on, there's got to be somebody around here who'll know something."

Lisette peered at me over the top of my commandeered sunglasses. "And how do we go about finding this somebody?"

"We ask. Hell, it's not like this place is Chicago. In a small town, everybody knows everybody. Even in a middlin' big small town like Baxter Springs, enough people are going to know enough people so it shouldn't be that big of a deal. Trust me."

I took a second to glance across at her. "Haven't you ever spent any time in a small town?"

"Gary was the smallest. And I didn't know a lot of people."

She went cold, silently warning me off the subject. Just like every other time I'd tried to probe into her past. The hatches would slam shut, and her wariness would return.

I let it ride as we blew past the sign welcoming us to Baxter Springs.

It was a quiet town with a contentedly worn-out and weary kind of peace about it, all crumbling brick and peeling white clapboard beneath the lush sycamores that lined its streets. There was a small business district, a shady little park, and a sign explaining that there weren't any springs anymore, but that before the mines there had been.

With Lisette tagging along at my heels, I couldn't drop in on the local cops like I had back in Saint Louis, but then I really didn't need to. Like I said, it wasn't that big of a deal. Excuse me, Sir Arthur Conan Doyle, but anyone, and I mean anyone, can be a halfways decent detective. All it requires is a degree of patience (stubbornness works just about as well) and the common sense God gave a doorknob.

We hit the local phone company. Sure, the number we'd been given was no good now, but it might have been once. A quick check in some of the old directories and, yeah, in 1947 there had been a Ruben Claster listed. The number matched, too. Reece hadn't been screwing with us.

Now we had an address. An old one, but an address. We checked it out.

It was rural, a short drive west out of town. And once we were out there, we found nothing: a tangle of wire in a ditch and what might have been the foundations of a house and barn in what was now a cow pasture.

But the land was there. A Claster had owned it once, and somebody else had to own it now. We drove a quarter-mile down the road to a prosperous-looking farmhouse and had a talk with a friendly, well-upholstered farmwife. Over a cup of coffee I fed her a line about how my new wife and I were looking for an old army buddy of my father's. In return, we listened to her tell about how her husband had picked up the land about eight years ago at a bank auction.

Gee, what had happened to the previous owner?

He wore out and died, leaving nothing but an unpaid mortgage behind.

Any of his kin still around?

There were a couple of sons. They were never much for helping around the place. They might still be around town somewhere.

Given the expression on the farm woman's face, she wasn't too happy about the idea.

We headed back to town and the local newspaper office. Reece had told us the Clasters ran on the wrong side of the law. Great! We asked to see the morgue files containing the last few years of the local police column and started cruising for Clasters.

It didn't take long to strike gold. It is written that Ruben begat two sons, and verily, they have sinned.

> Jubal Claster, Illegal Transport and Possession of
> Alcohol, September 1941, Six Months . . .
> Ira Claster, Theft of Farm Machinery, March 1944,
> State Youth Farm . . .
> Jubal Claster, Grand Theft Auto, September 1945,
> One Year . . .
> Ira Claster, Drunk and Disorderly, June 1951, Ninety
> Days . . .
> Ira Claster, Assault and Battery, Breaking and
> Entering, August 1954, One Year . . .

Neither of these guys appeared to be members of the Christian Temperance Union, so we hit the bars and roadhouses along the Galina–Baxter Springs corridor next. Leaving Lisette in the car, I went in and bought a few for some of the older regulars.

The State Line Tavern: "The Claster boys? Jeeezus! Their old man wasn't all that much good, but God, the two boys was hell-raisers. Pretty good with a motor when they felt like it, but that sure didn't make up for 'em the rest of the time . . ."

Andy's SmokeHouse: "Jubal and Ira. Yeah, I remember 'em. Jubal ain't around no more. Lit out back around '47 or '48, likely in some kind of damn trouble or other. Ira still comes in now and again. When he ain't doin' time, anyway."

The Old Trail Packaged Liquor Store: "Ira? Sure, he's still around. Got a mechanic's job out at that two-pump Texaco on the Melrose Road west of town. You can't miss it. He's likely out there now."

Piece of cake.

The service station was set in a patch of weeds and rusty car hulks. An army surplus Quonset hut with a couple of wood frame add-ons, its white paint losing the fight to a growing collection of rust stains. Turning into the shale rock driveway, I stopped the '57 just short of the bell hose. It was getting late in the day, and the sun was edging below a hazy horizon. Back up in the tanglewood, katydids screeched a protest against the heat.

"This is it, Princess; here's where we find the guy we need to talk to."

"But this is Ira Claster, not Jubal."

"Yeah, but who's more likely to know where this Jubal character is hanging out these days than his brother?"

"True." The girl nodded. "You were right, Kev. This didn't turn out to be that big of a deal." That speculative expression crossed her face again. "Where did you ever learn to be so good at doing this kind of thing?"

"You ought to see my collection of Hardy Boys novels." I popped the door and got out of the car. "Come on; let's go visiting."

She didn't move. Lisette just sat in the '57's front seat, arms crossed and with one elegant eyebrow lifted, waiting for satisfaction.

"Okay. I did a tour as an MP in the army. I watched our CID people do this kind of stuff all the time."

"I thought you said you were a paratrooper?" she asked suspiciously.

"I was. But I managed to get myself shot up in Korea and I lost my jump rating. I finished my hitch with the Military Police. That happens with a lot of ex-Airborne. The logic is that you need someone theoretically tougher than your average GI to keep your average GI slapped into line."

Lisette nodded and reached for the door handle. "Just curious."

The only sign, or rather sound, of life seemed to be coming from the station's single inside service bay. It was the slightly unsyncopated rumble of an engine radical enough to be investigated by the McCarthy Commission. We circled the building and, while Lisette hesitated at the open bay door, I went on in.

The hot mill was nestled in the immaculate engine compartment of a red-primered 1940 Ford pickup nosed inside the garage. A man leaned in beneath the open hood making an adjustment. Even given the loose gray garage coveralls he wore, I could see the classic chain gang build on him, lean but with powerfully muscled arms and shoulders. His hair was black and collar-length long, not out of style but out of don't-give-a-damn. His dark eyes were agate cold and indifferent as he looked up.

"Yeah?"

To tell the truth, I wasn't paying too much attention to the guy at the moment. My instincts had taken over, and I was focused on the engine.

It was one of the last of the flathead V-8s, a '52 or '53 24-stud Mercury, topped by an Edlebrock manifold and a gleaming quadruple-rank of Stromberg 97 carburetors. Aluminum-finned high compression heads had been installed along with custom-tuned headers, and the stock water pumps were gone. Replacing them was a single big positive displacement marine pump feeding into the block below the exhaust ports.

This last was the mark of a very serious engine indeed. Before the coming of the overhead valve, mills like this one had literally been the power and the glory of American hot-rodding. Even now, a full-house "Big Merc" like this wasn't anything to take for granted.

"You running a three-eight-by-three-eight configuration on her?" I asked.

Claster's eye became a degree or two less cold. "Yeah," he replied in a dry semisouthern twang. "I thought 'bout taking her out to three seven-sixteen, but I wasn't sure she could hold together."

"Smart move. She wouldn't be any good on the street. Get those cylinder walls too thin and you get all sorts of overheating

problems. You got a real haulin' Henry here as is. Damn! This
is nice!"

I meant it, too. Maybe Ira Claster was an ex-jailbird with a
long record, a bad attitude, and green teeth, but he had created
at least one little piece of perfection with this engine. He had
taken something and had reworked and refined it until it was
as good as it could possible get. Not many people in this world
ever do that.

"You ever run flatheads?" he asked, straightening and starting to wipe his hands on a piece of already-oily waste.

"No. No, I can't say that I have. But my first heap was a
'29 Ford roadster with a Model B four-banger in it. I ran a
Riley head and a pair of Winfields, and that little bitch was
hot. The V-8s would kill me once we got into high gear, but
man, for the first three hundred yards, there wasn't a car in the
world that could touch me."

We laughed then, just for a second, that odd little chuckle
that happens when one person's reminiscence triggers a sympathetic memory in another's mind.

"What you runnin' now?" he asked.

"One of the new Chevy 283 overheads in a '57 One-Fifty."

Claster's scowl returned and he took a second to spit elab-
orately on the concrete floor.

Obviously a Ford man.

"What'd you want?" he demanded, tossing the grease rag
behind him onto the tool bench that ran the full length of the
service bay.

"To talk to your brother, Jubal."

He hesitated for a second before turning back to face me.
"Jubal doesn't live around here anymore. He moved on 'bout
ten years ago."

"Well now, we know that. That's why we need you to tell
us where we can get ahold of him."

Claster's dark brows drew together, and his frown deepened.
His hand went back to the tool bench, coming to rest within a

couple of inches of a heavy-duty socket wrench.

"No big deal, man," I said levelly. "We're not cops. [At least one of us wasn't, anyway.] And we just need to ask him a couple of questions."

" 'Bout what?"

"About my father." Lisette had come up to stand beside me, lifting her voice to be heard over the rumble of the idling engine. "Ten years ago, we think that my father and your brother might have done some business together. I need to find out about that business. My name is Lisette Kingman."

She'd said the magic word, and the duck dropped. Claster's hand moved the last couple of inches to the wrench. "I don't know you," he growled, "my brother don't know you, and neither of us know what the hell you're talking about."

Oh, but he did. I could read it in his face. He knew who Lisette's father was. He knew why we wanted to talk to brother Jubal, and he knew just exactly what had happened one night on the Oklahoma prairie ten years ago.

"I don't want to make trouble for you or your brother," Lisette continued. "I just want to talk to him."

"Well, he don't want to talk to you, bitch, so you can quit lookin' for him!" The wrench came up in his hand, balanced for striking. "Get outta here!"

I shoved Lisette back behind me. I had a suspicion that this guy hadn't been listening when his momma had told him that deal about not hitting girls. "Hey, man! Take it easy! Like the lady said, we just want to talk."

"And like I said, we don't want to talk to nobody!" There was wild in this guy's eyes as I backed Lisette and myself down the narrow corridor between the idling truck and the tool bench. "Now you get the whole hell out of here, an' if I catch you asking any questions about Jubal around this town, you'll get your head busted open!"

"Okay, okay! Don't get the reds, man. We're gone." I lifted my hands shoulder-high, both as a diplomatic gesture and to give me an elbow to use for nudging a resisting female back toward the open door.

"Kevin, we have got to get some answers from this guy!"

"I don't think he has any he wants to give away," I replied, turning back toward the bright Kansas sunlight. "Be cool, Princess. Whatever he knows somebody else around here has to know, too."

Thinking about it, I realize now that wasn't the brightest thing I could have said at that moment.

Lisette, who had been looking back over her shoulder, gasped, and I heard the rasp of a boot sole on gritty concrete over the sound of the pickup's engine.

I was clear of the truck's tailgate by then, and I tried the spin kick, the one my old tae kwon do instructor said you could generally only land right by luck.

I was lucky. Claster was rushing up behind me with the wrench held low like a stabbing dagger. He planned on smashing the head into the small of my back, a move that could have laid me up for a month with a ruptured kidney or possibly paralyzed me for life.

Instead, the steel toe cap of my jump boot took the wrench out of his hand with the neatest little metallic *ping* you ever heard.

It stopped my attacker cold, and just for a split second it left him goggling at his empty hand. I went in on Claster in that split second, my right hand cocking back and pistoning forward, palm open, into his face.

The blow snapped his head back, the heel of my hand raking back across his features, crushing his lips and nose and throwing him backward into a sprawl between the workbench and truck. I'd hurt him, but guys like Claster get used to being hurt early on. He swarmed back to his feet, madder and no doubt meaner than he'd been before.

I had to go after him again. I couldn't let him get himself together. Tools make great ad hoc weapons, and there was enough potentially lethal ironmongery scattered on that garage workbench to stock half a dozen good East LA gang fights.

I tried to take him down with another kick, but Claster shoved my rising boot aside and it was his turn to come in at me. We were back between the pickup and the bench now, and there was no room to maneuver, just fist and skull and batter 'em down.

Brother Ira was bad news. He was as tough and stringy as old boot leather, and he had a pair of shoulders on him like a medium tank. He'd also obviously graduated from a pretty tough school of street and bar fighting. Well, so had I, but then I'd gone on to do postgraduate studies in paratrooper and cop.

I blocked a few punches and weaved around a couple more. Then I spotted him a wild swing that raked my jaw and put sparks in my vision. However, it also got me inside his defense far enough to drive a knee into his gut. Claster went green and gagged. Falling back against the workbench, he scrabbled for a rack of screwdrivers.

Not today, buddy. I peeled him off the bench, drove another fist into his belly, and spun him around. Wrenching his right arm up behind his back, I slammed him forward over the fender of his truck, his head extending out over the open engine compartment. I took a single deep breath and wished for a set of handcuffs.

Claster got his wind back, too, and began to struggle again, screaming some really interesting variations on a few of the more potent standard cusswords. Then another county was heard from. From the other side of the truck Lisette reached across the engine compartment and grabbed two handsful of Claster's lank hair.

"Where's your brother?" she demanded over the engine rumble.

Claster replied with a suggestion, something a lot of men would probably like to do with a lady like Lisette, but reduced to its ugliest gutter form.

The girl's eyes flashed and suddenly she wrenched his head

downward, pushing Claster's face toward the truck's spinning radiator fan.

Claster yelled and tried to rear back, but Lisette bore down with all of her strength.

"Where . . . is . . . your . . . brother!" It was a scream of anger to match Claster's scream of fear.

"Go to hell!" Claster's neck muscles bulged as he tried to lift his face away from the glinting fan blades. Lisette had the leverage, though, and she was merciless. Cold fire danced in her eyes, and her fine-lined jaw was set in a soundless snarl. Once more she shoved his face deeper into the engine compartment.

"Where!"

Jesus! She was meaning it! "You know, man," I said slowly, "you're probably really going to miss your nose."

Claster screamed as Lisette bore down again, but this time it was a single word.

"Arizona!"

"Arizona is a big place!" I prompted, tightening up on his arm.

"Peerless! West of Winslow!"

I didn't think he was lying, not two inches short of a face-lift by a '40 Ford engine fan. If he was trying to fake a fast story, he would have grabbed for some bigger, better-known city, not a whistle-stop in the middle of the Arizona desert. I met Lisette's eyes and gave her a nod. "Grab loose, Princess."

She released Claster's hair and stepped back from the truck, instinctively wiping her hands on the seat of her shorts.

"Listen to me, man," I said into his ear. "Like I said, we just want to talk. No trouble. You can tell your brother that. Now I'm going to turn you loose and everybody's friends, okay?"

Yeah, in a pig's ass. I could feel him still straining to break out of my hold, and I knew that the instant I backed off he was going to blow up all over me again.

I released him and stepped back.

Sure enough, he came off that fender and spun toward me, just about as pissed off as a freshly altered tomcat. I'd used that instant of time, though, to get my range and to get set. As he came around, I lifted him off the floor with a right cross that had all the steam behind it I could muster.

Claster slid under the workbench and went night-night for a while on an uncomfortable-looking bed of old oilcans. I switched off the pickup's engine—no sense in letting a really nice mill like that overheat—and we left him to his dreams.

Back in the car, Lisette had my Arizona road map dug out of the glove compartment in seconds. "Okay, we're set," she said. "There is a Peerless; it looks like just a little tiny place only a couple of miles off Route 66. It's right along where we're going. It couldn't be better. . . . What?"

She'd noticed that I hadn't started the engine yet. It was my turn to sit there studying her.

"Where in the hell did that move come from?"

She lifted her brows at me. "He wasn't going to tell us anything otherwise."

She had a point. "Yeah, I guess he wasn't."

Lisette shrugged demurely, her cool deb demeanor sliding back into place as smoothly as a sheath over a bayonet.

"This is one of those things above and beyond the quarter of a million bucks you were talking about back in Saint Louis. Finding this guy, Jubal, is a really big deal for you, isn't it?"

"Uh-huh, it is," Lisette replied with one of those sober little nods of hers. "More than you know. Maybe even more than I do."

It's never a good idea to hang around after a fight. Not that I was too worried about a guy like Ira Claster running to the cops about us. However, I did figure him to be the kind of guy who might just dig out a shooting iron and come hunting. We grabbed a sandwich and something to drink back in Baxter Springs and then moved on.

We crossed the Kansas-Oklahoma line just as serious dark

started to settle. We were beginning to leave the "Mid" part of the Midwest behind now; the terrain was flattening out, the hills shrinking down to just a low rolling of the land.

"Kevin, would you turn on the dome light for a second, please?"

Over on her side of the seat, Lisette had the Rittenhouse guide open again. I flipped the light switch to the right notch and watched out of the corner of my eye as she hunted up a page. The Princess looked somber.

"Okay," she said after a moment, "tell me when we've come two miles from the border."

I glanced down at the odometer. "We're just about there now."

Without being asked, I started braking the '57 to a halt. At the two-mile guidepost I pulled us off the pavement and onto the narrow shoulder of the two-lane.

There wasn't all that much to be seen. There were only the lights of the little reservation town of Quapaw gleaming in the dusk a few miles farther down Route 66. That and a single-lane dirt road that entered the highway on our left. Punching through a gap in a tangled wall of brushy ground cover, it led off toward a shadowy bluff to the east.

I guess that poets and other such five-dollar-a-word writers would call this part of the evening the gloaming. You could see, but not all that well. The scrub woods seemed to have a faint gray luminescence to them, and the sky overhead wasn't an honest black. It was more of a deep and dull green with an indefinable brassy tint to it, as if the zenith had been tarnished by the fiery passage of the day's sun.

I found myself wishing that the nightfall would get on with it so that a few friendly stars could show up.

Lisette indicated the side road. "We need to go down there."

For some reason, I didn't much dig that concept. "Why?" I asked succinctly.

"I'll tell you when we get there," she replied in a near-whisper.

The '57 didn't think much of the idea, either. As we nosed into the narrow lane, Car growled deep in her pipes like a wary police dog.

Bumping slowly over the ruts and potholes, we traversed a narrow passage through a laurel hell. Beyond that, things widened out again with barbwired pastures on either side of the road. The fences looked rusty and untended in the sidelobe of our headlights, and no livestock moved out in the fields.

Nothing moved except for a trickle of dry summer lightning along the horizon.

The road ran back a mile and a half to the base of the bluff. There it ended abruptly at an abandoned mine head. Our headlights swept beyond a padlocked gate and disintegrating rail fence to reveal a few warped and collapsing buildings and an expanse of torn, baked soil too contaminated with lead to even let the weeds and brambles invade. The towering gritty bulk of a tailings pile loomed on the edge of our perception, like a sand dune that had lost its desert.

I backed and filled, turning us around. If the urge suddenly struck to honk out of here, I wanted to be aimed in the right direction. I shut off the engine and the lights and let the silence flow in through the windows.

Quiet? Man, I'll tell the world. Even the tree frogs and katydids were keeping their mouths shut. And there was something out there . . . I dunno. Maybe it was the way the shadows back under the trees seemed to almost have a tangibility to them, like if you walked into one, you'd be stuck in blackness like a fly in amber.

"Okay, Princess," I asked, slouching back in the seat, "what's going on?"

"I'm checking out a notation in the guidebook," Lisette replied. She'd curled up in the seat with legs tucked under her, hugging herself, as if she were trying to keep out a chill. "You see, when my father stole his gang's war chest, it wasn't any spur-of-the-moment thing. He was working to a plan. Something he'd thought out and set up long beforehand."

"How do you know?"

"Because none of the notations he made in the Rittenhouse guide are random. He must have known that eventually they were going to move the money out to Los Angeles by car and that Route 66 would be the way they would go. He prepared for it. On his earlier trips out to the coast, he made notes about the ground they'd be covering on that last run."

She held up the little book. "He recorded them all in here. As we've been going along, I've been cross-referencing what's written in the guidebook with what we've been seeing along the way. I figure that if we can see how my father had his plans laid out and get a feel for what he thought was important, it might help us to find the money."

"Is that what we were doing with that Lincoln agency back in Springfield?"

Lisette nodded. "It was. There's a notation in the guidebook, 'Linc A.' It's shown up in a number of places, Springfield, Saint Louis, Joplin. In every one of those towns there's been a Lincoln agency. Dad was driving a Lincoln."

"I get it. He was keeping track of where he could get fast repairs made if he needed them."

"Exactly." I could see her as only an outline in the dimness now, huddled in the corner of the seat with her head lowered. "There are a whole bunch of other notes, too, relating to things like state police barracks, all-night gas stations, and what towns have doctors in them. All of them recording things a man on the run might need to know."

It made sense. Johnny 32 was a careful planner. He didn't like leaving things to chance.

"And he made a notation about this place?" I asked

"Yes. Between the Kansas and Oklahoma state line entry and the one for Quapaw. It just said: 'Two miles from border,' and it was underlined. And this road is all that's there."

"If your dad arranged to link up with his hired gun in Baxter

Springs, then he must have planned on making his move on the money somewhere right in this vicinity. This turnoff could have been the place set for the hit."

Could be? I was damn well sure it was. If you ever wanted a nice, quiet spot to 86 somebody, this was the place.

"I suspect it was," Lisette agreed bleakly. "I think my father's partners were probably killed somewhere right along this little road. According to the newspaper accounts, the bodies of Aaron Leopold and Nick Valessio were found just outside of Quapaw, Oklahoma, buried in a chat heap."

She glanced back over her shoulder at the looming mound of the tailings pile. "That could be the one right back there."

I gave a low whistle. "I've got to give your old man credit, Princess. He could sure pick a good place for a murder."

Lisette's head snapped up. "It might not have been murder!"

I gave a snort. "Okay, give me another name for it. You were the one saying they found your father's partners planted around here. What the hell else could it have been?"

"A lot of things!" Lisette spun around to face me. "Sure, I know that my father set out to rob his partners! But beyond that, a lot of different things could have happened. There might have been a fight over the money, and my father might have been forced to kill Leopold and Valessio in self-defense. Or maybe it was this Jubal Claster who killed them, maybe to keep himself from being identified. Dad might not even have been here when it happened. Claster is the only man who might know. That's why we have to find him as well as the money."

A desperation crept into her voice as she tried to make me see the subtleties of this thing the way she did. I understood the other piece of the program now. If Lisette Kingman was reaching out for the Leopold gang's war chest with one hand, she was grabbing for a straw with the other, hoping to find evidence that her father wasn't quite the total back-stabbing son of a bitch he appeared to be.

What could I say to that? Not a whole lot at the moment. Lisette looked away from me, gazing out into the newborn night beyond the windshield.

And gave a yelping little gasp.

I looked up as well. And man, I could actually feel my hair start to stand on end.

There were two of them, rising out of the ditch at the side of the road about a hundred yards away. Try and imagine an orange toy balloon, but with a lit candle inside of it. A candle that burns with a particularly clear and crystalline white light. Lazily they began to bounce back and forth across the dirt ruts of the lane as if some kids were playing a slow-motion game of catch with a pair of luminescent basketballs.

Only there weren't any kids out there. There wasn't anybody there except for Lisette and me, and we were all of a sudden wishing we were somewhere else.

The Princess became a scared little girl, sliding across the seat to huddle against me "What are they?" she asked in a strangled whisper.

Hell, I didn't know what they were! Although for a second I had some pretty wild suspicions about *who* they might be.

Then the good old *National Geographic* magazine came to my rescue. And am I glad that I actually read the articles instead of just looking for pictures of topless native girls.

"Easy, Princess," I said, putting my arm around her. "It's okay. They're called spook lights and they're just something that comes with this part of the country."

Lisette straightened a little, not all that much reassured. "But what are they?" she insisted, warily eyeing the flickering spheres as they bobbed and weaved above the road.

"Nobody knows. They crawl all over the place down here where Missouri, Kansas, and Oklahoma butt together. The Army Corps of Engineers did a study on them right after the war, but all they ever came up with was 'mysterious lights of undetermined origin.' You've got all your usual legends about phantom Indian maidens looking for their lost lovers and decapitated Civil War soldiers looking for their heads with a lantern, but for sure nobody knows."

As if showing off, one of the spook lights shot a hundred feet into the air, then descended in a slow spiral. Its partner contented itself with rolling slowly along the top wire of the left-hand fence.

"What do these 'spook lights' do?" Curiosity was replacing fear in Lisette's voice, so I knew she was going to be okay. She didn't seem to object to having my arm around her shoulders, though, and I didn't object to leaving it there.

"I guess about what they're doing now. They pop up after dark in an empty field or along a deserted road somewhere, zip and bounce around for a while, then disappear. They've been reported in these parts ever since the middle of the last century. Some scientists figure that the start of the mining operations might have had something to do with stirring them up. On the other hand, they may have been here for a long time and there just wasn't anybody around to see 'em."

We sat there and silently watched the eerie interweaving display. If you stared at them long enough, the twin balls of light almost seemed to display a kind of intelligence. They'd sidle away from the road to play hide and seek in the scrub woods for a time. Then they'd bust back into view, racing closer, but never quite close enough to let you see if there was a shape or form behind the glow.

After a while, Lisette shivered a little in the curve of my arm. "I guess we should get going," she said.

"I guess so."

The spook lights hovered low over the dirt ruts of the road as I fired the '57 up, pulsating, as if ready to block our escape.

"Can we get past those things?' Lisette asked a little nervously.

"No sweat. If you get close to a spook light, it just goes somewhere else."

At least according to *National Geographic*.

Even so, we cranked our windows up and I charged us down that cow path a little faster than I normally might have. The spook lights held position as if daring me into a game of otherworldly chicken. I kicked on our high beams, and the clean white light glare of the '57's headlights reached out toward the luminescent orbs. As it touched them, they suddenly stopped being, snuffing out of existence like twin candles on top of a birthday cake.

As we passed through the spot where the spook lights had been, I thought I felt something brush me. Something like a faint chill or a low-grade static shock. Then again, maybe it was just my imagination.

Still, as we bounced out through the barrier of the laurel tangle to the highway, it was hard not to wonder, just a little.

Aaron Leopold and Nick Valessio. Is there any chance at all that it might actually have been you back there? Could this be the sentence handed down when you couldn't beat the rap at the last big trial? Three to five eternities hard time, chained to the spot where you were betrayed and killed by your partner?

As we turned onto 66, I thought I caught a last lonely flicker of yellow-white light in my rearview mirror.

Good luck with the parole board, guys.

We lay over for the night in Vinita. I conned a price reduction on a couple of side-by-side units out of a grandmotherly motel keeper. (I'm taking my fiancée home to meet my parents.) She did make a point, however, of making sure the connecting door was locked. I humored her.

While Lisette soaked contentedly in the bathtub, I yelled in to her that I was stepping out for a cigarette. And, in fact, I did light up as I waited for the long-distance operator to put me through to California.

Jack wasn't home. However, Sheila, his wife, was. She told me to, for God's sake, call the office on the double. I dropped another dime and went through the routine with long distance one more time.

"Jesus, kid, where are you? You okay?" the Bear's voice roared out of the earpiece.

"Oklahoma, and yeah, I'm fine. What's going on? How come you're still downtown?"

"Captain Faraday ordered me not to leave this desk until I'd gotten a report in from you."

"The captain! Aw, Jesus, Jack! I wasn't ready to go to the captain with this thing! I'm just starting to get it pieced together out here!"

"Hell, kid, I didn't have any choice in the matter. You were about two seconds away from having an all points bulletin put out on your head."

I hurled my half-smoked smoke to the ground with my free hand. "What's the deal, Jack? What's going on?"

"This morning the captain came out of his office breathing fire and asking what in the hell my crazy punk kid partner was doing back in Saint Louis!"

"How'd he find out?"

"A real hot rocket that came in over the wire from the East Saint Louis PD. It seems like yesterday some hotshot who matches your description was going around flashing an LA County star and asking a whole lot of questions about a local citizen named Calvin Reece."

"Yeah, we looked this guy up. So what about it?"

"So, early this morning Calvin Reece was found shot to death in the alley behind his bar."

OKLAHOMA

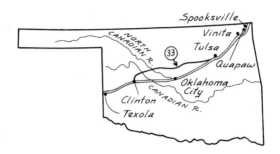

*The road for the next 100 miles is good: with wide
shoulders, generally grassy. The hills are low, the countryside almost flat with patches of wood . . .*

The connecting door between the rooms swung open, its old
Yale lock yielding more quickly and quietly to my knife blade
than it would to its own key. I stood stock-still for a full three
minutes, giving the occupant of the bed plenty of chance to
slip back into a deep sleep.

During that time, I indulged myself, studying Lisette in the
faint light that glowed in through the room's curtains. It was
a warm night and she lay bare, a single sheet drawn up to the
smooth curve of her hips and her arms curled around one of
her pillows, cuddling it to her chest. Her tousled ponytail was
looped around her throat, and her face held a relaxed innocence
I had rarely seen when she was awake and coping with her
world.

The empty expanse of bed beside her looked awfully good,
too.

When we'd said good night, I'd mentally mapped out the position of all of her possessions within the motel unit, as well as its furnishings. Now it took me only three silent sock-footed steps to reach and retrieve her shoulder bag.

Back in my unit, I sprawled on the bed and went through the Rittenhouse guide, page by page, looking for where Johnny 32 Kingman had written. "Here's where I buried the loot."

Nothing, or at least nothing I could recognize as important yet. As Lisette had pointed out, there were mileages and notations, stars and check marks, all of which must have meant something to a man ten years in his grave but didn't mean anything to me.

There had to be another part to this. And shit, sure there was! She was sleeping next door right now. Lisette had lived inside this thing all her life. She said she'd been asking questions, digging up old stories. She must be able to look into this book and see things that I couldn't.

Then again, maybe not. Maybe Lisette was running blind herself, hoping the pieces would come together as we got farther west along her father's trail.

Granted that the girl next door really was Lisette Kingman in the first place. Jack's trace on Lisette was still dead-ending. Officially, the paper trail on Lisette Marie Kingman began with her birth in a Chicago hospital and ended when her mother had carried her out of the door.

Damn it! What had happened to the other twenty years of her life? What had put the demon I had seen this afternoon inside her and was there any way to get it out again?

Damn it all entirely.

I slid the girl's art pad out of its pocket in the shoulder bag and flipped it open, studying the additions she had made today.

It was turning into a visual log of our journey. There was a simple landscape that contrasted the lifeless elephant backs of the chat heaps with the verdant growth of the scrub woods. There was an outline sketch of the old stone mansion library in Baxter Springs and another of Claster's one-horse service station. There was also a drawing of the '57.

She'd made a couple of false starts on that one. I don't think Lisette had done many car studies before. But in the end, just as she did with people, she'd caught the essence of the machine. The cock of the half-turned front wheels was just right. Also the subtle angle of the upsweep of the tail fins. I wondered how I could con this drawing out of her without giving away the fact that I had been snooping in her stuff.

And on the last page . . . Damn, was that supposed to be me? I never look that good to myself when I stare into the shaving mirror in the morning. Thanks for the compliment, pretty girl, but I think you've got a little too much Prince Valiant in there.

This wasn't getting me anywhere. I returned the guidebook and sketch pad to her shoulder bag and quietly returned it to her room, taking one more moment for myself to look at the slender form curled on the bed.

I left the door between the units unlocked. I had to start covering her better. I couldn't take the chance of Spanno getting her alone, whoever she might be.

Suddenly the motel room seemed unbearably hot and stuffy. I tucked the Commander back into my belt and turned out the reading lamp by the bed. Then I stepped out through the unit's door into the motel's central court.

The '57 dozed in her parking slot in front of our rooms, her paint dulled in the moonlight by an accumulating layer of road dust. I quietly promised her a wash job just as soon as the rush was over, and I leaned back against her fender.

The motel and the town slept. Even 66 was quiet at one in the morning, the traffic stretching out to one or two tire-whispering passages a minute. Across the highway, a cluster of fireflies danced defiantly in the treetops, refusing to believe in the coming first frost. I lit up a Lucky and flashed an acknowledgment to them with its glowing tip.

If there was anything at all good about this thoroughly screwed up situation, it was that I wasn't losing any more vacation time. As of now, I was officially back on the county payroll. The death of John Kingman had ridden on the books for the past ten years as a cold case. But the books never get closed all the way on murder.

By a freak set of circumstances I'd stumbled across a trail that might lead to the resolution of four killings that had taken place a decade ago. And maybe to a fifth barely twenty-four hours old.

Captain Faraday had reluctantly agreed to let Jack and me play this thing out for a while. I was way the hell out of my jurisdiction here and running without any backup. On the other hand, I was the only cop in the right place at the right time to maybe break this case open.

I'd flow with the investigation, seeing where it would lead and collecting the evidence as it came along. I'd report back to Jack, and when the time felt right we'd call in the local law to make the arrests. I'd worked solo undercover operations like this before, and that's how I'd work this one now.

The thing is, most cops who die in the line of duty generally die when they're alone. And brother, I was alone out here, alone except for a girl who carried a big load of secrets around with her.

I took another drag and exhaled. Somewhere out there, a fast black car was running through the night. In it were three men who had taken the life of Calvin Reece as a testament, a pledge to the will and desires of Mace Spanno. Spanno wanted the money and the girl, and he was willing to pay a blood price for them.

He must be putting the pieces together the same way we were, remembering the past and following the trail of his late partners down Route 66. We knew he was out there, and he knew we were out here. And sooner or later, we'd cross.

I flipped my dying smoke onto the pavement. I didn't pray for Calvin Reece, but if he was out there anywhere in the dark,

I wished him well. I also promised that I'd try and make things even with the guys who had iced him. I figured that was the kind of religion he'd appreciate.

I hope he got at least one good punch in before they put him down.

We'd knocked off the hundred and fifty miles to Oklahoma City in the cool of the morning, slowed some by our passage through Tulsa and by the Friday traffic flow between Oklahoma's two big towns. The brushy hardwood forest that had cloaked the land ever since Saint Louis was growing ragged, the patches of pasture and cultivation growing larger the farther west we went, heralding the return of the prairie. With the concrete rolling away beneath her willing tires, the '57 pulled Oke City in over the horizon.

"The guidebook have anything to say about Oklahoma City, Princess?" I asked, slaloming us around an elderly and laboring Plymouth.

"Yep," she replied, sliding over closer to me on the car seat. "It does. There are the usual notations about a car agency and a hospital and so forth, and one special one. See?"

I moved the book and her hand down out of my face in time to avoid the looming back end of a Greyhound bus. "I'll take your word for it. What's it say?"

"Just three letters: WRK. In capitals and underlined three times."

"WRK? What the hell does that mean?"

Lisette frowned and shook her head. "I have no idea. There's no other entry like it anywhere else in the book."

"Think we should have a look around?"

She nodded. "Yes, I think this might be something important. Do you still have your friend with the Ouija board?"

"I'll see if he's home."

We passed a sign reading: OKLAHOMA CITY BUSINESS LOOP 2 MILES.

*   *   *

I apologize, Sir Arthur. If Sherlock has a little free time on his hands, we could sure use him in Oklahoma City about now. After a long hot afternoon, we'd hit a blank wall. Hell, we'd damn near beaten ourselves to death against it.

WRK underlined, something that meant something important to John Kingman. No phone number. No attached address. I'd tried all of the standard investigative techniques. We'd hit the city library and gone through the old phone books and city directories, trying to connect the three letters up with some business or company name. We'd found a few matches, too, but why Johnny 32 might have had a sudden overwhelming need for a bakery or a shoe store in the middle of Oklahoma was beyond us.

We'd gone through the newspaper files, trying to match the letters up with some event or noteworthy person within that time frame. That had turned up nothing outstanding. We'd checked out the phone book. There were all sorts of matchups there. A lot of people live in Oklahoma City. Too many. What do you do, dial up Mr. Walter Richard Klausburg and ask him if he'd numbered a well-known Chicago gunman among his acquaintances ten years ago?

I even checked to see if the letters *WRK* might have been the call sign of a radio station broadcasting out of Oklahoma City in 1947. They weren't. We ended up cruising the city streets to see if anything might leap out at us. Nothing did.

In the end, we parked the '57 beneath the shade trees of a small neighborhood park. Sprawling on the grass, we listened to the sprinklers hiss and considered our options.

"Let's work on the *K* again," I said, staring up at the sky. "It's the last of the letters; it could be the initial for your last name. Did your dad have any relations who might have lived out this way? Any Kingmans at all."

"Like I said about four hours ago, none that I ever heard of." Lisette lay on her stomach a couple of feet away, her flats kicked off, her sketch pad open in front of her, and a grass stem tucked in the corner of her frowning mouth.

"How about your mother?"

"Mom was from northern Italy. She didn't have any family in this country." Lisette picked up her pad and aimed a sketch in my direction. "What do you think?"

I glanced across at it. "Shorten the skirt."

"This is supposed to be a business suit. No woman is ever going to buy a business suit with a skirt that comes up to midthigh."

"Sounds like a good idea to me."

"Men!" Lisette flipped the pad shut and rolled over on her back, mimicking my position. "This isn't getting us anywhere."

"It doesn't seem to be," I agreed.

"Maybe this *WRK* thing isn't important after all."

"But maybe it is. You thought so this morning."

"I know I did."

"So what do we do next? You're the boss."

"Damn it, Kevin!" She yanked herself up into a sitting position angrily. "I know I'm the boss . . . and I admit it. I don't know what to do next."

I came up on one arm. "You open for suggestions?"

"Yes."

"Then let's get back on the road. You're right: maybe this *WRK* notation isn't such a big deal after all. Or maybe we can do without it. Either way, it's not good for us to hang around any one place for too long."

She nodded. "You're right. It's not good a idea at all." She flipped her notepad shut and reached for her shoes. "Mace will be after us, Kev. I know it."

Damn straight. So did I.

I got to my feet and offered her a hand up. She accepted it, offering a thank-you smile in exchange.

Her hand felt good. Why is it that the feminine thermostat is set differently than that of the male? A girl's skin is always about ten pleasant degrees cooler or warmer than her surrounding environment, depending on the season.

It also felt good to fire the '57 up with the intent of moving on. Oklahoma City was starting to feel itchy, kind of like a bad patrol zone along the DMZ or a dark alley in Long Beach. I heard a rattle and a rumble coming up behind me and caught movement in my rearview mirror. I hesitated before pulling out into the traffic stream to let the truck pass.

There wasn't anything much remarkable about the vehicle. A massive and grimy ex-army deuce and a half, loaded down with a tangle of rusty appliances, scrap pipe, and crumpled bicycle frames. Some junk dealer headed out to the local . . .

"WRECKING YARD!"

It was right out beside 66 on the city loop, right where any inbound traveler would see it first thing. We'd driven straight past the place without making the connection. Twenty acres of scrap, the handling cranes lifting above the expanse of rusting and crumpled metal like the necks of a pack of browsing dinosaurs.

The yard crew had knocked off for the day, and the small office parking lot was almost empty as we got out. There was all of the usual stuff beyond the chain-link fences: metallic city junk, girders and plumbing from demolished buildings, old cars. I winced at the sight of what had been the perfectly good body of a '32 Ford five-window, crushed under a stack of lesser automotive corpses.

The yard had a few specialty clients as well. We were in oil country, and apparently this was where old drilling rigs came to die. There were miles of battered piping and casing, piles of rusty valve and pressure heads, and a row of old stacking towers, lying over on their sides like steel Christmas trees in some giant's off-season lot.

"What in the heck could your dad have wanted here?" I asked.

"I haven't the faintest idea," Lisette replied, coming to lean beside me against the '57's fender. "I don't suppose it would do any good to try and ask around?"

"For what was probably a onetime stop ten years ago? I doubt it." I crossed my arms and shook my head. "We'll have to figure this one out ourselves."

"If this is actually what he meant," Lisette brooded.

Hello, wall. Fancy meeting you again.

"Anything I can help you folks with?"

A man came out of the small office building behind us. He wasn't the kind of guy you'd generally associate with a junk-yard. Lean, neat, and on the short side, in his fifties, his hair and precisely trimmed mustache were gray as were his (my God, were they pressed?) JCPenney's work shirt and pants. Shrewd-looking brown eyes glinted out from under a canvas fishing hat.

" 'Bout to lock up here," he said, "but if there's anything special you need?"

Lisette hesitated and then got her purse out of the front seat. "Maybe. Have you worked here long?"

"Ever since the war. Took the job when Tom Jardine went off with the Air Corps. Tom never come back, so I kept on here at the office. There a problem?"

Lisette held out her father's picture. "This probably sounds awfully funny, but by any chance, do you remember this man? He might have come through here a long time ago.?"

The old-timer glanced down at the picture and studied it for a moment. "He did. Around ten years ago or thereabouts. An easterner. City man. Good-looking fella. What would you like to know about him, young lady?"

"It was the car that made it stick in my mind," Hawk Carby continued. He'd invited us in to the comparative cool of the wrecking yard office. Settling in a well-lived-in chair behind a battered but mathematically neat desk, he went on with his story. "Pretty damn thing. Bran'-new Lincoln coupe, cream-colored. One of those twelve-cylinder jobs. The boys here in the yard talked about it for a couple of days after. That was right after the war, and we were just starting to see new cars again. That and the suit.''

"The suit?'' Lisette prompted.

"Yep. You don't see many men poking around a scrapyard in a new suit. Pants of it, anyway. Left the jacket in the car, as I recall.''

It was my turn to prompt. "Can you remember what he was looking for?''

"Sure. Pipe. A chunk of three-inch-diameter oil line, oh, about yay long.'' Carby held his hands about four feet apart. "Threaded at both ends. I remember that 'cause he picked up a couple of end caps for it too.''

Lisette and I swapped glances. "He didn't say what he wanted it for, did he?'' she inquired.

"I didn't ask and I don't recall him saying. We mostly handle bulk metal here, but every once in a while we get some fella coming through looking for some little bit of junk or another. Boss lets us sell 'em off out of the office here for coffee and doughnut money.'' The yard man nodded toward a massive chrome coffee urn in the corner. "Just not too many of them drive Lincolns or wear suits.''

I swore I'd never play poker again. In finding this guy I think I might have used up my entire quota of good luck for the rest of my life. "Okay, did he pick up anything else while he was here?''

Carby considered methodically. "Yeah, he did. We had an old shed out there then with a bunch of stuff in it. He looked around some and got a jar of some kind of old grease or something. Axle grease, I guess. Got some of it on his shirt, but he didn't seem to give a damn. And I think an old bucket of red lead. Paid two dollars for the whole shootin' match. I wasn't going to argue.''

Things were coming together in my mind real fast now. I nodded to Lisette. We had what we needed. I flipped open my wallet and stuffed a couple of bills into the coin-loaded coffee mug beside the urn. "For you and the crew, okay? Thanks a lot. You've been a big help to us. You don't know how much."

"No problem, son." And no more. The old gent had been born and bred in a country where excessive curiosity was considered bad manners.

We started to leave, but his voice caught us halfway to the door.

"I just couldn't do it."

Lisette bumped up against me as I looked back toward the desk. Carby was looking off toward the office wall reminiscently. "He wanted me to just dump all that dirty junk into that Lincoln's trunk, but I just couldn't do it. I had to put down some newspapers first. *Pretty* damn thing!"

We mounted up and I moved the '57 out of the yard's parking lot. But I pulled over at the first turnout along the road, thinking hard.

"Well?" Lisette demanded.

"We know what we're looking for, Princess. And we know a lot more about where we should be looking."

"You think so?" she asked excitedly, coming up to kneel on the car seat beside me.

"I'm sure so. Look; we know what your dad must have been thinking when he hid the money. He was on the run, and that much cash is hard to run with. It's bulky, you run the risk of getting separated from it, and man, does it attract attention."

"Uh-huh?"

"So he caches it somewhere safe. That frees him up for running. It also gives him a bargaining chip, just in case the law or his ex-partners ever nail him. And if things really screw up for him, maybe he can get word about it back to you and your mother."

"That's all obvious. What does that have to do with a piece of old pipe?"

I looked over into her face. "That's his strongbox, Princess. Durable, plenty of room to stow the dough in, and it won't attract a lot of attention even if somebody falls over it."

Lisette nodded, thinking now just as hard as I was.

"It's watertight, too," I went on. "That's what the axle grease was for, to seal the cap threads. He was planning to stash it out-of-doors or somewhere else exposed to the elements, probably somewhere near the highway where he could get at it fast."

I swear to God, I saw it happen. Something clicked behind Lisette's eyes, and all of a sudden at least one person in this world knew where Johnny 32 had hidden his last big score.

Very carefully she looked away from me and sat back into her seat. "That's good," she said after a moment. "At least we've got something to go on."

"Yeah," I replied with equal care, popping the '57 back into gear.

We both scrambled frantically back from the thin edge of excessive truth.

There must have been something in the Rittenhouse guide, some clue that I must have just bumped over. But Lisette had made some kind of connection that made sense to her. And no, she wasn't going to tell me about it yet. I couldn't blame her much, either. She'd been playing with a junk hand for a long time. Now, at long damn last, she had a fighting card to call her own. She wasn't going to be casual about throwing that away.

Like her dad, this girl was smart. And like her dad, she was going to hold on to the money's location, just in case she needed a bargaining chip, too.

I wondered if, unlike her dad, it would do her any good.

As in Baxter Springs, we'd finished up in Oklahoma City at the drag end of the day. We could still make some miles that evening, though, and that itchy feeling about this town was coming back. I treated the '57 to a load of gas and a quart of Pennzoil, and we cut back through town. Weaving through the tail end of the going-home traffic, we planned on grabbing a fast burger on the way west.

"Kev, what's red lead?" Lisette asked. She lounged, frowning, with one arm over the passenger-side door. Obviously still doing a lot of thinking.

"A kind of heavy-duty paint," I replied absently.

"I wonder what he'd want paint for?"

"Well, just as a guess, I'd say to paint something with."

"That I could guess, goopy! But what?"

"Probably to mark where he hid the money."

Lisette rolled her eyes. "Oh, sure! I can see the sign now: 'Two hundred thousand dollars buried here. Please keep off.' "

"I'm serious, Princess." I flipped my right hand off the wheel for a second. "Out here in the West there are about ten million and one stories about the outlaws who knocked off a hot stagecoach and went to hide the loot somewhere. They stuck it in a cave or a hollow tree or some damn place, figuring on coming back later to divide it up. Only when they do try to go back they find that there's been a flood or a range fire or something and they never can find the spot again."

"That's just *Death Valley Days* stuff, isn't it?"

"No. It's happened out here. We're getting on toward the high plains now, and that country can fool you. Given your dad had the brains God gave a groundhog, he'd have planned on marking his hiding spot in some way that wouldn't mean anything to anyone else but would stand out for him."

Suddenly I realized that I'd lost my audience. Lisette had gone absolutely rigid in her seat, staring into the rearview mirror. Her expression was that of someone who had felt a sting on her leg and looked down to find a coiled copperhead and a couple of bloody fang marks.

"Oh my God," she whispered. "He's found us."

I didn't fool with the mirror. I twisted around and looked back.

There was a hearse black 300-C Chrysler riding our rear bumper like it was chained there.

"We're okay," I said.

"He's found us!" There was a rising shrillness in her voice.

"We are okay!" I reached out and grabbed her left wrist, giving her something outside her panic to anchor to. It worked. My grip broke the past's hold on her. She came back into herself, scared but functioning.

"How, Kev? How did he track us down?"

"Damned if I know. They must have been following us down 66, and we stayed long enough in one place for them to catch up. To hell with that, however. We're going to have to bust loose from them again."

"That won't be easy."

Tell me about it, Princess. My eyes kept flicking to my rearview mirror. I could make out Nate Temple and Randy Bannerman in front, Bannerman driving. Behind them, in the Chrysler's backseat, was a third, more massive silhouette.

I knew what he was trying to do. Over the last couple of days I'd started to piece together a working image of Mace Spanno. The man was a blunt object. Intimidation and threat were his stock-in-trade. A cagier character might have tried to trail us to an ambush site. Not Mr. Spanno, though. He moved straight on in, trying to bluff us into surrendering or panic us into doing something stupid. If we tried to run, he'd chase. If we stopped, he'd take us.

Not today, buddy. Not today.

"We're okay, Princess," I repeated.

I refocused my attention on the road ahead. Route 66 was one of the main drags through Oklahoma City, and along the magic mile road businesses fronted on the highway. Pallid neon promotions for motels, bars, and restaurants were flicking on in response to the fading day.

Traffic was dropping off as well. However, there were still enough people on the streets and sidewalks to keep Spanno and company from trying anything too flagrant, like waving hardware around or forcing us into the curb. I wouldn't put a boarding action past them, though, especially if we got pinned down at a light. I looked ahead for the next set of traffic signals.

I spotted the next intersection, and I also spotted something else. It took only about half a block for the entire plan to come together and gel. Suddenly I was grinning like an idiot.

"What's wrong?" Lisette asked.

"Not a thing, Princess. You know, in a situation like this, there's only one thing for us to do."

"What's that?"

"Have dinner."

I whipped the '57's wheel hard to the right without signaling. Our tires chirped in protest as we made the turn, wheeling into the driveway I'd targeted. Braking hard, I blocked the path in over the curb. Behind us, the Chrysler's rubber squawked as Spanno's wheelman instinctively slowed to avoid a collision. Horns blared behind them and the traffic flow shouldered the black coupe on past before its occupants could react.

Phase one complete.

"Kev, what are we doing?" Lisette demanded.

"We are going to drive ol' Mace totally screaming out of his mind," I replied, rolling us into the drive-in restaurant that was going to be our bomb shelter.

It was a warm summer's evening and a Friday at that. And the joint, as the saying goes, was jumping. It was a nice place, an art deco classic belonging to the old Texas Pig Stand chain, its name climbing a tower above the central restaurant. A whole horde of vehicles were trying to squeeze in beneath the aluminum sunshades that radiated out from the circular building.

I got lucky and a slot opened up just as I circled through the parking area. I swung the '57 into it, easing her into place between a sleek Lincoln green Rebel Cruiser and a veteran Dodge pickup truck that carried more rust on its fenders than paint.

"Kevin, you're the one who's gone out of his mind!" Lisette managed to scream in a whisper, an interesting effect. "Mace has found us!"

"I know he has. And that's why we're stopping here." I lifted my hands off the steering wheel and killed the engine. "Just cool your jets and look around. What's he gonna do?"

She picked up on it then. There might be a busier spot in Oklahoma City, but you'd have a hard time naming what it might be. Every parking slot in the lot had a car in it. There were a few youthful families treating the children to a night on the town, but mostly it was the high school crowd. The town and country kids were gearing up for the weekend. A steady stream of cruisers circled through the lot, making the scene before going out to drag Main. More kids jammed the inside booths or sat at the white-painted picnic tables lined up on the center strip beneath the sunshades. All local, happy, and young.

"Get it? What's he gonna do? He and his goon squad would stand out in this crowd like nuns in a nudist camp. He'd have an easier time snatching you off the stage of the Hollywood Bowl during a Liberace concert."

Lisette's tension eased as she realized that, yeah, we were okay, its release taking the form of a short, quasi-hysterical giggle. "I guess you're right."

"Damn right I'm right. We'll just fort up here for a while." I dialed in to the local Top 40s station, merging our speakers in with the ad-hoc open-air stereo of ranked car radios. "So Rare," Jimmy Dorsey and his last-gasp salute to the big bands. "Now, sit back, relax, and look cool. We got this wired."

The drive-in had one of those newfangled intercom ordering systems, and I reached out and punched the button.

"Whachaunt?" a filtered Oklatexan drawl inquired back.

I remembered my Southron cuisine from the days when Dad had been working down at this end of the GM&O line. "A couple of pig sandwiches, shoestrings, and a couple of Wacos."

"Y'all got it, partner."

"What in the world did you just order?" Lisette asked, curiosity overwhelming her edginess.

"Barbecued pork sandwiches, French fries, and a couple of Dr. Peppers. It's a regional institution down here. You'll love it."

You know something funny? I felt pretty good. Oh yeah, I did have a pack of proven killers sitting out there on my tail, but I still felt pretty good. I suspected strongly that we, or at least Lisette, now had the tip that could lead us to the money. I wasn't quite sure when she might be willing to share the word on that, but at least she'd keep us aimed in the right direction.

And as for Mr. Spanno, well, like I said, I had a plan.

A minute later the Chrysler reappeared, looping back around the block to pick us up again, a black steel barracuda swimming past in the street. Nate Temple, Spanno's lieutenant, rode shotgun in the front seat, his head turning continuously, watching for trouble. The big man himself was at the coupe's rear window, those cold, cold eyes tracking us as they drove past. God, how it must have galled him to be rendered so impotent by a bunch of cheerleaders and farm boys.

I saw Lisette shiver under that gaze. Very deliberately, I extended my arm along the seat back and slipped it around her shoulders, gathering her close. It was a move for her and for him. I was throwing it right back in Spanno's face. *Yeah, you asshole. I got her, and what are you going to do about it?*

A childish gesture? I guess it was. But then a lot of the moves people make in this world seem kind of childish at times. Why should I be any different?

To another blare of horns, the Chrysler whipped into a U-turn. It parked at the curb across the intersection from us, positioned so that its passengers could keep both of the drive-in's exits under observation. They were going to wait us out.

"I hate him," Lisette whispered. "Oh, how I hate him!"

Her soft words were a weird contrast to the laughter and light music that saturated the dusky evening around us. It seemed to wall us away in a cool little room inside the '57.

"Do you know for sure he's the guy who killed your dad?" I asked.

I was already sure of it myself, but it seemed like a good lead-in for another probe into her past.

"In my heart I am. Mace never said so, never in so many words. But I could feel it. And beyond that, he gave us so many other reasons to hate him."

"Us?"

"My mother and I. But she started to hate too late. She could never do anything with it."

Despite the warmth of the evening, Lisette nestled into me slightly, as if she was cold. I've done enough interrogation work to sense the door opening. She was all the way back in her past: open, vulnerable. I could take advantage of that now and make a note to feel shitty about it later.

"What happened to your mom, Princess? You told me once that she was dead."

The girl nodded, not taking her eyes off the parked Chrysler. "She is. They were polite about it and they didn't call it suicide, just an 'accidental death.' Too many sleeping pills and too much alcohol.

"And they were right. She wouldn't have left me alone. She knew what would happen. Mom just wanted to get away from the hurt and the hopelessness for a while, and she went too far and couldn't get back. It wasn't her fault. It was mine. I wasn't fast enough. I didn't get this set up in time."

That dumb-ass pat phrase, "it wasn't your fault," was at the back of my throat, and I choked it back down. "What are you talking about? You mean about tracking down the money?"

"Yes. I was going to use it to get us away. We'd managed it once before when Mace was sent to prison for a while. Mom and I got as far as Cleveland. It wasn't easy. We didn't have much money, but we managed." A little ghost of a sad smile touched Lisette's face. "Mom found a job in a restaurant, and I went to a regular high school. We were almost like real people."

She took a deep shuddering breath. "But Mace got out and found us. That's when I got serious about trying to learn about the money my father had taken. With it we could have run so far and so fast that he never could have found us again."

All of a sudden a pretty blonde carhop bustled up with a loaded tray, popping the bubble of isolation that had formed around us. Lisette and I both jumped a little, and I had to fumble with my wallet. The hop's eyes widened as I tossed her a five spot and told her to keep the change. To hell with that now; I wanted to get back to Lisette and her story.

It was too late. The moment of vulnerability was gone. I was a little surprised when the Princess accepted the sandwich and drink I passed her. Then I saw the anger in her eyes. She was back in full possession of herself, refusing to let the man in the black car deny her even her own appetite.

"That's why this money's so important," I said, trying to start the talk cycle again. "It'll let you get a life away from Spanno."

She shook her head. "No. That was the plan when my mother was alive."

"So what's the plan now?"

"I'm going to have him killed," she replied matter-of-factly.

I was the one who suddenly lost my interest in food. "You are shitting me, right?"

Lisette shrugged and shook her head again. "Not at all. I tried doing it myself once, but it was no good. Mace is fast and tough and smart. It will take a pro to do the job. Besides, I like the idea of his own stinking pack turning on him and tearing him to pieces. That will be justice." There was a cold satisfaction in her voice as she savored the thought.

"Do you know how to set it up?"

She arched her eyebrow at me and took a bite out of her sandwich. "I'm the daughter of a Chicago gangster," she replied after a moment. "I've lived in their world all of my life, and I've learned a few things. I know who I need to contact, and I know how I want to arrange it."

Again that cold satisfaction crept into her voice. "A ninety-thousand-dollar open contract on the head of Mace Spanno. And a ten-thousand-dollar bonus if you can prove to me that he died screaming." She took another deliberate bite of her sandwich.

We have a whole new ball game here, sports fans. I stared across at the faces in the black Chrysler, who were busy staring back at us. If she got hold of that 100 Gs, Spanno was going to find some of the best hit men in the world lining up in his back alley, matching nickels to see who got the first shot.

I was dreading the answer I might get for this next question. "Does he know about this new plan of yours?"

She nodded again. "I'm afraid so," she replied quietly. "One night, while he was standing over the bed, I screamed it right in his face."

Fan . . . damn . . . tastic! And if Spanno knew this girl at all, he'd know that she meant it. When someone like Lisette says that she's going to kill you with that kind of intensity, you'd better start picking out your casket lining.

The big man wasn't just greedy. He was scared.

"Who is he, Princess? What the hell is he to you?" I had to ask it.

"No!" She shook her head decisively, her ponytail brushing lightly against my arm. "Don't ask me that, Kevin. When Mace Spanno dies, a whole part of my life dies with him. It will be gone and no one is ever going to be able to remind me of it again."

Time passed, the evening darkened, the neon buzzed, and the standoff continued.

"We can't stay here forever, Kev," Lisette said, "and if we try to leave, they'll be right behind us. I hope you have some kind of plan to get us out of here."

"I do, and it's in full swing even as we speak."

"Excuse me, Mr. Pulaski, but you don't seem to be doing anything."

"That just goes to show you how appearances can be deceiving. I happen to be sitting here awaiting developments . . . and here comes one up the street right now."

My development took the form of a black-and-white Ford Fairlane sedan with a set of flashers on its roof and an Oklahoma City Police badge on its door. Twenty minutes before, I'd seen it make a pass west on the arterial. Now it was sweeping back in the other direction.

Only this time, as it approached the parked 300-C it slowed down. I couldn't see into the shadows beneath the Ford's roof, but I could tell that the cruiser crew was giving the Chrysler the eye.

"Ha!" I slapped the '57's steering wheel. "God, I am proud of myself! Stand by; we're going to be taking off in just a minute."

I kicked over the engine, warming it up.

The police cruiser was back. Circling the block, it made another slow run past the 300-C. This time I could make out the cruiser's observer speaking into his radio mike.

So could some other people. As soon as the police car was clear, smoke jetted from the Chrysler's exhausts and its headlights flicked on. Signaling, Spanno's car sedately pulled out into traffic, rolling east well below the speed limit. The Oklahoma City cruiser went to the curb to let the black coupe pass, then pulled back out again, trailing the 300 down the street.

The second they were out of sight, I switched on my headlights and honked the horn, calling for a fast tray pickup.

Totally lost, Lisette watched the brief automotive ballet. "What did I miss?" she demanded. "What just happened?"

"Just what I knew was going to happen, eventually, when I pulled in here," I replied, backing us out. "It's a Friday evening and this place is popular with the local kids. I noticed the hot rods turning in here as we came up the street. The local beat cops always keep an eye out for trouble at joints like this on a weekend."

"But Mace and his people were just sitting there. They weren't doing anything."

"Three older men in an out-of-state car loitering around a teenagers' hangout at night? That would spell trouble to any street cop in the world. It's too much to hope for that Spanno might have any wants and warrants out on his personal wheels, but I bet that cruiser will stay on his tail clear to the edge of its patrol sector. By the time Mace and his boys get back here, we'll be long gone."

But not on the highway.

One of our problems was that we were stuck with being linear. Everywhere we needed to go and everything we needed to know was strung out along Route 66 like a string of beads. Spanno obviously knew this and could use it. No matter how often we might shake him off, he could either just catch up to us or blow past and wait for us to catch up with him.

Tonight, though, we might be able to do an end-round.

I took us out on a northbound Oklahoma City arterial, riding it beyond the city limits until it became a county road, crossing over the 66-bypass loop and the Santa Fe tracks that paralleled them. Only then did I start looking for a turn west.

We were out on the true prairie now. The only trees that remained either grew along the stream banks or clumped protectively around the scattering of homesteads. Grazing land and fall-turned fields stretched out toward a widening horizon. This was farming and ranching country, and there's always a set of back roads. Maybe they aren't detailed on any map, but they'll get you to where you're going. You just have to be a little patient and not mind doing some winding around.

It was beyond sundown as we went on our way. At first on pavement, then on gravel, and then just on graded blood-colored dirt. The red dust in the hard-packed ruts of the road muffled the rumble of the '57's tires. Swirled up by our passage, it glowed double scarlet in the ruddy flare of our taillights.

Ahead, an occasional rabbit scurried across the tunnel blasted in the darkness by our headlights. And once, a coyote crouched in the dried grass beyond the ditch, its eyes burning golden.

I navigated by my dashboard compass, occasionally having to divert and cast along a north–south cross road until I could find another stretch heading west again. To the south we could occasionally make out the cars on Route 66 or the big headlamp of a train running on the rails beside it.

Eventually, though, our course angled us away from the interstate, leaving only the lights of an occasional farmhouse to remind us that we weren't alone under the black and empty sky.

After a while, we ran out of farmhouses, too.

The only radio stations we could pick up were the big "skip" stations that cranked up their power after sunset. Meant for the long-haul truckers and other such lonely travelers in the night, they were country western mostly. Bonnie Guitar's cool contralto serenaded us on our way with "Dark Moon."

On toward midnight, a solid line of cottonwoods cut across our path, marking the flow of the North Canadian River. We swung north, running parallel to its course. After a while, I found a trace of a turnoff leading down toward the water. Slowly, I eased the '57 into the overgrown ruts and we bumped into the deeper shadows beneath the trees.

Our headlights swept over the leaning and overgrown ruin of what had been a small house and a collapsed pile of lumber that might have been a barn. Someone had tried to make a stand here once, some farm family with a dream of making it on a place of their own. Likely they hadn't been able to make it through that grim time back in the 1930s when the skies and the banks both had dried up. They'd been dusted out, and no one had ever come back to try again. All that was left was this little clearing, marked by the tire tracks of the occasional local who used it as a turnaround or a fishing access.

I shut Car down and clicked off her lights. Silence except for the ticking of the engine as it started to cool and the chuckle of the North Canadian flowing beyond the tree line.

"Why are we stopping?" Lisette asked, her voice instinctively going to a whisper.

"To spend the night," I said, popping my door open.

"Here? You're kidding?"

"That's just the way I hope old Mace is thinking at the moment," I replied, climbing out of the car. "He's a city boy, and he thinks town. Right now, I'm betting that he's either back there taking Oklahoma City apart looking for us or tear-assing up 66 on what he thinks is our tail. The one place I doubt he'll look is out here in the boondocks. Even if he did, there ain't no way in hell he's going to find us."

Just to make sure, though, I took my old crook-tubed army flashlight out from under the seat and walked back up to the road. From the turnout I played the light toward where we'd parked, checking for any glint of chrome or glass that might be visible through the brush. There wasn't any.

I was willing to bet that it was impossible for anyone to have followed us here. I hadn't seen a set of headlights behind us for the past ten miles. On the other hand, sometimes it pays to make sure that the impossible really can't happen. I took one more long last look back along the road. Just in case.

When I returned to the car, Lisette was standing beside it, gazing up at the sky. "Oh, look at all the stars!" she said with all the awe of a little kid at her first fireworks display.

I glanced up as I came to stand beside her. "Yeah, that *is* somethin'. But wait until we get a little farther west on the high desert. You won't believe it. Sometimes, when we're running time trials out at El Mirage, we sleep beside our cars out on the dry lake bed. You look up and you don't think that there's a number big enough for all the stars you can see."

That brought Lisette's attention back to more immediate concerns. "Uh, where are we going to sleep?" she asked cautiously, crossing her arms and looking around. "There's only one sleeping bag, isn't there?"

"Yeah, and it's yours. And in return for that gentlemanly sacrifice, I'm claiming the backseat. Either you can take the front seat or I can put a tarp down on the ground beside the car and you can stretch out on that. The smart money for a good night's sleep would be the ground."

I saw Lisette uneasily eye the seriously black shadows under the trees. "But aren't there snakes and stuff like that around here?" she asked.

I had to nod. "That does sort of come with the territory, yeah."

"I'll take the front seat."

There followed the inevitable Three Stooges minus one routine you get whenever two adult human beings try to bed down in a conventional automobile, for either sleep or recreation. It could have been worse, I guess. I only almost removed my kidney with the hammer spur of my pistol once, Lisette only got her foot caught in the horn ring of the wheel twice, and we only swore at each other three or four times apiece.

It's only in situations like this that I ever seriously consider buying a Rambler.

Finally, there was that last big mutual *flump* of positioning that indicates both parties have settled down into their least worst compromise for the night.

For me, that was with my feet over in the floor well on the passenger side and with my head propped back in the corner of the rear seat and the side panel. My B-4 bag on the floor beside me widened things out a little, and Lisette's wadded-up car coat made a pillow. It wasn't the plushest bed I'd ever slept on, but then it was a long way from the worst, either.

To make these kinds of accommodations work, you have to ignore the bad, like how my knees were already cramping up, and focus on the good, like the fresh prairie wind flowing in through the '57's half-open windows. I could smell the moistness of a dewfall starting. We wouldn't have to worry about rain tomorrow. And somewhere off in the distance, someone had gotten into an argument with a skunk.

I positioned the Commander on the rear window shelf a short grab away and pulled my leather jacket over me.

"Kev?"

"Yeah?"

"Will you be all right? Won't you get cold before morning?"

"I'll be fine. I've been to Korea. Cold doesn't count until your toes start to fall off."

"Oh, okay. Good night."

"Night, Princess."

I settled down to think myself to sleep. Okay, Pulaski, let's assume that we, or at least Lisette, do have a fix on the location of that money. What does that do for us?

Not a whole hell of a lot, really.

It was a major point on Lisette's agenda, but I couldn't see how it put me any closer to getting the goods on Spanno for Johnny Kingman's murder. Lisette had said that Spanno had never admitted in her presence that he had killed her father. She seemed to be running on instinct and circumstance, neither of which is worth a damn in a courtroom.

Maybe she had more, though. There were a whole lot of connections missing here. Lisette and Spanno were tied together in ways I didn't understand yet. She hated him for reasons way beyond just the death of her father. Maybe if I could only ask her the right questions I could get the right answers. The ones that would start Spanno on that last long walk to the gas chamber and stop Lisette from becoming a murderess in her own right.

The problem was, that would mean breaking cover. But hell, I was going to have to do that eventually anyway to recover the money.

Wasn't I?

The car rocked a little on its springs as the girl shifted in the front seat. "Kev?"

"Uh-huh?"

"Why do you call me Princess?"

"Because that's the first thing I thought of when I saw you back there at the Dixie. I'll knock it off if it bothers you."

"No. That's all right. I like it."

TEXAS

160 mi. (113 mi.) Cross TEXAS–OKLAHOMA STATE LINE. At once the road improves and a decorative stone marker welcomes you to this vast state . . .

The opening car door woke me. But a couple of quiet words from Lisette took the edge off the event, and I sprawled in a comfortably drowsy daze for a few minutes longer. Eventually, though, the sun in my face brought me fully back alive. Pulling myself upright in the backseat, I rubbed the grit out of my eyes and acknowledged the complaints being filed by assorted muscles and vertebrae.

The sky was cloudless and the growing heat of the morning stewed a cooking jam scent out of the blackberry tangles. Back up in the cottonwoods, the songbirds were expressing a lot of confidence in the new day.

Lisette wasn't in sight, but her shoulder bag and drawing pad lay on the front seat beside the wadded mass of the sleeping bag. Just for the hell of it, I reached over the seat back and scooped up the pad, flipping through to her latest entries.

Hm, she had fooled around with giving that suit a midthigh skirt. My, wouldn't that be an interesting development in the business world. But Lisette was right; women would never be that generous or men that lucky.

I turned the next page. A quick Hank Carby. Hi, old-timer. Thanks for the help yesterday, and may God bless you and that carved-in-granite memory of yours.

Lisette must have been awake for a while, because the next sketch was of the abandoned farmhouse across from us in the clearing. Its gaunt outline was shadowed heavily as it might have been seen in the early light of dawn.

And finally there was another of her quick portraits, a special one this time. I took a second to verify the identity of the smiling man from the photograph in Lisette's purse.

Hello, Johnny 32. I'm trying to take good care of your daughter, granted that's who she is. I hope you approve. I do wonder, though, why Lisette drew this row of question marks in under your picture.

I returned the photo and pad to their places. I felt kind of funny going through Lisette's sketches that way. There were bits of her thoughts, dreams, and emotions locked up on that paper, a kind of graphic diary. The thing was that there might also be some clues to the stack of mysteries that kept piling up in front of me. This morning, though, there were no answers, just more questions.

The intriguing sound of splashing started to come from

down toward the river. Getting out of the car, I followed the sounds to their source.

Finding a pretty girl's clothes lying discarded on the grass is one of the better ways to start your morning.

The lazily flowing stream hooked around the grove where we had spent the night. Lisette was out in a deep pool, joyfully discovering the simple kid pleasures of skinny-dipping in the creek. She didn't notice she'd gained an audience. The same intense morning light that danced fire off the ripples around her made the shade back under the trees inpenetrable. I hooked my thumbs into the belt loops of my jeans and leaned against a cottonwood trunk, savoring the chance to watch her as she played.

Oddly enough, sex didn't come into it, at least not at first. It was just kind of nice seeing her be so—I guess the word is innocent—for a little while. For this one moment she wasn't having to think about running or killing or dying. She wasn't having to think at all. She could just be happy enjoying the feel of the warm sun and the cool water on her skin.

Eventually, though, Lisette's casual nakedness began to catch up with me. The twinned curves of her pale, firm breasts as she stood waist-deep for a moment, the flash of her long, sweet legs as she dived forward, the flow of her dark wet hair down her back. Oh, yeah. The urge to stop watching and go down to her began to build fast, real fast.

But I didn't.

I was coming to realize that I'd started a strange and complicated dance with this girl. A number of different threads were getting tangled together here, and I had no idea where they all were leading yet or where they all would end. But I did know that I didn't want to risk a misstep. Not with her. Not for a lot of reasons.

I walked back to the parked '57. I needed to touch its cool steel. I needed something I could get a grip on.

I began to field-strip Car the same way I would my side arm. I checked all the fluid levels again, running the dipsticks between my fingers to feel for any traces of metal or gasket fragmentation, visually studying the oil for any hint of that chocolaty look that might mean coolant water contamination.

I checked and tightened the battery cable and hose clamps. I checked the cables and hoses for weak spots and worn insulation. I used a scrub brush on the radiator, clearing away the bug accumulation of the past few hundred miles and I checked the levels in the oil bath air cleaners.

Check the wheel lugs. Check the rubber for cuts or bulges. Check the brake cables and shift linkage and the suspension mounts. Check it all, brother, because we were going to the wars.

I'd gotten sloppy the last day or so, lax about the threat Mace Spanno might represent. He'd taken me by surprise last night and I couldn't afford to let that happen again.

A pair of slim ankles appeared at my eye level as I started to slide back out from under one of the wheel wells. "Is the car all right?" Lisette inquired, looking down at me.

She looked damp and pleased with herself and about fourteen years old in her travel-grubby blouse and shorts.

"We're fine, Princess. I'm just checking a few things out. We're set to go."

"Too bad," she replied with a regretful smile. "In a funny way, this was nice. I've never camped out before, and I almost wouldn't mind having to stay here for a while."

"If we did, I'd have to go out and shoot a cow. It's time for breakfast and I'm starving to death."

"Me, too," Lisette replied, digging my suitcase out of the backseat. Rummaging around in the bag, she procured my last clean T-shirt and, with supreme female self-assurance, proceeded to dry her hair with it.

"Enjoy your swim?" I asked with a certain degree of irony.

"It was terrific!" She paused and peered out accusingly from beneath the white cotton. "You didn't peek, did you?"

I shrugged. "At what?"

I slid behind the '57's wheel, grinning at the faint feminine snort that sounded behind me.

I hit the ignition. The 283 turned over and fired, the needles on the Stewart Warner instrument gauges snapping to attention at the first barking growl of the exhausts. Lightly feathering the throttle, I made those needles dance sinuosly to the engine's song.

I let her warm for a full minute. Then, with the oil pressure in the right range, I leaned into the gas pedal. The decibels grew to match the revs on the tachometer. Thunder filled the grove and Lisette pressed her hands over her ears. As we passed through three thousand RPMs, the secondary barrels of the dual Carter carburetors slammed open. The shrill, rising scream of air through the venturies merged with the roar of the exhausts to form a single composite howl of power.

I pushed the needle around the tach face until it hovered just short of the 6,000 rev red line, and I held it there for a slow count of ten, feeling the vibration of the hammering pistons resonate through my rib cage. The '57's iron soul whispered to mine over the bellow of her mill, *Yeah, boss. It's all here.*

I let her drift down to idle, and she backed off with a final decisive crackle of her twin pipes. Killing the ignition, I gave her a light slap on the dashboard. We were ready.

"Why is it so much louder?" Lisette asked, curiously peering in through the window.

"I pulled the header plugs while I was underneath. That bypasses the mufflers and reduces the engine backpressure. It'll mean a lot more noise, but it'll also give us an extra ten or eleven horsepower."

She nodded with sober understanding. "In case of Mace."

"You got it. He's up with us now, and he knows that sooner or later we've got to go back to 66. He'll be trolling for us. Last time we were able to outfox him. Next time we might have to run for it."

I got out and secured my tool roll in the trunk. "That's it," I said, slamming the lid. "We're ready to roll."

"Not quite yet."

Lisette handed me my slightly soggy T-shirt and a well-used

sliver from one of those miniature bars of hotel soap. "I've made my contribution to general hygiene this morning. Now it's your turn. The river is just over that way, and the water is fine."

"You have an interesting set of priorities, woman. We're supposed to be running for our lives from the Mob here."

"I'm fully aware of that, and as special dispensation I'll let you get away with not shaving until we can get to some hot water. However, I'm not going to ride around in the same car all day with a stale male. We're both going to be whiffy enough as is."

She had a point. That's another area where movies separate from reality. Grace Kelly and Cary Grant never seem to run out of fresh laundry.

Lisette pointed pointedly. "Go!"

"How do I know that you won't peek?"

"At what?"

We crossed the Canadian on Oklahoma State 33 and cut down to reacquire Route 66 at Clinton. We were getting well out into the short-grass country, and the hills had cured golden and dry after a long, hot summer. There were fewer farms and more ranches, less cultivation and more cattle and oil. Nodding grasshopper pumps shared the pasturage with grazing herds of Hereford cattle.

66 was changing as well, throwing us longer and longer straightaways as it porpoised west over the low rolling countryside. Towns and traffic were spaced out with more miles of highway for fewer people. Even the paving was different. The concrete took on a pinkish hue, the red rock of the western lands having gone into its composition. The '57 ate it up like candy, the ground covered spinning away behind us.

Wind roar and engine snarl boiled in through the open windows. Battering at first, it became almost hypnotic as you focused past it. With my sunglasses propped on her nose, Lisette drowsed across the front seat, her bare feet propped on the passenger side doorsill and her perspiration-damp back nestled comfortably against my shoulder.

Foss . . . Elk City . . . Sayre. . . . Small towns roofed by fluffy white clouds and sun-faded blue sky, a water tower rising above each of them like an H. G. Wells Martian on sentry duty. Quiet towns. Nice places to stop for a rest if you didn't have anyone on your tail. My eyes kept flicking to the rearview mirror, watching for a glint of polished black behind us.

Erick . . . Texola and the Oklahoma-Texas line . . . Shamrock . . .

At Shamrock, we pulled in under the spire of the U-Drop-Inn café and service station for a cold Nehi and a tank of gas. I also made a point of filling both of the one-gallon water bags I carried in the '57. A "just in case" move, since we were now heading into serious dry country.

As I slung the bags upright in the trunk, the inevitable finally happened.

"Hey, let me drive for a while?" Lisette asked, beating me around to the driver's side of the '57.

I winced inwardly. I'm one of those people who'd rather let someone else use his toothbrush than his car. A lot of hot rodders are like that. We have this ingrained suspicion that if we ever let some uninitiated individual lay her eager little hands upon our personal wheels, we'll see that finely tuned piece of racing machinery disintegrate into elephant snot right in front of our eyes.

Only with me, it's not a suspicion. I'm sure of it.

"Why?" I asked in considerable pain.

"For a lot of reasons," Lisette replied, sliding in behind the wheel and slamming the door. "Because it's not fair for you to have to do all of the driving. And because it would be a good idea for me to know how to handle this car in case I had to drive it in an emergency. But mostly, because I want to."

"And if I say no, you'll likely go all girl on me and moan, bitch, whine, sulk, and complain for the rest of the day."

She gave it a moment's sober consideration and then nodded. "Very probably."

"Right."

I tossed the keys on the seat beside her and got in on the passenger side. "I'm not even going to try and fight this. Car, this is Lisette. Lisette, this is Car. Whatever happens next between the two of you is none of my responsibility."

She actually had at least one pretty good point. She might have to drive herself or us out of somewhere if I stopped being lucky. And it made sense for her to get the feel of the car now, before she had to do it while running away or being shot at. Anyway, it wasn't nearly as bad as I had expected.

Lisette had apparently cut her driving teeth on some pretty hot iron. Beyond a mild tire chirp or two while she was getting used to the stiff clutch, she didn't grind any hunks off my transmission. And unlike the growing number of Dynaflos-damaged in the world, she actually knew what a stick shift was all about.

She also wasn't intimidated or casual about all those horses under the hood. She just put them to work like God and Zora Arkus-Duntov intended. After about the first ten miles, I began to let my weight down a little.

A little bit beyond Allenreed, we climbed the eroding caprock breaks that mark the edge of the real West. Suddenly we were driving across a sea of land. Route 66 arrowed almost die-straight across a great flat ocean of golden grass, speckled with tufts of stunted rabbitbrush. No more hills. No more valleys. No more trees. The next high ground would herald the coming of the Rocky Mountains.

This vast prairie had so spooked our forest-raised forefathers that they had called it the Great American Desert. They'd lied to themselves about it being worthless, and they'd cowered at its eastern edge until a new generation could be bred: the plainsmen. Like their close cousins the seamen, these were people who could tolerate looking out across a little piece of eternity.

On its southern edge, the Conquistadors had another name

for it: the Llano Estacado: the Staked Plains. When they ventured out into it, they drove stakes into the ground at intervals to mark the trail, fearing that they might just sink into all that emptiness and disappear.

Our modern-day trail had been staked out as well, although not quite for the same purpose. This stretch of the highway was a roadside advertiser's dream. You had to read the billboards just to keep from going stir-crazy.

Phillips 66, Burma Shave, the black-and-yellow crouching rabbit of Arizona's Jackrabbit Trading Post, the sexy cowgirl of Winslow's Store for Men, and the smiling fat man of Santa Rosa Club Café.

Granddaddy of them all were the siren calls of an entire city: TUCUMCARI TONIGHT in an orange-and-red visual scream, backed by the alluring whispered promise of two thousand motel room beds. Posted at regular intervals, the massive garish billboards bashed at the subconscious with an invasive brainwashing that made North Korea's best look like kindergarten stuff.

Those were just the big boys, though. The little guys tucked in between where they could. GAS 30 MILES! CLEAN REST ROOMS! SLEEP OFF THE HIGHWAY! AIR COOLED! HOME COOKING! FREE ICE! DESERT ZOO! LIVE RATTLESNAKES! EXCITING! EDUCATIONAL!

"Who in the world ever came up with the idea of a roadside snake pit in the first place?" Lisette asked, her lips curling.

"The snake pit is a child of the depression, Princess," I replied, slouching over on the passenger side with my arms crossed and my eyes half-closed.

"You mean like with *The Grapes of Wrath* and the dust bowl refugees and all?"

"Yeah. That's the way I understand it. When things got really bad back here in the thirties, Route 66 was a way out for a lot of people. Like with the Joads going out to California and all. But the old Mother Road also helped to keep alive a lot of the folks who stayed behind as well. Money was going through on the highway, and if you were smart, you could get ahold of some of it. If you could scrape together a few bucks, you could open an auto court or a café or a gas station. If you had absolutely flat-ass nothing, however, you set yourself up a snake pit."

"Geyuck!"

"Think about it."

"I don't want to!"

"It was the only roadside business you could start with a zero cash investment. Your star attractions could be picked up for free out along the rimrocks. Rattlers, coral snakes, copperheads, and maybe a few Gila monsters on the side if you wanted to be exotic. Sure, you might lose a slow cousin or two collecting 'em, but hey, that's show business."

"Kevin! That's awful!" Lisette shuddered.

"The upkeep was minimal, too. You just ran a trap line out in the barn. Throw them a nice dead rat every couple of weeks, and the majority of your employees were happy. In fact, I'm informed that after a while the snakes even started coming to you. A slot in a good snake pit was considered a pretty plush position if you happened to have been born a dust bowl diamondback."

"Kevin Pulaski! I am warning you!"

Oh, the simple masculine pleasure of making a squeamish female squeam.

"Anyhow," I continued. "You knocked down the chicken coop for the wood to build your pens, and you used your leftover barn paint to make your road signs. You leased a Coke cooler to serve up cold drinks, and you charged the rubes from back east a nickel apiece for a good case of the creeps. If your old man had the hands to throw a little three-card monte on the side, you could stay alive."

"I'd rather have gone west with the Joads!"

"You don't dig snakes, huh?"

"Not until they've been made into handbags."

I chuckled and settled lower on the base of my spine.

Now that I was used to it, it was kind of nice having some-one else herding the wheels down the highway for a change. The heat of the day and the rhythmic clicking of the tires strik-ing the expansion joints in the pavement sank into me. After a few minutes I found my eyes closing and my head sinking forward on my chest.

Why not pile up a few Zs while I had the chance? It wasn't as if I'd been getting all the rest in the world these past few nights. And anyhow, what the hell could happen out here in the middle of nowhere?

I was just fading out when I heard the sound of another engine overriding the steady growl of the '57's mill. Gaining on us, it sounded like. Given the rate of knots Lisette was turning, not many people had been trying to pass.

That little instinctive card file in the back of my head tried to match the burbling rumble to a specific power-plant type. Sounded like a souped-up flathead. Maybe a Big Merc. A Big Merc? Where had I seen one of those lately?

My eyes snapped open and my head whipped around.

"SonofaBITCH!"

My left foot came over the transmission hump and smashed down on Lisette's right foot and the gas pedal. The '57 surged forward and the shotgun blast that was meant to take our heads off didn't.

Instead, the fist-sized buckshot pattern from the fully choked Winchester blew in one rear side window and out the other, spraying us with fragments of safety glass. Over in the cab of his '40 Ford pickup, I could see Ira Claster mouthing a curse and fumbling one-handed with the weapon's pump action.

He'd really meant it back there in Baxter Springs. He didn't want anyone finding his brother.

"What do I do?" Lisette's voice was taut but steady. There was no panic there, just a request for instructions.

"Stand on it!"

She did! Lisette socked the spurs to the 283 horses under the '57's hood, and we pulled away from the pickup. For a few

seconds, anyway. A puff of smoke streaked back from the
Ford's laker pipes as Claster poured it on and came after us.

I twisted around in the seat, drawing my gun. My attention
was divided, my eyes fixed on our pursuer and my hearing on
the rising scream of our own engine.

"Watch your tach!" I yelled. "Hold her at six thousand revs!
Push her over the red line and you'll blow the mill!"

"Okay!" Lisette was yelling, too, but her voice was almost
lost over the sound of the engine and the hurricane's worth of
wind blasting in through the open windows.

My thoughts were racing almost as fast as the car. We had
to keep moving. If we stopped, it would be my automatic
against Claster's twelve-gauge, and one shotgun outnumbers a
whole lot of pistols.

Out here on the road, though, Claster would have a problem
in the confining space of his truck cab. His shotgun looked like
a hunting weapon with a full-length tube. The only way he
could shoot was one-handed and out of the passenger window,
the gun barrel braced against the frame. That gave him only a
narrow effective field of fire: his passenger side to our driver's
side.

If we knew what was good for us, we had to have to stay
out of that killing zone. It would be a two-dimensional dogfight
on an eighteen-foot-wide-strip of concrete. And just now,
brother Ira had the position advantage on us.

The experience advantage, too. The Claster boys had probably been outrunning revenuers in the third grade, while this
was likely Lisette's first time at driving at real speed.

"S curve!" Lisette called out.

I whipped my attention forward. "She can take it at seventy!
Don't brake yet. . . . brake now! Keep your revs up! Accelerate
through the turns . . . Now punch it! Go! Go! Go!"

The '57 didn't like the untrained hand at her wheel. Rubber
sobbed where it should have drifted, and she shook her tail fins
angrily as we tore a ragged path through the curves. Lisette
fought through it, though, her hands white-knuckled on the

wheel, her eyes coolly flicking between the wavering tachometer
needle and the road ahead.

Claster cornered more cleanly and went for our flank again;
the hoarser bellow of the Ford's engine overrode the higher-
toned howl of the Chevy's mill as he started to pull alongside.

I tried to line up on the truck's radiator, aiming through the
shattered rear window on the driver's side. The .45 would be
going off right behind Lisette's head, and I prayed that I
wouldn't take out one of her eardrums.

"Watch it! I'm taking a shot!"

The Commander roared and a spent shell casing ricocheted
around the '57's interior for an instant before flicking out
through the window with a brassy glint. I wasn't rewarded with
an eruption of steam from the Ford, but Claster slowed
abruptly and swerved in behind us.

Okay, you hick-town asshole. You didn't figure on us shooting back, did you?

Throwing myself over to the passenger-side window, I
leaned out into the slipstream. Aiming back with a deliberate
two-handed grip, I laid the front blade of my sights on the
silhouette behind the truck's wheel.

"Watch it!" It was Lisette's turn to yell a warning. The '57
danced sideways and I got a blurred impression of a bronze
Pontiac station wagon and a cluster of terrified faces as we
blazed past. We drifted over too far and ticked the gravel
shoulder of the left lane. Just for a second, we fishtailed wildly,
one notch short of losing it all.

Lisette dragged us back onto the pavement again. That same
fighting snarl that I had seen back at Claster's garage was on
her face. Her fingernail marks were probably permanently
carved into the steering wheel.

"Bitchin', Princess! You're doing good!"

She gulped on a dry throat and managed to nod a reply.

Claster had snaked around the station wagon as well and
was closing with us again. I drew a bead once more. But I
hesitated. One of the things they teach you as a lawman is that

you can't just worry about shooting at the bad guy. You have to worry about shooting at what the bad guy is standing in front of.

To the left and right there wasn't anything except open desert. To the front and rear, though, we were sharing this highway with other cars. A slug from the military-spec hardball ammunition I was using could carry almost a mile and still have enough velocity to kill. A miss on my part might just blow away some poor damn vacationing dentist from Paducah along with his whole family.

Abso-friggin'-lutely fan-damn-tastic!

I twisted back around and faced front again. "Pour it on! We have to outrun this guy!"

Again the '57 cranked up and again we pulled away. But again the primer-red pickup only drifted back so far. Slowly it began creeping up on our rear bumper once more.

Shit! That was a flathead back there! A mean one, but still a flathead! We had to be able to take him! I glanced down at the gauges. The stock Chevy speedometer had its needle buried at a hundred and ten, but on the tachometer we still had room under the red line.

"Come on! Lean on it! Give her the gun!"

"I can't!" There was no panic in the girl's voice, but she shook her head decisively. "I can't!"

I understood then. Lisette had hit her own personal red line.

It's a whole new deal the first time you take a car beyond a hundred miles an hour. The dashes of the center line hose at you like tracer bullets, and you can sense the aerodynamics lifting the frame off the suspension. Your sense of solid control fades until you're skating on stainless steel and you feel like the brush of a butterfly wing will tip you over the edge. Lisette was taking us as far as she could go.

Unfortunately, Ira Claster could push it a little bit further. The red-primered Ford was creeping up on our hip once more. The shotgun barrel slid out of its passenger window like a pirate ship's cannon clearing its gun port.

"Block him!"

Obediently Lisette slid us over into the left lane, cutting him off. I could see Claster's lips move as he swore.

I kept my cursing internal. *Come on, you son of a bitch! We can play this game all day. Hurry up and get impatient. Try and pass us on the inside so I can stick this .45 in your ear.*

Claster refused to get stupid. Instead, the Ford lunged forward again and our bumpers kissed. Lisette cried out as we bucked under the impact. It was a square shot. He hadn't figured out yet that an off-center impact might flip us off the road. It would only be a matter of time, though, before he did. Risk of a miss or not, I had to take him out. I leaned out the window again and tried to aim. However, before I could squeeze the trigger Lisette screamed my name.

I whipped back around in the seat. The land had fooled us. It had looked as if we were thundering along on an empty straightaway across a level plain. But there had been a hidden swale out there, a depression large enough to hide something the size of a tractor-trailer truck.

The big rig had surfaced out of the desert like a submarine blowing ballast. We were coming at him head on, in his lane, at a combined speed of close to two hundred miles an hour. We were all about one heartbeat away from starring in one of those "Don't let this happen to you" horror films they use in the driver's-ed classes.

Lisette froze and I couldn't blame her. Claster swerved wildly back into the right lane, cutting us off. The diesel jockey couldn't do anything at all except aim a fast, "Hey, Chris! Save my ass!" prayer at the medallion hanging from his cab roof.

And that left me.

The only thing I could come up with was to grab the wheel and turn it . . . to the left. I didn't even bother to look. If we had a broad shoulder out on that side of the road, we were living. If we didn't, we weren't.

We were living. We hit gravel with a roar like a thunderbolt. Lifting a roostertail of dust and thrown pebbles behind her, the

'57 clung to the edge of the shoulder by the grace of God and Goodyear. If it weren't for her reinforced interceptor suspension she would have shaken herself apart. It was a good thing I'd left her in her stock factory colors, too. The thickness of an extra coat of paint would have killed us.

There was a gray steel and black rubber blur outside of my windows, a fragment of a second of stillness as we punched into the vacuum created by the truck's passage, and then, WHOMP! We blasted past and were battered by the turbulence of the wind wake.

The '57 was beyond being steered by then. I could only hint to Car that she might be happier with her tires back on the pavement. Being the sweet lady that she is, she accepted my suggestion. We slithered back onto 66, caught traction with a puff of rubber smoke, and lunged forward once more.

Only now, a few things had changed. The red Ford pickup was in front of us. Claster hadn't lost as much speed as we had out playing in the dirt. Now we were in the kill slot.

Lisette's hands were back on the wheel. She was ghost-pale but with it again. We were also dipping across the swale, and we could see a long, empty stretch of road ahead of us. It was time to finish this.

"Stand on it! Get around him!"

The girl nodded. Gritting her teeth, she punched the gas pedal and made the '57 wail.

Claster had lost us when we had cut around the far side of the truck. He was slowing and I saw his head frantically turning between his side and rearview mirrors, trying to see where we'd disappeared to. He didn't realize until too late that we were already riding in his blind spot. As the sound of our engine began to leak past his, he looked over his shoulder and right back into my eyes.

He was unshaven and his black T-shirt was soaked with sweat. His face was still marked up from our previous set-to, and all in all, brother Ira didn't look too good. He was going to look worse presently, because we were screaming down on him like a Hellcat diving on a Zero. He saw the blue-steel glint of the automatic in my hand, and his face distorted with fear.

I could have killed him. I had the justification and the setup. But what the hell, maybe the guy was just trying to cover for his brother. Besides, filling out the paperwork afterward is a pain in the ass. Aiming out of my window, I laid the sights of the Commander on the center of Claster's left front wheel and braced my shooting wrist with my free hand. As we swept past him, I emptied the .45's clip in a six-round burst.

The ricocheting slugs tore the tire and tube clear off the rim in an explosion of rubber and cord. Suddenly there wasn't anything holding up one corner of the red Ford. Lisette stayed on the gas, and we clawed clear, leaving Ira plenty of room to have his wreck in.

Even in the harsh noon sunlight, I could see the explosion of sparks as the ruined wheel gouged into the concrete. There was no way in hell Claster could control the wild left-handed skid that threw the pickup across both lanes of 66 and out into the desert. To even try would've put the vehicle into a death roll. Brother Ira was strictly along for the ride.

Shedding parts and bucking like a berserk bronco, the truck tore out through the greasewood, angling away from the road. About fifty yards out, it must have encountered a little arroyo running parallel to the highway. The Ford vanished in a massive burst of red dust, like a prop in the trick of some high plains magician.

Lisette backed off on the loud pedal and we started to slow, the '57 grumbling a protest at being reined in. Sorry, Car, but the speed limit was going to look pretty good for a while.

A couple of miles down the road we came on a Texas Highway Department maintenance turnout. Lisette pulled into it, parking us out of sight behind the massive gray heap of fill gravel. I reached over and switched off the ignition. The girl just sat behind the wheel, vibrating like she had a broken motor mount.

To tell the truth, I was doing a little vibrating myself. It took a couple of tries before I could fit a fresh clip into the

Commander's butt. I didn't even attempt to return the pistol to the Maqui loop on my belt. I just left it on the seat and went around to the trunk.

En route, I checked out my busted car windows and the dings in my rear bumper. God damn it all to hell entirely and back again! I should have availed myself of the opportunity to blast Claster's malignant little pea brain right out of his skull. I could only hope that greasy-haired sociopath ended up holding his friggin' perfect engine in his lap!

There wasn't anything I could do about it for the moment, anyway. I popped the trunk lid and got out one of the water bags. After taking a long pull of the canvassy fluid, I splashed a couple of palmfuls into my face before taking it around to Lisette.

She had the driver's door open by then and was sitting sideways in the seat, trying to take advantage of the occasional puff of hot Texas wind. We didn't say anything. I just held the water bag for her, pouring into her cupped hands so she could drink. Like me, she sluiced a little over herself, craving the soothing coolness.

I capped the bag and knelt down in the open door. "You want a cigarette?"

"Yes, I guess so."

I got her purse from behind the seat and dug out her pack of Fatimas. Lisette's hands were still shaking, so I slipped the cork tip of the cigarette between her lips and struck a match for her. For several seconds she tried to mate the wavering end of her smoke with the flame. Then she reached up and tossed the cigarette away. "Oh, to hell with it. I only smoke the damn things for effect anyway."

I don't think she meant it to be funny, but I laughed. A second or two later, she joined in. It was a foxhole laugh, a shared release of tension between two people who had looked over the edge into the dark together. Humor really isn't involved; you're just celebrating being alive.

Lisette's usually immaculate plume of brown hair looked as

if she'd had raccoons nesting in it. Her face was raw and wind-
burned, and her blouse was mud-streaked where dust and water
had mixed.

All in all, she looked pretty damn good.

I really didn't plan it, but my hand curved around the back
of her neck and I drew her face to mine. There was a moment's
instinctive resistance, and then she yielded to the kiss, first just
melting into it, then replying with a growing urgency of her
own, her small, soft tongue darting.

Our positioning was poor and the setting was far from ro-
mantic, but as our lips parted I think we both had come to the
same conclusion. That with a degree of practice and a little
dedication on both our parts, we probably could get really good
at this.

"I'm bored," she murmured, nose to nose with me.

"What?"

She responded to my explosion with her laziest feminine
"gotcha" smile. "With driving. You can take it for a while
again."

We hit Amarillo in time for lunch. Following Amarillo Boulevard over San Jacinto Heights, we dropped down to West
Sixth Street and pulled into an open and not too busy Chevrolet
agency on the west side of town. I wanted to get those blown-
out windows replaced. Not only would we have trouble in bad
weather, but busted glass in a car can draw the attention of the
local justice merchants.

I also wanted a telephone and a little privacy. I was way past
due checking in. Jack does not wait well, and by now he was
probably chewing up his desk blotter. Lisette, on the other
hand, would probably get real leery real fast if she caught me
making cryptic calls to mysterious strangers. Take a note, Mr.
Scientist. If you ever get a free moment in between inventing
the better H-bomb and all those new, new, NEW and im-
proved toothpastes, how about coming up with a phone a guy
can carry around in his hip pocket?

The repair work gave me my excuse, however. I got Lisette installed in a greasy spoon café across the street, and then I cut back over to the garage "to see how they're doing." They had a pay phone in their waiting room, and I did the long-distance deal.

"Pulaski, you little prick! I ought to kick your ass!"

"Hello, Jack. I love you, too, but I'm a little rushed for time here, so let's skip the fond pleasantries. All right?"

"Where are you? And where were you last night?"

"I'm in Amarillo now, and last night I was somewhere where I didn't have a goddamn telephone, okay? Now copy this down: Ira Claster, white adult male, age twenty-eight, height six-one, weight about one-seventy, black hair, brown eyes, dark complexion. Resident, Baxter Springs, Kansas. He has a local rap sheet as long as your arm, minor felony and heavy misdemeanor. Last seen on Route 66 about seven miles west of Lark, Texas. Armed and dangerous."

"Got it. Now what do I do with it?"

"Get on the horn to the Texas Highway Patrol or the Texas Rangers or whoever the hell has jurisdiction out there and get this guy picked up on two counts of attempted first-degree homicide."

"Were you one of these attempts, kid?"

"Yeah, I was, but I don't have time to go into it now. Just have the locals pick this guy up. I'll file a report and officially swear out the warrants as soon as I break cover, but I need this guy off my back now."

"You got it. Now, what else is going on?"

"I have an update on Mace Spanno's location. As of last night, he was in Oklahoma City. An Oklahoma City patrol car might have filed a field event card on him. Black '57 Chrysler 300-C, Indiana license Able Charley Delta six three nine."

"Got it."

"Good. Now tell me that they've also got a nice juicy arrest warrant out for this guy."

"No joy there," Jack replied regretfully. "We passed the

word on Spanno back to the East Saint Louis police. They're looking for witnesses who can place him and his boys anywhere near the scene of the Reece killing at the time of the murder. So far, they don't have anything they can take to a judge."

"Great." I let the air hiss out of my lungs and leaned against the waiting room wall. "Okay, Jack. There's one thing more you can do for me."

"What's that, kid?"

"Work the hell out of the Lisette Kingman angle. I need all the dope I can get on this girl. I need to know who she really is and what she's really about."

"Shit, I can give you everything you need right now. We got the kickbacks in last night. I could have told you then if you'd just phoned the hell in like you were supposed to."

"Yeah, yeah, yeah, sure! Whattaya got?"

"Why we had trouble tracking her down before. Your girlfriend underwent a name change about nine years ago."

"What are we talking about here, Jack?"

"Well, it seems that about a year after her late husband's untimely demise the Widow Kingman remarried, an old family friend. Shortly thereafter, her new husband adopted little Lisette, formally bestowing his name upon her."

I felt my jaw drop. My partner couldn't really be about to say what I thought he was.

"Jack, what are we talking about here?"

"Lisette Kingman's legal name is Lisette Spanno. She's Mace Spanno's stepdaughter."

NEW MEXICO

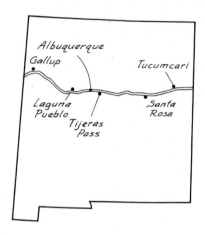

Since the region is often very arid, it is wise to carry a spare container of water for your car and drinking water would come in handy too. Don't turn off on any side roads without inquiring locally as to road conditions . . .

Oh, shit! In no uncertain terms.

I should have known. I'd been given the tip-off all the way back in Illinois, on that first night in the parking lot of the Dixie Trucker's Home. "This is a family affair," Spanno had said. "My family."

He'd meant it. And it made sense in a weird kind of way. This was the connection that brought a whole lot of stuff together. The dominating role Spanno had played in Lisette's life. The way she'd been held so deeply inside of his world. The way she'd known so much about that world. The hate.

That was why Lisette was so terrified of the man. She wasn't afraid of dying at Spanno's hand; she was afraid of having to live with him.

And as for Mr. Spanno himself, my partner, Jack, had said it: "Mr. Spanno is kind of possessive."

Layers upon layers of motivation were working here. Beyond greed. Beyond fear. Beyond hate. Hell, Johnny 32's lost money was the least of it.

That past Lisette wanted to destroy along with Spanno. Those things she'd refused to talk about last night. I sensed I was brushing close to something big and ugly and unclean.

Lisette was still waiting over in the diner. She looked at me funny as I came in, and I guess I looked a little funny, too.

"You okay, Kev?" she inquired.

"Yeah, sure," I replied offhandedly. "Have you ordered yet?"

"Just coffee. This place doesn't exactly inspire my appetite."

"I'm not all that hungry, either. They'll have the car ready pretty soon, so let's skip the lunch for now and make some more miles. We still have a long way to go."

I felt her eyes follow me as we walked back to the garage.

Out on the highway that afternoon the wind through the windows didn't cool; it just circulated the heat so you were baked by it from all angles. Route 66 was a wavering stream of molten silver flowing across the desert, exploded truck tires curling along its shoulders like overcooked strips of bacon charring in the pan. The only things that moved in the sun shimmer were the patiently patrolling flocks of road crows, waiting for something to be a little slow in crossing the pavement.

There was the engine and the slipstream; that was all. We didn't talk. We didn't listen to the radio. We just existed while the '57 doggedly assaulted the forever of the road.

Bushland . . . Wildorado . . . Vega . . . smaller, rougher, farther apart. I started riding the dashboard gauges: engine temperature, oil pressure, fuel level. Water and gas wasn't something that was just down the road anymore. I mentally plugged into the sound of the engine, trying to separate any real aberrations from the imaginary taps, rattles, and vibrations the gremlins produce whenever you're driving across the big empty places.

The little town of Adrian, Texas, was outstanding for one thing. It's the exact halfway point of Route 66, the halfway point of our journey. The milestone rolled past unmentioned.

As the afternoon passed, the blue of the sky began to pale into a hot milky hue. There wasn't enough wind to stir the cheat grass, and an oppression began to build beyond the heat.

Glenrio and the Texas–New Mexico border. The edge of the Llano shattered, and we dropped off the great plain into a growing jumble of caprock and tableland. Endee . . . San Jon . . . Tucumcari. By that time, I was so sick of those TUCUM-CARI TONIGHT signs that I wouldn't have taken one of their two thousand damn rooms if Mamie Van Doren and Bettie Page both were waiting in it for me along with a roll of complimentary quarters for the Magic Fingers massage bed. I kept the hammer down, and we burned through, heading west, chasing the retreating sun.

Eventually Lisette cleared her throat delicately. "Excuse me, but I think I'm ready for lunch now."

I glanced down at the dash clock. Five thirty-seven.

"Oh, Jesus! I'm sorry; I've been thinking about some stuff, and I didn't realize that it was getting on like this."

"I know," she replied. She was curled up over in her corner of the seat, studying me, her shadowy eyes the only cool things in this part of the world. "You've been scowling about something all afternoon, and I haven't wanted to interrupt. What's wrong?"

"I've just been studying on this run. Things are kind of getting complicated."

"I know. More so than even I expected." Her gaze dropped to some point on the upholstery between us. "Look, Kev. If you want out of this, I can't blame you. I can more than understand. If you want, just drop me off at the next town. I'll be okay."

"No, you wouldn't be, and what makes you think I want out?"

She looked up again and I realized that I would have to be careful with my face for a while. She peered at me with that catlike intensity of hers, trying to read me. "Look, Kev," she said softly. "You've been really good to me. I'd have never made it this far without you. But you are just a nice guy who happened to walk into my problems. How far do you want to go just for the promise of some money that may not even be there?"

I wanted to reply that the damn money hadn't been in the equation from the first damn second. But I couldn't. Not without saying a lot of things to her that I wasn't sure I could even say to myself yet.

"Hell, I'm going as far as I have to," I replied. "I made a deal with you back there in Saint Louis. I don't back out of my deals. I also don't run out on my partners just because things start getting a little raunchy. You and me, Princess, we're doing this all the way. You dig?"

It was her turn to be careful with her expression. "I dig." She nodded. "All the way."

Up ahead, buildings materialized out of the heat shimmer. A little patch of humanity notched into the side of the road.

It was one of those little travelers' survival places, a modern-day oasis in the desert. A Phillips 66 sign and a couple of pumps. A white cinder block café with a sheet metal Pepsi thermometer beside the door and a cardboard sign in the window assuring that YES, WE ARE OPEN. A couple of scrubby cottonwood trees surviving on seepage from the well. Everything, even the trees, a little sun-bleached. Only two or three cars and a single tractor-trailer rig stewed in the gravel turn out, leaving me plenty of room to park the '57 out front where I could keep an eye on her.

The place was about what you'd expect under the situation.

A scarred counter and row of stools. A row of three-sided booths around the walls and another couple of tables centered in the room, the tabletops covered in checked oilcloth. The Mixmaster, the battered coffee urn, and the chalkboard offering up the special of the day.

The place didn't run to air-conditioning, but it did have a set of desert coolers, big burlap-sided boxes mounted outside of the windows at either end of the dining room. Hoses trickled water onto the burlap, and powerful electric fans drew the outside air in through the wet cloth. They didn't actually make things cool, just less hot. Any improvement was appreciated, however.

A lone, wilted waitress was on duty, dealing off the arm with the two heat-fretful families and the pair of truck drivers who shared the place with us. She still managed a couple of pleasantries, though, as she brought us our menus and glasses of alkali-tinged ice water.

Generally in a place like this, you're safe with a hamburger and fries. And we were. Fresh meat, a fresh bun toasted on the grill, and the lettuce, tomato, and onion kept in the refrigerator until just before being served. As a longtime burger gourmet, my compliments to the chef. The menu also boasted about their king-sized, genuine ice-cream milk shakes. Lisette and I spilt one, she getting the glass while I got the half remaining in the aluminum blender canister.

I was just taking a pull out of that canister when I looked up right into Mace Spanno's face.

He filled the front door of the café, a mountain in a sweat-limp white shirt and gray suit trousers. His coat was draped over one arm, and his tie was yanked down a couple of inches. The same fedora he had worn back at the Dixie shaded his eyes.

Lisette went absolutely rigid beside me.

There was movement at the back of the room as well. From there, a short corridor led back to the rest rooms and to the restaurant's side door. Nate Temple, Spanno's backup gunner, appeared at the entry to that passage, sealing off the line of retreat.

They must have spotted the '57 from the highway. Turning off short, they must have cut around behind the building out of our line of sight. We were boxed in, but good.

Deliberately I finished taking my pull on the shake then set the canister down in front of me. Spanno crossed to our booth and loomed over us. The big square-faced man was going for intimidation again, the principal from hell about to chastise the two cowering truants. His clothes looked as if they had been lived in for seventy-two hours straight, and his face was hazed with the start of an iron gray beard.

I just nodded toward a chair from one of the center tables. "Sit down and take a load off. It's a hot day."

Nothing stirred in those dead eyes, but the corner of his mouth quirked up about half a millimeter. He drew the chair up and sat down at the front of our booth, his right arm, the one with the coat draped across it, held in his lap. I sat facing him at the back of the booth, and as he settled into his chair Lisette huddled closer to me.

I saw emotion in Spanno then, for the first time. One brief, hot flash of rage played across his features. That massive jaw tightened, teeth glinting in a snarl for an instant. Lisette glared back defiantly, the air between them so charged it would have registered on a Geiger counter.

"You have made me a lot of trouble." Spanno spoke the phrase to Lisette as if he were passing sentence.

"Yeah? Well, we're sorry about that," I said. I wanted to get that inclusive "we" in there just so all parties involved would understand where I stood in the negotiations.

Spanno's head turned toward me like a traversing tank turret. "As for you, boy, I warned you once that you were sticking your nose in my family affairs."

I nodded in agreement. "I recall you saying something about that. I also seem to recall not giving a damn."

"Then you'd better start now. This is your last chance. Get

up from this table, go out that door, get in your car, and get out of my life."

I shook my head. "Can't do it. I haven't cleaned my plate yet."

The big man's eyes narrowed. "I guess you still don't know how much trouble you've bought yourself."

"Oh, I know lots of stuff, Spanno. Maybe more than you'd expect. Among other things, I know that I'll be leaving with the lady I brought."

"My daughter is going with me."

I faked the appropriate startled glance in Lisette's direction.

"No, I won't, Mace," the girl said in a low voice. "I am not your daughter and I am never going with you anywhere ever again."

Spanno's hand, his left one, darted across the table and caught Lisette's wrist. "You *are* my daughter!" he spit with venomous intensity. "You have my name and I raised you!"

"I'm a prisoner in your damn house, and I never wanted your rotten name," Lisette hissed back. "The only reason you ever married my mother was to get even with my father. He took your damn money, and killing him wasn't payback enough! You bullied my mother into marrying you, and then you adopted me, all just so you could torture us both! All to get even with Johnny 32!"

"And why the hell not!" Spanno growled back. "Your father was a back-stabbing son of a bitch and he owed me! He owed me for the money, he owed me for the lives of my partners, and he owed me for my life! The life I could have had if he'd played it square with us! You and your slut of a mother were poor-enough payback for that!"

Spanno kept his voice low despite his intensity, and the rumble of the cooler fans blurred his words. They didn't spread beyond our booth. No one noticed out in the rest of the room. A harried mother coped with a two-year-old's spilled milk. An overweight salesman argued over the bill with the cashier. A trucker laughed at his driving partner's joke.

How many times has this happened in your life? How many times in a restaurant or on a bus or in the street have blood, death, and murder been discussed just a few feet away and you never even realized it?

"If it's such a bad deal, big man, why don't you give up on it?" I cut in. "If you don't think she's worth it, why not save yourself some trouble? Let her go."

Spanno's eyes slashed at me. "Shut the hell up, boy."

His gaze returned to the girl. "Listen to me, Lisette. You've had clothes, money, school, a town house, even a maid. I've given you what you needed and what you wanted. Me, I've done that for you. You can't say that you've had it so hard. You're the one that's given me the grief. But maybe I can forget about that."

And then, for the second time, I saw emotion in Mace Spanno's face. It was far back there in his eyes, a faint warped specter of the way a man should look at a woman like Lisette. The desire, the passion, the . . . no, I won't spot him that last one.

"Just come back with me," he said. His grip on her wrist eased almost to a caress. "Stop making this trouble. Forget this punk and your father's money and come back with me. I'll be able to forgive you after a while. Things will be good. I can make them good for you. Just come home, Lisette."

It wasn't the kind of speech a father makes to a daughter. There was something grotesque in the softness of the big man's words. Like Frankenstein reciting love poetry.

Lisette's eyes burned hard and cold like black ice. I hope that no woman ever looks at me the way she looked at Spanno just then. "Why?" she asked. "So you can fuck me in my own mother's bed again?"

She'd carefully chosen the vilest word she could have used, and with equal care she'd thrown it in his face.

Spanno's face went bloodless and his lipless mouth peeled open in a snarl. His hand clamped onto Lisette's wrist again, the skin of her arm going pale as he bore down. A low whimpering cry escaped her as the bones strained to the breaking point.

"That's it!" I growled. My right hand closed on his wrist, just as his had closed on Lisette's. And it wasn't about laws, cops, or money or anything else. For a few long seconds we held that lockup, and it was Spanno who grabbed loose first.

"That is it, man," I repeated through gritted teeth, releasing him.

He sank back in his chair. At least I'd managed to drag the big man's hate off Lisette and onto me. "Oh, yeah," Spanno hissed. "That's it. You bought this, you little bastard, and now you're receiving."

From under the table, where his right hand had been hanging out all during this conversation, there came the deliberate metallic click of a pistol hammer cocking back.

"Now listen," Spanno continued, keeping his voice down. "We're going to get up and go out the back door. Stay in front of me. Don't give me any shit and nobody gets hurt."

I grinned at him. "You set this up real good, Mace," I replied. "Keeping your piece out of sight under your jacket and everything. You've got your ace man over there covering me, too, and neither one of you have taken your eyes off my right hand here, my gun hand, for a second."

Slowly, and using that right hand, I reached across the table and picked up the aluminum shake canister, giving them something to watch. "And that's cool," I continued, taking a quick drink, "but let me clue you in on something. You see, I'm what you call ambidextrous, and neither of you have seen my left hand since you walked into this place."

There was another metallic click under the table. The sound of a Colt .45's safety being thumbed off.

I had to hold Spanno now. I had to be the only thing in his world if this was going to work at all. I had to look right straight into those dead oyster eyes and not glance away for a second.

"I can read your mind," I whispered. "You're wondering if

you can tip the table over and knock my gun down. Forget it. The table's bolted to the floor."

Spanno's only answer was a twisted whisp of obscenity.

"Now," I went on, "you're thinking about firing up through the table and putting a bullet in my brain before I can shoot. Forget that, too. This heavy plywood tabletop would probably deflect a round from that snubnose you're carrying. You can't be sure of killing me instantly with your first shot. We're stuck. There's not one single thing either of us can do except sit here, face-to-face, and blow each other into dog meat."

"Don't be stupid, boy. Put the piece down or you're dead!"

"You think I just fell off the goddamn turnip truck?" I replied coldly. "I know about you, man. I'm dead no matter how you cut it. I've spit in the face of the great Mace Spanno. If I go out that door, I get taken for a ride. If I stay here, I'm dead, too. But this way, I get to take you with me, and Lisette goes free. It's no contest, man. *No friggin' contest!*"

Just now I was clinging desperately to some words of wisdom bestowed upon me by Mr. Jack Le Baer, street cop and profound student of human behavior. "Kid," he had said, "sometimes the only way you can deal with some of the psychos you'll meet in this business is to make 'em think that you're crazier than they are."

At the edge of my vision I saw Nate Temple straighten from his lounged posture in the passage back to the side door. He sensed that something was wrong with his boss but he couldn't see the problem. No one could. There were just three people talking around a table.

"You set this up too good, Spanno," I continued, keeping my voice in a hypnotic monotone. "You've got me backed into a corner, and I've got nothing left but death or glory. You've got all the choices. You get to walk away and try again."

I could feel the perspiration running down my spine. And why not? I was sitting here with a gun aimed at my balls, banking on the residual sanity of a proven sociopathic killer.

The only ray of hope in sight was that the sweat was standing out on Spanno's brow, too. A droplet trickled down into the corner of his eye, and the lid twitched.

"What the hell do you think you're getting out of this?" he demanded, his words grating. "The money? That money's mine! It's been mine for the past ten fucking years! Just like that little bitch sitting next to you is mine. And once something is *mine*, it stays that way. You're not getting a piece of either one."

The serrated grip plates of the Commander burned in my hand. "What I'm getting out of this, Spanno, you'd never understand in ten million years."

We were right on the edge now, and I had to take us even closer. "Look, man; my burger's getting cold and my shake's getting warm and I'm getting sick of looking at your face. Now, either get the hell out of here or let's get it done."

It was a sure-money call that no one had ever wanted me dead as much as Mace Spanno did at that moment. The question was which he wanted more, my life or his.

"Having trouble deciding?" I whispered. "Okay, let me give you a hand. We go on the count of three. One. . . ."

Lisette sat to one side, her lips parted, frozen. She'd be okay as long as she wasn't hit by a loose round. Spanno's boys probably would be more concerned with getting away after our private hell broke loose than they would with fooling around with her. I wish I could have told her about Jack out in LA. He could have helped her.

"Two . . ."

That's how many pounds of pressure it takes on the trigger of a cocked pistol to trip the sear and drop the hammer.

"Sorry it took me a minute to get back to you, folks," the waitress chirped, bustling up with a menu under her arm. "Get you a cup of coffee, sir?"

It was a good thing that it was over by then. "No thanks, ma'am," I answered for Spanno. "The gentleman's just leaving."

Spanno stood up. His eyes swept from me to Lisette, making a silent vow to piss on our graves. Then he turned, brushed past the waitress, and headed for the side door. Perplexed, Temple followed his boss down the passage and out into the desert sun.

"Anything wrong here, folks?" the waitress asked dubiously.

"Nah," I replied. "It's just the heat. It gets to some people."

I'm glad she was satisfied and turned away. After making that statement about the temperature, I'd have had a tough time explaining why I suddenly started to shiver.

Evening is the worst time for clouds to come in over the desert. During the day, a little overcast is a good thing. It can take the edge off the sun. But with night coming on, a cloud layer can act like insulation, trapping the heat on the ground like a smothering blanket until you give up hope of ever feeling cool again.

A miniature dust devil swirled past the café. It snatched up the smoke of my cigarette, whipping it in with the sand and cottonwood fluff it carried. A hundred feet away, poised under the parking lot arc light, the black Chrysler eyed me like a hungry shark. So did the three men it carried.

Nate Temple leaned against the car, loose and relaxed, a smoke of his own between his fingers. Like any good hunter, he knew all about patience and about not wasting your energy. His face was emotionless as we swapped stares.

Not so the kid wheelman. It was getting to him a little. Bannerman kept shifting his position in the driver's seat, one thumb tapping time on the steering wheel to some nervous internal rhythm. He never met my eyes; he just kept looking out toward the road as if he were the one seeking escape.

As for Spanno, out there in the backseat, I couldn't even guess what he was feeling just now.

This standoff had lasted for two hours. It couldn't go on for much longer.

"Anything wrong, son?" The establishment's cashier–cum–

pump jockey came up behind me in the café's side door.

I snubbed out my smoke on the door frame. "Nope. Just waiting for it to get a little cooler before we head out again."

The old desert hand peered out at the dark copper sky. "It's not likely to get all that much cooler, at least until the rain breaks. You watch yourself out there. There's going to be some weather out on the highway tonight."

"Yeah, thanks. I will." I let the screen door swing shut on its spring and went back into the café. It was dinnertime and the little place was about as full up as I imagine it ever got. Half a dozen tables and booths were filled. Enough people so that we were ignored over in the corner. Enough witnesses so that Spanno and his boys would hold off for now.

It wouldn't last, though. Soon it would be just us, the café workers, the night, and the desert. Spanno wouldn't wait forever, and what were two or three more corpses to dispose of?

I slid into the booth beside Lisette. Her drawing pad was open on the table in front of her, but there wasn't any picture, just row after row of aimlessly spiraled loops. "Any change?" she asked.

"Nope," I replied, ignoring the flat Coke in front of me. "They're still out there."

"What are we going to do, Kev?"

"I don't know, Princess. I plain don't know."

The bitch was that I actually did know what I could do. I could walk over to the pay phone, call up the local state police barracks, and whisper the magic phrase. "Officer in need of assistance." Shazam! In about fifteen minutes I could have everything short of the New Mexico National Guard out here backing me up.

But then what? The whole op would be blown to pieces and what would we get out of it? What the hell could I stick on Spanno as it was now? A weapons charge? Attempted kidnapping? A parole violation? Hell, I hadn't actually even seen a gun in his hand. I could hear his pet lawyers puking in court already. "My distraught client pursued his spoiled and erratic stepdaughter across the country because he believed she had fallen in with some young tough. Ladies and gentlemen of the jury, what loving parent could do less?''

He'd walk. He'd be out on the street in no time, and where would that leave Lisette?

Come to push the point, where would that leave Lisette and me? I found that I really wasn't looking forward to that moment when I'd have to turn to her and say, ''Excuse me, but I'm really a cop and I've just been stringing you along and screwing you over. Sorry about that.''

No. I was not looking forward to that at all.

I guess Lisette mistook the reason for my grim expression.

''Kev?'' she said, rather carefully studying the tabletop.

''Hm?''

''I'm sorry.''

'' 'Bout what?''

''I'm sorry about not telling you that I'm Mace's stepdaughter. It's not something I'm particularly proud of.''

I could only shrug. ''Don't sweat it. I can see why you wouldn't want to talk it up too much. I would like to know just how in the hell your mother ever got tangled up with Spanno in the first place. Especially after what happened with your real dad.''

Lisette gave a bitter smile. ''It's safe to say that love didn't have a whole lot to do with it. My mother was an only child, like me. Her family immigrated to the United States in the thirties, and her parents both died shortly after she married my father. Then Dad was killed and she was left alone with no family in this country. She was a young widow with a child. She had no means of support, no one she could turn to. You've seen her picture, Kev. She was a very beautiful woman. And in case you haven't noticed, Mace Spanno can be very, very forceful when it comes to getting what he wants. I can't blame her for any of this. She was never given a choice, or a chance.''

''No. I guess she wasn't.'' My eyes drifted out towards the café's front windows. The oncoming storm was killing the remnants of the day fast. The cars out on 66 had their lights on.

Lights . . . lights . . .

"Kev, I want you to know something else, too."

"What's that, Princess?"

"I never said yes to him. If you ever believe anything about me, believe that. I never said yes to Mace."

I glanced over at her. Lisette was still keeping her eyes lowered. There was the faintest tremor in her voice, like you might feel in an overloaded two-by-four just before it snaps. On the chance that it might give us a weapon against Spanno, I had to ask. I had to.

"How did it happen?"

Lisette shuddered for a moment; then she began the story. "I think Mom saw it coming. She had always been Mace's primary . . . target. But I think she noticed the way he was beginning to look at me. She tried to protect me. For the first time since we ran away when he was in jail, she stood up to Mace. She insisted I be allowed to go to college. She was trying to get me out of the house, to keep me out of sight."

The girl shrugged. "In the end, after she'd paid the price for confronting him, Mace let me go. Why not? He knew that as long as he had a handle on one of us, he had control of the other as well. That was how he always worked it. That was why he adopted me formally. It gave him more control."

Studying Lisette's pale, perfect features, I could see how this dark and convoluted relationship had come to be. Driven by rage instead of love, Mace Spanno had claimed the family of his traitorous partner as a prize of war. But then, as his partner's daughter had grown into the full beauty of her womanhood, Spanno had found himself trapped as well. Love and hate became two sides of the same coin.

Another cluster of cars passed out on the highway, headlights starring in the newborn darkness. Lights . . . I found myself splitting my attention between Lisette and what was going on out there in the night.

The girl didn't notice. She was some distance away in a not very pleasant place.

"Mom managed to keep him away from me for a while," she went on quietly. "But then Mom died. And after her funeral, Mace wouldn't let me go back to school. He made me move back in with him. And about a week later, after dinner one evening, he told me that it was time for me to assume the duties of the 'lady of the house.' And then he went on to describe, in detail, just what those duties would involve. And then I tried to stab him to death with a pair of scissors."

She laughed a little, soft and wild. "Obviously, I didn't succeed. And then he beat me for the first time the way he'd beaten my mother. And he took me up to their bedroom and he took me . . . and took me . . . and took me . . ."

I rested my hand on her shoulder. "God, Princess," I whispered. "Why didn't you go to the cops?"

"It wouldn't have done any good. I talked to a lawyer, very discreetly, and he told me that cases of incest rape are among the most difficult to successfully prosecute. I didn't have any evidence. Hardly even any bruises. Mace is an expert when it comes to certain things. He can beat you to death with his bare hands and scarcely leave a mark. It would be my word against his. And even if it got to trial, I'd never live to see him convicted."

Her head sank down tiredly onto her crossed arms, as if the weight of my hand was too much for her to support. "That's when I knew that just getting away from Mace wasn't enough," she finished, her voice muffled. "That's when I knew that I had to destroy him. It's not just a matter of escape, Kev. For my mother and me, it's a matter of justice."

"Yeah."

For Lisette and me, though, it was a matter of escape. And suddenly something started to come together.

"Princess, get the book out."

"What?" She looked up, confused.

"Get the damn guidebook out! I need to know something about the road west of here."

She didn't ask further questions; she just dug the Rittenhouse guide out of her purse.

"What do you want to know?" Her voice was all business again.

"Anything they have on this immediate stretch of highway." I kept my eyes fixed out the front windows of the café, watching for more travelers out in the night.

She riffled rapidly through the pages, looking for the little line maps.

"Amarillo to Albuquerque . . . Tucumcari . . . Montoya, we passed there. . . . okay! West of Montoya the road winds and climbs through country which becomes more rugged, with rock ledges, mesquite, and stunted trees. Tourists with trailers often camp along here . . ."

"Okay, that's it! That's what I needed."

"Do you have an idea, Kev?"

"Yeah, I might." It was pitch-dark outside now. Perfect. I needed one more thing, just one more specific thing. Come on. *Come on!* They built better than a million and a half of them last year. There's got to be another one out there tonight!

And there it was, flickering past on the road, its familiar shape outlined for an instant in the café's outside lights.

"Okay," I said quietly. "Here's the deal. We're getting out of here in a second. When I say go, we're going to get up, go out, and get in the car. Move fast, but don't run. Got that? *Don't run!*"

She didn't speak an answer. She just stowed away her sketch pad and looped the strap of her purse over her shoulder, alert and ready.

"Let's go."

We got up. I dug out my keys and tossed some money on the table. The eyes of the café crew followed us as we headed out the door. I suspect that we were going to be the prime topic of speculation around that place for some time to come.

Since I'd parked her where I could keep an eye on her, I'd left the '57 unlocked and with the windows partially down. It took us only a second to slide into the front seat. I had the engine cranking before the doors slammed shut. Around on the side of the building, more car doors were hastily closing and another power plant was turning over. Our headlights blazed on and the Chrysler's did as well, matching us move for move.

I backed away from the building, and I headed us out. But I didn't burn rubber. I swung the '57 around slowly through the fan of Spanno's headlights, giving him plenty of time to look us over. Then I pulled onto 66, heading west at the speed limit, as if I didn't give a damn in the world that he and his retinue would be following.

I was banking hard on the psychology of the pursuer. It's like dealing with a mean dog. Run from it, and it chases you by instinct. Confront or ignore it, and frequently you'll confuse it. You aren't acting right, so it doesn't know what to do.

Spanno and his boys were our mean dogs. We'd kept them out there for a couple of hours, wired up and waiting for us to make our break. But when we finally did make our move, we didn't bolt; we ambled.

They followed, of course, pulling out on the highway behind us. But they hung back about a quarter-mile, looking us over, trying to figure out what the deal was. They wouldn't stay back there for long. But maybe long enough for me to stage another disappearing act.

This one wasn't going to be easy. Route 66 was almost the only game in town out here. A single narrow strip of concrete heading into the wild. No towns. Few side roads. No second chances.

We were in mesa country. The intermittent bursts of heat lightning that played around the horizon outlined slab-sided rimrock and scattered gnarled patches of mesquite and desert cedar. An occasional wind gust shoved impatiently at the side of the car, and tumbleweeds skittered across the road.

If I was going to pull this off, I was going to have to bring a number of different factors together at the same time. My eyes flicked from the headlights in my rearview mirror to the darkened road ahead. Carefully I eased my speed up another ten miles per hour. You see, I was chasing someone, too.

Lisette sat curled in her corner of the seat, her eyes large in the dashboard glow.

"Okay," I said. "Dig my spare box of shells out of the side pocket of my suitcase. Stick it in the crack between the seat backs so it won't drift around, but where I can get at it in a hurry."

She didn't waste words; she just obeyed, procuring the ammo.

"What's up?" she inquired.

"Just doing some contingency planning in case I'm not as smart as I think I am," I replied. "Look, if I bitch this move and we end up in a fight with Spanno, you run. Don't argue. Don't try and be brave. Don't look back. You just get your little tail somewhere else as fast as you can. Head east. Stay under cover. Don't walk on the highway, but keep it in sight. Keep moving. You listening to this?"

"Kev . . . yeah, I am," she replied in a dry-throated rasp.

"I wish I could have gotten you a water bag from out of the back, but it's too late to worry about that now. If you don't come to a ranch or something by morning, go out to the road and flag down a car. Get to a phone. Call the state police. Then call a guy named Jack Le Baer out in LA, *L-e-B-a-e-r*. He's in the book. He's a friend of mine, and he'll take care of you. Got it?"

"Le Baer. Got it."

I just hoped she wouldn't need it.

Suddenly, as we came around a curve, we caught up with the first part of my plan. There was a twinned flash of red ahead of us, the taillights of another car. Specifically, they were the lights of the 1957 Chevy Nomad station wagon that I'd seen roll past the café a few minutes before, two distinctive vertical crescents glowing scarlet in the darkness.

Identical to the taillights of my own car.

I pulled in tight behind the station wagon, probably earning me a dirty thought from the Nomad's driver, but also masking it from the occupants of the Chrysler that trailed us a couple of hundred yards back.

Now I just needed the terrain to cooperate a little.

"Make sure you pull that seat belt tight, Princess. We're going to be doing something kind of wild here in a minute."

The '57 gave me the first warning, lagging down a little as she started to climb. Then I could feel the grade, too. We were going up a shallow hill, just the kind I needed. Now if only the eastbound lane would be clear.

"Grab a good hold!"

We crested the hilltop and started down the other side. The lights of the Chrysler disappeared from my mirrors as we broke line of sight.

"This is it! Hang on!"

I stood on the brake pedal and spun the wheel hard over to the left. In the vernacular, it's called a bootlegger turn, so named after the gentlemen of the hills who developed it as an escape from Revenuer roadblocks. You can turn a fast-moving car around 180 degrees within its own length. There are side effects, however; rubber smokes, tires scream, and gravity temporarily turns sideways.

Lisette gave a startled yip as the '57's tail lashed around. One second we were headed west and downhill in the right lane; the next we were going east and upslope in the left. I grabbed the floor shift, dropped down a gear, and floored the accelerator, bringing us back up to highway speed. Then I kicked my headlight beams up high.

Another set of headlights glowed just beyond the rise. I backed off on the gas so the roar of our unmuffled engine wouldn't give us away. Almost exactly at the crest of the hill, we flashed past Spanno's car, heading in the opposite direction.

It depended on a number of things now. Did they figure on our being able to turn around in the few seconds we were out of sight? Did the glare of our high beams dazzle them enough so that they didn't recognize our car as we went by? Would they stay focused on that other set of '57 taillights that still beckoned out there ahead of them?

We'd know in a second. That big 300-C would come swarming back over that hillcrest, and the chase would be on.

The rearviews stayed dark.

I gave Lisette a thumbs-up. She smiled at me. We resumed breathing.

This respite wouldn't last, though. Pretty soon, Spanno would order his wheelman to make a run on the car ahead of them and they'd discover that the hardtop they'd been chasing had magically turned into a station wagon. After blowing a few gaskets, Mace and his merry men would be after us again, this time breathing fire. Before that happened, Lisette and I had to find a nice deep hole to crawl into.

The weather was working for us, anyway. The parched night wind was rising, carrying streamers of dust and cutting down visibility. On the run out from the café I'd been mentally checking off the turnoffs along this stretch of 66. I bypassed one pretty good gravel road and a couple of what looked like ranch accesses. Then we came to a dilapidated highway-side cattle guard and a couple of ruts that led south through a scattering of scrub cedar.

That was the hole I'd chosen. No lights were in sight in either direction as we got off the highway and headed back into the trees.

It was slow going for a road car. I had to watch for potholes and for high centering. The only cheerful thought was that Spanno's vehicle was slung even lower than mine. I doubted he'd be able to make this road without leaving his oil pan draped on a boulder.

The track ran south for more than a mile and then swung west, paralleling the base of a looming cliff side. When it threatened to become totally impassable, I eased the '57 over into a rocky little turnout and shut her down.

The night wind smelled of dust and cedar and ozone. It rocked the car lightly on its springs and whined around the coachwork like a hungry animal. I put my arm out and gathered Lisette to me, and we let exhaustion catch up with us. We'd come a hell of a long way from that Oklahoma riverside.

Jesus God! Had that just been this morning?

I rested my cheek against Lisette's silky hair and tried to remember how she had looked playing in the stream.

"Kev." Her voice was muffled against my shoulder. "Can I ask you something? And will you tell me the truth?"

"Sure, Princess. And I'll try."

"Does it make much difference, those things you learned back there at the café?"

"You mean about Spanno being a shit-eating son of a bitch?" I replied. "No, not really. I'd pretty much figured that out on my own."

"No. I mean about Mace and me?"

"Like I said, Mace Spanno is a shit-eating son of a bitch, and that's about all that needs to be said on that subject."

I guess Lisette agreed, because she didn't speak again; she just nestled closer.

After a while, I scraped together enough energy to start moving again. It would be another night in the car. Out on that highway in the dark, there'd be too much chance of running into an ambush. Let Mace and his boys burn themselves out looking for us.

I dug the water bag out of the trunk, and we each took a nightcap swig. Then I got Lisette bedded down, lying on the sleeping bag in the front seat. It was still way too hot for her to think about getting into it.

I assumed my station in back. By the glow of the flashlight I took a minute to look over the Commander. I didn't dare take the pistol down completely for a full cleaning, but I checked the action and the magazines and ran a lightly oiled cloth over her. The Colt had served me well twice that day, and it would be bad joss to reward that service with a lack of attention.

Shutting off the flash, I set the pistol up on the rear deck and stretched out as well as I could.

Boy, it was a truly lousy night out there. The rising wind made the scrub trees surrounding us writhe and lash and in a couple of instances, I suspect, even get up and walk around.

Intermittently a few pinpoint spatters of rain fell on the roof, but never enough to quench the thirst of the night and bring the cool. With the windows down, the dust swirled in. With the windows up, the skyrocketing temperature pulled the sweat out of us like a magnet. I didn't think the sky was sucking quite enough air for there to be a tornado funnel in the immediate neighborhood, but we were sure in the middle of a classic high plains summer storm.

It wasn't heat lightning anymore, either. It was the genuine cold-fired article now, blue-white, hard-edged, and forking across the sky, burning starkly lit images of the rimrocks onto your retinas and blazing a path for the thunder to follow.

And damn, the thunder. A crack like a mountain splitting and a rolling roar like a battery of eight-inch howitzers firing for effect. It was a hell of a show when there was nothing between it and you but a little glass and sheet steel.

I'd made do with less, though. During the four years I'd been a soldier, I'd lived out in just about every kind of weather you could name, from blizzard to typhoon, and mostly with no more shelter than a field jacket. That was one edge I'd have over Spanno tonight.

Sure, he and his boys were big, tough gangsters with a gun in each fist and a spare up their ass. But the city was their world. They'd seen their lightning dimmed by smog and heard their thunder muffled by concrete. Tonight, though, they'd be out here under the real stuff, straight from the bottle and without a chaser.

Grown men afraid of a little storm? Yeah. It happens. They'd never admit it to it, though, especially to themselves. But deep down in their bellies, Spanno and his boys would be just a little afraid. The fear would manifest itself in their finding good, logical reasons not to stay out searching for us. It would motivate them to find solid, manly excuses for getting four walls around them. It would justify three fingers of whiskey and a blaring jukebox.

You see, on a night like this, they'd be reminded about God.

Blow on, Brother Storm. Lay me down some covering fire. Chase the scum back under the rocks so my Princess and I can rest safe awhile.

The thing was, I'd forgotten that there was someone else around here who'd never been out under the raw-edged sky before either.

"Kev," a small voice asked from the front seat. "May I crawl in back with you?"

"Sure."

The backseat was tight for one person. It was claustrophobic for two, even with the front seat backs flipped forward. We did the best we could, though. We used the sleeping bag and my suitcase to fill in as much of the floor space as we could, leveling us out a scrap of a bed. Then I gathered her in close and she tucked her head under my chin and we let the storm roll over us.

The heat was volcanic. Our sweat-damp clothes bunched and chafed, and perspiration prickled wherever our bodies touched. We didn't notice, though. No more than we noticed the clamor of the storm or the limited room. We were becoming too aware of each other just then, our heartbeats, our breathing, our being, to pay attention to details.

After a while, it started to happen. A random movement of my fingers extended into a caress down her flank. A shift of her position changed into a responsive writhe, the firm softness of her breasts molding against my chest. I felt Lisette's face tilt up, her lips brushing lightly across my face, seeking mine.

It had been a hell of a few days, a continuous string of emotional highs and lows, adrenaline surges and shared fears, enforced intimacies and half-acknowledged exhaustion. And always that perpetual hungering presence on the edge of each other's space. It was a mixture that had become as explosive as a pool of gasoline. Now we flicked a match into it.

Blouse and shirt, jeans and shorts, panties and underpants, all were torn off by one person or the other and thrown into the front seat. There was a last moment of sanity as I dug out the little cardboard box with its payload of small foil packets. Then Lisette and I both went slightly crazy.

She was all raking teeth and nails and urgent, voiceless demands. She offered and then took back. She resisted and then yielded on her terms. I had to capture her and pin her down into the narrow angle of the seat and there lift her up and out to the edge of this fire we had ignited and beyond.

And it was never enough. We'd collapse back into each other's arms, panting and exhausted, thinking that it was over. But after only a minute or so, our hands would begin to explore and caress again, moving beyond our will, and once more we'd start the long climb. We were a couple of young animals trapped in a rutting season, driven to mate again and again until we both reached total satiation.

It was the storm that finally saved us from ourselves. The rains broke, roaring down out of the skies, toning the wind down into a clean, cool breeze that flowed over us, bringing us back to our senses.

We slipped out of the car and stood naked on the hard packed sand, holding each other close and swaying through a couple of dance steps born out of some music that only we could hear.

I looked down into Lisette's face, and a last lightning flicker showed me her ironic and infinitely lovable smile. "I guess we don't have to worry about getting two rooms anymore?" she said.

Damn straight we didn't.

We helped each other bathe in the sweet rainwater. Then we crawled back into the '57's rear seat. Once it had felt like a coffin built for two. Now it was a cozy den. We built our abandoned clothing into the bed, bare skin being a lot more comfortable than damp denim in a situation like this. Also during the past couple of hours, we'd learned a whole lot about the best ways to fit our bodies together. With Lisette snuggled against me like a drowsy kitten, I tugged a corner of the unzipped sleeping bag over us.

This time we slept.

We awoke next morning to a clear sky and a brushfire sunrise out over the plains. On one side, a towering streak-sided mesa loomed over us, night shadow still cowering in its rim canyons. On the other, a broad and rolling valley glowed dry-grass gold and cedar green in the dawn light.

That's the funny thing about New Mexico. People just go around living in places beautiful enough to be declared a national monument anywhere else.

I dug my pants, shirt, and boots out of the boar's nest in the back of the car, leaving my space to Lisette. With a drowsy grumble, she hugged the sleeping bag to herself and burrowed into the corner of the seat, leaving the morning to the '57 and me.

That was okay. I didn't mind having a few minutes to myself. I had a lot of things to think about.

I ambled around to the front of the car and leaned back against the fender, stretching the kinks out and enjoying the experience of breathing. God, the air was something else. Cool and so clean that it was almost scary to an LA boy. The rain had refreshed the cedar grove around us, and the little trees were pumping out so much oxygen you felt like you were running on a personal supercharger.

That supercharge, though, reminded me that we were going to be doing some serious climbing today. "You're going to need your jets reset, Car," I commented to the '57. "We're getting into some altitude, and I don't need you fading out on me. I'll go under the hood and have a look at those carbs before we haul out this morning."

"Just warm your hands first, hotshot," the '57 replied in a muffled feminine voice.

Since my vehicle is far too dignified to make that kind of wisecrack, it had to stem from another source. Lisette leaned bare-shouldered out of the rear window, smiling at me. "Do you always go around talking to your car like that?" she asked.

"Sure. Don't you?

"Uh, no."

"Well, then, the next time it won't start for you on a cold morning don't wonder why."

I stepped back to the girl and hunkered down to meet her at eye level. I started to say good morning, but then I remembered that we had better ways to communicate now. Lisette's good-morning-it's-nice-to-be-with-you kisses were fully as good as her good-night-and-thank-you ones.

"Sleep well?" I asked her as we paused for breath.

"Eventually," she drawled back.

"The accommodations weren't exactly the Waldorf Astoria."

"I've stayed at the Astoria," she replied, "and this was nicer. A much better grade of clientele." She drew herself up a little farther. The sleeping bag slipped to the car floor, leaving her kneeling sleek and nude on the seat.

"Aren't you a little cold, Princess?" I inquired, sighting down her back.

"Nope," she replied, glancing at herself. "It feels good. So good, in fact, that I might give up wearing clothes altogether. Would you mind terribly?"

"I guess I could learn to live with it after a while."

We shared a chuckle and a nuzzle. Lisette crossed her wrists on the window frame and rested her chin on them. "Kev, can I tell you something?"

"Sure. Anything you like."

"Last night is going to be my first time."

I didn't know exactly what she meant, so I didn't exactly know how to answer. Lisette's experiences with Spanno must have left a massive raw place torn inside of her. I wasn't sure what I could touch without causing her pain.

"That . . . stuff with Mace didn't count," she went on, a shadow of sadness crossing her face. "That will all go away after he's gone. But last night I'll remember."

She slipped one of her hands out from under her chin and reached out with it, gently stroking my hair. "I didn't get to choose the first time and place I was ever with a man. But I did get to choose the first time and place I ever made love, and that was here, with you. No matter what else happens, Kev, I want you to remember that. It's important. Okay?"

I traced the outline of her cheek with a fingertip. "That's an easy promise to make, Princess."

When we crept down out of our hideout, we found 66 clear of traffic, hostile or otherwise. In Santa Rosa, we yielded to the grinning blandishments of the fat man on the Club Café advertisements and stopped for a short stack and a side. Topped off on gas, grub, and water, we headed out on the hundred-and-twenty-mile haul to Albuquerque. As we pulled the long subtle climbs west to Cline's Corners, more ranked mesas rose out of the scrub forest ahead of us, stone-sided battleships cruising a green sea. To the north and west was the shadowy promise of the more serious mountains to come.

We cleared Tijeras Pass at seven thousand feet, with the peak of Cerro Pedernal towering buckled and broken on our right hand. Then the downgrade and fifteen miles of twists and dips into Tijeras Canyon and, finally, the valley of the Rio Grande.

Albuquerque itself was good for another refuel, a stretch, and a cold quart of milk shared out of the bottle in the meager shade of the market building. Then we moved out again. We were getting within striking range of Arizona and of a place called Peerless.

West again, into a hot, parched pastel world. Pale vermilion cliffs, pale yellow sand, and pale gray sage under a pale azure sky, tangled with frost-colored contrails.

Correo . . . Mesita   Village . . . Laguna   Pueblo . . . Paraje Trading Post. The Indian trading posts along the stretch of the highway weren't tourist traps. They were the real thing. We were skirting the vast Laguna, Navajo, and Zuni reservations, and there wasn't a Made-in-Japan rubber tomahawk in sight.

Grants . . . Prewitt . . . Thoreau . . . the Continental Divide and the highest point on Route 66. Then the final decent to Gallup, hiding down in the wind-carved sandstone bluffs near the borderline.

It was midafternoon when we rolled into town, and the asphalt smoked under the glare of a sadistic sun. The biting heat gave us the excuse we'd both been looking for to stop early.

Things had been different in the car that day. We'd ended one kind of dance last night, and now we were beginning another. Suddenly it was safe to let a casual touch turn into a caress, a look become a kiss. Lisette didn't ride over in the corner of the front seat anymore. She sat beside me, her thigh brushing mine, her hand lightly resting on my shirt collar, her head free to rest on my shoulder whenever she liked.

I was incredibly aware of her as well, the look of her, the feel and the scent of her, the wondrous secrets hidden beneath her scant summer clothing. And then there was the realization that all of it was open to me now. Lisette's gift, freely given.

It was hard to keep my mind on the road or the job. And it would be incredibly easy to tell Spanno and the Los Angeles Sheriff's Department and the entire world in general to kindly go to hell and leave us alone for a little while. The Princess and I wanted some time to explore the new steps and rhythm we were moving to.

We hadn't gone totally hormone-happy, however. Before settling down, we cruised the narrow western-flavored streets of Gallup, scouting for anything black, shiny, and ominous.

There hadn't been any sign of Spanno and company all day, although the drive through the mountains and desert had left them plenty of good openings for an ambush. Once, out beyond Barton, we'd nearly jumped out of our skin when we'd come booming around a blind corner to almost rear-end a dark Chrysler. However, it turned out to be a navy blue New Yorker and a gray-haired retiree couple en route to Vegas with a back-seat full of hangered evening wear.

I wasn't sure which was worse, having the bad guys hanging on my hip, where I could at least keep an eye on them, or having them out there somewhere, out of sight, setting something up.

Eventually, I took us back to the old El Rancho hotel.

I'd heard about El Rancho clear out in LA. The big old brick-and-native-stone hotel is Gallup's finest and the base camp for a lot of the movie crews doing location work in the area. Framed photos of some of the biggest names in Hollywood, personally autographed to the hotel, were displayed around the big two-story lobby, along with a sizable collection of southwestern art.

With Lisette secure behind locked hotel doors, I took the car to the service station across the highway. There I got the '57 up on the rack for a lube job and an oil change. I slipped the attendant a couple of bucks to let me do my own work. I slipped him a couple more to let me keep my car parked out of sight in one of the service bays until the next morning. I used one of my better lines, the just-between-us-guys one about my inattentive son of a bitch of a boss, his obliging and warm-natured wife, and a discreet little rendezvous that I didn't want disrupted. I suspect I made that pump jockey's day.

A shower and a shave felt good, and considering the company I was keeping, I didn't even mind digging out my sports jacket and the one pair of dress slacks I had along. Lisette wanted a sit-down dinner that evening in the hotel dining room, and she was busy at the esoteric task of making herself even prettier than usual. Naturally, I was ready in about a quarter of the time she needed. Taking advantage of the fact, I told her I had some things to do and that I'd meet her in the lobby.

There were a couple of phone booths down there, and it

didn't take long to get through to our office in LA. I brought Jack up-to-date, and his response worried me. He didn't do any roaring and raging.

"Kid," he said quietly, "I think we might want to pull the plug on this one."

"Pull the plug! Jesus, Jack! I haven't gotten anything yet!"

"I know. And you've been sticking your neck way the hell out for that load of nothing. Look, yesterday this guy Spanno had a gun in your guts. You managed to bluff him, once. You ain't going to be able to do it again. Next time, he's gonna pull the trigger."

"Next time I won't give him the chance. Hell, this is no worse than any other undercover job we've ever worked."

"The hell it ain't, kid!" Now the Bear growled. "These guys are pros! The real Chicago article! And you are out there without one damn bit of cover. You do one thing wrong, and we'll never even find your damn corpse. Hell, screw that! You could do everything right and still end up dead!"

"Come on, Jack; give me a break here!" I replied. "I'm solid inside the setup, and I'm still rolling the dice. I just need some more time to work this thing. I know I can produce some solid evidence on Spanno. We have to put this guy away!"

"Why?" Jack asked flatly. "I want you to tell me why it's so important that we put this one particular hood down."

"What do you mean, why ?"

"Let me put it this way, kid. Has Spanno's daughter dropped her pants for you yet?"

"*Jack, you son of a bitch!*" I came to my feet in the confined space of the booth so fast that I almost knocked out the door.

"Take it easy. Take it easy." Jack suddenly sounded old and tired. "You just answered the question. God damn it, Kevin! Haven't I taught you anything these last three years? When you're out there working undercover, you don't get involved! You don't become part of the crime!"

"That's bullshit, Jack! I'm handling this!"

"The hell you are, Pulaski! The second the job gets personal instead of professional, the second you stop thinking cop, you are *not* handling it!"

What could I say? He was right. Somewhere back along the road this deal had become more than just a job. Maybe it was about time that I started admitting that to myself.

"She's a good kid, Jack," I said into the phone. "And she's in bad trouble. I can't bail out on her now. If Spanno ever gets his hands on her again, it's going to be something really ugly. I'm asking you to stick with me on this, partner. I need a little more time."

"Aw, shit!"

But it was a resigned, "Aw, shit!"

Jack's voice went wry. "Okay, kid. It's your neck. We'll hang on this thing awhile longer. I've got a picture of the Spanno girl on the desk in front of me now. Maybe if I didn't have Sheila and I was twenty years younger, I might be tempted to make a goddamn fool of myself, too. What's the play for tomorrow?"

"We're moving in on the older Claster brother, Jubal, in a place called Peerless, Arizona," I replied. "It's a little hole-in-the-wall out between Flagstaff and Winslow. According to dope we got on this guy from Calvin Reece, he was involved in the killings of Leopold and Vallessio back up in Oklahoma. By the way, any word out of Texas about the younger brother, Ira?"

"The Texas Highway Patrol found the truck and the shotgun about where you said they'd be. No sign of this Ira guy, though. They figure he must have hitched a lift out of there to one of the local towns. APBs are out in Texas and all adjoining states. No kickbacks on him yet."

I nodded to myself. "Okay, let's just hope he hasn't joined up with his brother, Jubal, or that they both haven't taken off."

"Hey, kid. How 'bout we contact the Arizona Patrol and have them put a couple of cars in around this Peerless place? Just in case."

"Nah, that's no good, Jack. If I remember right, the country out that way is as flat and empty as a pool table. Even a plain-clothes car would stand out like a sore at a short arms inspection. The Clasters are real twitchy about this whole Kingman situation. If Jubal's still there and if the girl and I go in alone, maybe we can get him talking. But if he even gets a sniff of anything funny, I'll bet he'll either bolt or start shooting. Let's just make the scene and play it cool."

"Whatever," the Bear grumbled. "You're calling it. But this is one hell of a way to run a police operation."

"I know, but it's my way."

I heard him sigh heavily into the phone. "Will you at least do me one favor?"

"Sure. What is it?"

"*Listen to me!* Stick your dick back in your pants, clean the wax out of your ears, and listen to what I'm about to say!"

"I'm listening, Jack."

"Do not trust the Spanno girl! Take her out, take her to bed, take her home to meet your friggin' Aunt Angeline, but do not trust her! Maybe she is on the square, maybe she is feeding you a straight line, but don't count on it! She's the daughter of a hood, and she's the stepdaughter of another hood. She's been raised in a world where loyalty is for suckers and a stab in the back is just how you do business. She could sell you out or turn on you in two seconds flat if it becomes necessary or even only convenient!"

There was a silence on that phone from both ends for a lot more than two seconds.

"You hear me, kid?"

"Yeah, Jack. I'm hearing you. I have to go, man."

I left the phone booth and lit up a smoke, just because I needed something to do. Crossing the flagstone floor, I leaned against polished timber rail of the lobby stairway.

Yeah, I heard you, Jack. And I really wish I could tell you to go to hell. The problem is that in the three years you've been my partner I've never known you to give me a bum steer about the job.

A special voice called from the top of the stairs, and I jammed the mass of doubts and suspicions that had suddenly come crowding around me back in the closet. For a while anyway.

The dust-stained tomboy that I'd been tear-assing around the country with for the past couple of days was gone, and the Princess was back in her full regal glory. She was in her heels and a bright print summer dress she'd been holding in reserve ever since Saint Louis. Strap-shouldered, full-skirted, and a long way from being expensive, Lisette made it beautiful because she was beautiful in it.

She knew it, too. She paced proudly and gracefully down the halved-log steps, her eyes bright and her head lifted high. She wore her long and sheening brown hair like an expensive stole, bound back with a scarlet ribbon and swept forward over her shoulder with provocative casualness.

I found myself praying that just this one time, Jack might be wrong.

We had a drink before dinner in El Rancho's cool pine-paneled bar. As we were shown to our table, there was a hesitation in the flow of conversation around the room. I'd noted Lisette producing that effect before. Men got that faraway look in their eyes while other women gritted their teeth and thought about dark alleys and blunt objects. Lisette was aware of it, too, and she smiled a slightly smug and eternally feminine smile beneath lowered lashes.

A few ancient and atavistic instincts of my own were in play as I held her chair for her and beamed a silent warning to the other masculine onlookers around the room. Something to the effect of, *No trespassing, you bunch of losers! This claim has been staked!*

After the barmaid had brought us a couple of screwdrivers, Lisette lightly swirled the hem of her skirt. "Like it?" she asked.

"I do, Princess. But I thought this morning you were swearing off clothes."

She arched an eyebrow. "I'm closer to it than you might imagine. The only two pairs of panties I have to my name are in the hotel laundry just now. If you see a breeze coming, for God's sake yell."

"I'll make a note of it." I struggled past some very intriguing mental imagery and got back on the job. "It seems like you started out on this jaunt awfully short on resources. How come you didn't set yourself up better?"

"I didn't plan it this way," Lisette replied grimly, swirling the ice cubes in her glass. "Believe me. When I decided to go after my father's loot, I started stashing away running money for a car and traveling expenses. I almost had enough, too, when the ceiling fell in."

"What happened?"

"Mace got wise to what I was up to. I think that's one of the reasons Mace forced Mother to marry him. I think he always suspected that we knew something about where the two hundred thousand was hidden. Sometimes when he was mad about something or had been drinking, he'd . . . question her about it."

Lisette's jaw tightened and she took a long pull at her drink. "Anyway, word must have gotten back to him that I was talking to some of my father's old acquaintances and asking questions about the lost Leopold gang war chest."

"So Mace guessed you might be making a try for the money?" I prompted.

"He must have. The day before we met, I came home and found that my room had been torn apart. I'd taken to carrying the guidebook with me at all times, but I'd had some notes and newspaper photostats hidden away there. They were gone and so was all my money. It was just sheer luck that I'd come home unexpectedly early that day. If Mace or one of his boys had been there waiting for me, I don't know what would have happened."

"What did happen?"

"When I came out of my room, the housekeeper was just

hanging up the phone. I knew what that meant, and I knew I had to get out of there." Lisette gave a cool smile. "She tried to keep me from leaving, but I decked her with the best right cross I've ever thrown and was out the door like a scared rabbit."

"And then?"

"I had nowhere to go and nothing but what I stood up in. I knew that Mace would have every one of his men out combing the streets for me, so I hid out in a movie theater, sitting through the same bill over and over again. When the theater closed, I drifted from one all-night café to the next. By the next morning, I realized that I didn't have any choice. I had to go after my father's money right then, just as things were."

"You were taking on pretty long odds."

She shrugged her slim shoulders. "A little chance is better than no hope. I sneaked out of Gary into Chicago and then headed south. I ran out of bus fare in Pontiac, and I started hitchhiking. That's how I ended up at that truck stop looking for a lift to Saint Louis."

I shook my head. "How in the hell did you ever figure on making it clear across the country?"

"I'd have managed," Lisette replied, regarding me somberly. "I know what I look like, Kev. I wouldn't have had much trouble getting money and favors out of men along the way. I just would have had to pay for them."

A smile lit up her face then, and she caught my hand in hers. "But it turned out I didn't have to. A genuine Sir Galahad came to my rescue." Lifting my hand to her face, she gently pressed my palm to her cheek. "For a long time," she murmured, "I thought knights in shining armor were only something they wrote about in storybooks."

I'm sorry to disappoint you, Princess, I replied silently, *but I'm afraid they are.*

A film crew was in residence at El Rancho, shooting an oater called *Fort Massacre,* and Lisette was as excited as a kid when we were seated across from Joel McCrea and Forrest Tucker in the hotel's compact dining room. If this had just been a date, I could have told her some of the wilder Sheriff's Department stories out of Hollywood, the ones that *Photoplay* and even *Confidential* were scared to pick up. Instead, after we had ordered, I had to maneuver our conversation back around to tomorrow.

"Do you figure this Jubal Claster might have some clues about where your father stashed the war chest?"

Lisette shook her head. "I'd doubt it. Dad didn't say anything to Calvin Reece about his plans, or even to my mother. I don't think he'd let anything on to some hired hand he'd picked up along the way. And Claster wasn't with Dad when he hid the money. My father was traveling alone by the time he reached Oklahoma City. We know that from the wrecking yard."

"Are you sure he's worth bothering with then? The Claster clan seems a little edgy about the whole Leopold question. When you consider the way little brother Ira flipped out over the matter, you have to wonder how big brother Jubal is going to react when you introduce yourself. Chain saws and dynamite?"

Lisette stared down at the tabletop, tracing an outline on the cloth with the tines of her fork. "I know it's stupid risking our lives just to try and ask this man some questions he probably won't answer. But this is important to me, Kevin. I wish I could explain it so you could understand."

I whistled a couple of soft notes to bring her eyes up to meet mine. "Hey, just keep going. This is old Sir Galahad over here, remember. You can talk me into anything. Just give me the word on this."

She hesitated a moment, then went on. "I know that my father was responsible for the deaths of his two partners back there in Baxter Springs, I accept that. But I need to know how they died. I need to know if it was a robbery that went wrong or a murder that went right. Jubal Claster is my only chance to find out."

"Hell, Princess, putting it bluntly, dead is dead. Does it really make that much difference at this late date how those two guys bought it?"

Lisette flinched a little at my words. "It makes a difference to me!" She hesitated a long second, hunting for words. "Look; when I was a little girl, my dad was just . . . Daddy. He was a big man who was away lots of the time, but who smiled and laughed when he was home. He brought me nice presents and told me funny stories, and he was good for a hug and a cuddle whenever I wanted one. That was all that was important. It wasn't until later, after he was killed, that I began to realize what the word *criminal* meant."

The girl twirled the fork moodily between her fingers. "Even then, for a long time I couldn't accept the reality. I tried to visualize my father as a kind of modern Jesse James or Robin Hood, different and superior in some way to Mace and the others. You know, a 'gangster with a heart of gold' like James Cagney used to play in the movies. But as I started to look deeper into my father's past and into his world, I began to learn that real gangsters don't have hearts at all. They just have a big dark hole in their chest where they pour the blood of innocent people."

The fork tinkled down on the table amid the other tableware. "That's what I need to learn, Kevin," she finished softly. "For my own peace of mind and for any future I'm ever going to have. I need to know if I have any daddy left that's worth remembering or if both of my fathers are just lousy murdering hoods."

Our steaks showed up and I was damn glad to have this line of discussion interrupted. Lisette didn't have much appetite at first, but I got to work running the train of conversation over any track except the one that led to Peerless. I dug out some of my old army stories, like the one about the night my squad and I sat out maneuvers in a North Carolina roadhouse. I filled her in on the truth about the "Hotsy-Botsy" baths in Tokyo and about my one memorable leave in Honolulu, or at least the parts that happened before I passed out. I had her laughing again by the time the mountain-blueberry cobbler showed up.

We lingered at the table, killing off the last of the wine we'd ordered with dinner. Then Lisette stretched languorously. "I think I'm ready for bed," she sighed.

"Sleepy, Princess?"

She gave me a long and level-eyed look across the table. "I didn't say that I was sleepy, darling. I said that I was ready for bed."

En route back to our room we passed the "trading post" gift shop just off the lobby. As is just about mandatory in Arizona and New Mexico, it was jammed with the usual selection of Navajo blankets, pottery, and kachina dolls for the tourist trade. And even aroused passion couldn't get Lisette past the displays of handmade Indian jewelry blazing under the showcase lights.

I stood next to her as she oohed over the trays, waiting for that inevitable sideways glance in my direction. What the hell, I was starting to run a little tight on money, but I had an emergency ten spot tucked away in a corner of my wallet.

Her eventual selection was a burnished copper barrette that suited the sheening brown of her hair.

"What do you think?" she asked cautiously. "Do you like it?"

"Hell," I replied. "Do *you* like it? That's what's important."

She shook her head emphatically. "No. You're buying this for me, and you'll see me wearing it. You have to like it, too."

"Then I think it's beautiful."

"Truly?"

"Truly."

It was a done deal all around, and the young Navajo woman behind the counter grinned knowingly as she packed the barrette in a little white jewelry box and passed it to Lisette.

The Princess studied the box in her hand for a long thoughtful moment. Then she smiled as well.

"Here," she said, pressing the box into my hand. "Give me the room key and you take this. Bring it up in five minutes and we'll try it on."

Then she was gone in a quick swirl of skirt.

It was a long five minutes.

Our room was at the end of the cool and curving brick-walled hallway on the second floor. The door's safety chain rattled off in response to my knock. "All right," she whispered through the door. "Come in."

The room was darkened and I took a second to secure the door behind me.

The drapes had been drawn back and the windows had been opened to admit the moonlight and the breeze coming off the mountains. The bed was turned down, and Lisette's dress was draped over the back of a chair.

She stood in the center of the little room, clad as she had been that first night back at the Coral Court, in her hair ribbon and my old white shirt. Only now, none of the buttons had been done and the shirt was held closed only by a strip of shadow. "Did you bring the barrette?" she asked.

It took me a second to remember. "Oh, yeah. Still got it," I replied, balancing the little box in my hand. Despite the open windows, it seemed to be getting a little hard to breathe.

"Would you put it on me, please?" Deliberately she reached up behind her head, untying her ribbon and letting a dark cascade fall loose around her shoulders, allowing the front of her shirt to open with the lift of her arms.

Lisette let me have a long look at that perfect ivory body. Then she turned away, presenting her back and her glossy fall of hair, silently demanding her present.

My fingers felt stiff and clumsy just at a time when I wanted them to do something perfectly right. I fumbled the barrette from its box. My hands picked up a touch of the wild rose perfume she'd brushed through her hair as I gathered the warm, living silk at the base of her neck. Containing it with the clip, I snapped the clasp shut.

I'd given her something, and now it was only fair that I take something as well. Slipping my hands down to her shoulders, I took her shirt away, leaving her in nothing but moonlight and the single gleam of red-gold.

"How does it look?" she asked huskily, her voice sounding as if she was having a little trouble with her breathing, too.

My only answer was to brush her ponytail aside, lifting it over her shoulder so she could experience the liquidy caress of her own hair flowing down over her bare breast. Lisette gasped and I sensed the shiver that rippled down her spine. I leaned down and kissed the starting place of that shiver, just between her shoulder blades. With another sound, half-snarl, half-whimper, she spun around and threw herself into my arms.

Some sweet and interesting times later, Lisette lay curled up beside me, making that soft little purring buzz that's as close as she gets to a snore. I should have been asleep, too, but I wasn't.

I hadn't seen a real bed for two days, I'd had enough alcohol to take off the rough edges, and I'd just finished making prolonged and satisfying love with a very playful, passionate, and enthusiastic young lady. By rights, I should have been out like a light. But sometimes, in these quiet, dark hours beyond midnight, thoughts you can escape during the day can sneak up on you.

This operation was dangerously close to exploding in my face. We were just two states out from the coast, and I still didn't have a line on the money or on how I was going to take Spanno down. It's all well and good to say that you're going to wing it and await developments, but man, I was running out of miles and time.

I also had no idea about how I was going to tell Lisette the truth about myself, nor could I even guess about what might happen between us afterward.

I was dangerously close to whispering some very special words to this wild and wondrous little person who slept naked at my side. Words that I guess I'd said but never really meant to any woman before in my life. I think I might have already if it weren't for the little matter of trust.

Love and trust need to be in the same sentence. And the moment, with Lisette and me, they weren't even mentioned in the same chapter.

Lisette trusting me? Hell, that was a nonstarter. She was still holding out about the location of the money.

Me trusting Lisette? Besides the money, what else was she holding out on? Tonight, she'd frankly said that she'd been willing to do whatever was necessary to reclaim her father's lost fortune. And back in Saint Louis, she'd tried to buy my services with that beautiful body of hers. Maybe she was buying them now but just using a little more sophisticated kind of payment plan.

The Bear had been sooo right. A lawman can't let the law become personal.

I rolled over to the edge of the bed. Glancing down, I noticed Lisette's shoulder bag sitting on the bottom shelf of the lamp table.

A long time ago, when I was a kid, my father told me, "Sometimes if you can't think your way out of a problem, work your way out of it. Do something constructive, anything; just don't sit around and brood." I sometimes suspect that Dad came up with that bit of wisdom just to help get the lawns mowed, but I was willing to give it a try tonight.

Reaching down, I opened the clasp on the bag and eased out the Rittenhouse guide. Being careful not to wake Lisette, I got off the bed and went into the bathroom. I'd been wanting to take another look at that little book, and now was as good an opportunity as any. Turning on the light, I assumed my best "The Thinker" position on the pot and began studying pages.

There were a lot fewer now to be concerned with, just Arizona and California. Essentially desert, no major cities, few small towns, few people at all until you hit LA. Just lots and lots of empty space to hide $200,000 in. And maybe, some-where in this book, there was one tiny hint about where.

I didn't find a thing on my first read-through. Doggedly I flipped back to the start of the Arizona section and began again. Lisette had figured out where the money was, but Spanno hadn't. This guidebook was the sole information source that Lisette had that Spanno didn't. Ipso facto, the key clue was here in the book.

Barring, of course, the very real possibility that somebody, somewhere, wasn't feeding me a line of total bullshit.

I didn't see anything on my second go-round, either. I con-sidered saying to hell with it and going back to bed. But then I decided to give it one more shot. This time, though, I didn't try to read; I just leafed through the pages and looked.

That was when I spotted it.

The paper of the hard-used little guidebook had darkened some over time. But around one entry on page 116 of the Cal-ifornia section the paper was just a shade lighter. Maybe as if something had been erased off of it.

Carefully holding the book parted at that place, I rapped the bottom of the spine against the edge of the sink. A few crumbs of rubber fell out of the binding. I rolled a finger over them. They were still soft, fresh. Something had been erased on that page and recently.

The entry concerned a desert stretch of Route 66 out be-tween Needles and Barstow. It had been underlined, but the pencil marks had all been carefully removed. I couldn't help but remember the big art gum eraser Lisette carried in her purse.

195 mi. (174 mi.). Here you pass close to Mount Pisga Volcanic Crater, whose lava flow comes to the very edge of US 66(L). If you did not visit Amboy Crater, it is worth your while to stop for a few minutes to walk over and examine this lava flow . . .

Johnny 32 Kingman did not give a howl in hell about volcanic geology. He'd been using this guidebook as a blueprint for a heist. Every notation he had made had a direct connection with some concrete aspect of his plan. A fast recheck verified that there was only one other notation in the book that didn't involve a location in a city or town.

And that was the murder site outside of Quapaw.

I remembered my own words back in Oklahoma City: ". . . out-of-doors . . . somewhere near the highway where he could get at it fast." Lisette must have remembered this entry, and my thinking out loud must have made the connection for her. This was it. This had to be it!

I could visualize Johnny 32 grinning at his own inside joke as he underlined the passage ten years ago. I could also visualize his daughter rubbing those lines out just a couple of days back, sealing the secret away for herself.

I took a minute to memorize the entry and the mileage notations; then I switched out the light and went back to bed. I returned the guidebook to Lisette's bag, and I was just easing down onto the mattress when the even tempo of the girl's breathing broke.

"Everything all right?" she asked drowsily.

"Everything's fine. I'm just a little restless, I guess."

"Let me help." She nestled against me, a flow of bare satiny skin molding against my back from shoulder to the knee. Her arm lightly hooked around my chest, and I felt a gentle hug and the brush of her lips against the nape of my neck. "I'll keep you warm."

"Thanks, Princess. Go back to sleep."

She already had. I could feel her slow, even breathing riffle my hair.

I stared out into the room's darkness again. So there was one of my problems solved. I'd broken the secret of the guidebook, and now I knew where the two hundred grand was hidden.

Big friggin' deal.

ARIZONA

173 mi. (69 mi.) Stafford's Café, including gas, gro-
ceries and a curio shop, comprises the town of Allen-
town here. Soon the trees grow more sparse and you
begin to enter a stretch of over 125 miles of almost
barren country . . .

Back at the dying end of the last century, a wagon track met a
mean dry wash out on the Arizona desert. Here a bridge was
built, and so was a town. Dreaming boomers' dreams of growth
and prosperity, its founders called it Peerless.

Peerless didn't grow, however; nor did it prosper. It just
survived through the searing summers and freezing winters on
the flats just east of the San Francisco range, a one-horse supply
stop for the local ranchers and miners.

Years passed and times changed. Mr. Ford's Tin Lizzie gave
the locals a new mobility. The ranchers and miners started
going up to the bright lights of Flagstaff whenever they needed
to restock, and Peerless found itself deprived of its justification

for existence. Soon even survival looked questionable.

But then, in 1927, some crazy government men came through, posting signs along the gravel road that ran across the bridge and through the little town, proclaiming it officially part of something called "US Highway 66." They predicted big changes coming.

But not right away. The depression came first. Throughout the thirties, Peerless lingered, staying alive on the droplets of blood left behind by the dust bowl refugees fleeing for the theoretical refuge of California and from the crumbs dropped by the upper crust experimenting with this new amusement called motor touring.

Things began to turn around after the CCC boys brought the paving through. Diesel fuel and black coffee were added to the town's inventory as America heard war talk and the big rigs started to roll again, riding the wave of rearmament. And after Pearl Harbor the troop convoys trudged past. On their way to combat, a million men caught a fleeting glimpse of a gaunt little desert town and never even knew its name.

When the war ended, the changes did come. The men came home and started families and bought the bright new cars rolling off the assembly lines. They wanted to enjoy the freedom they'd fought for. They wanted to see the country they'd defended. And Peerless was part of that country.

Good times, man. Mary was kept busy in the kitchen of Mary's Café. High-octane flowed in a river from the Peerless Flying A. The Tom Tom Trading Post produced an unending stream of postcards and "genuine Indian" beadwork. And the Grand Canyon Auto Court was full almost every night during the season, even when their advertised "air cooling" turned out to only be an electric fan on the dresser.

Then, about the time the present deponent was arguing with a bunch of moody Marxists over around Pyongyang, the aging two-lane bridge over the wash west of Peerless was taken out by a flash flood. This was bad enough, but then some bright young engineer in the State Highway Department noticed that if a replacement span and a bypass were built just a few miles downstream, a meandering northern loop could be cut out of Route 66. The driving time from Winslow to Flagstaff could be reduced by a good fifteen minutes. No doubt feeling proud of himself, he reached down and drew a little line on the map.

He couldn't have destroyed Peerless any more thoroughly if he'd called in a bombing mission.

The traffic on the highway had become the lifeblood of the town. Deprived of that bloodflow, gangrene set in rapidly. No one came to eat Mary's hot beef sandwiches. No one pawed through the beads and trinkets in the Tom Tom Trading Post. No one stayed at the Grand Canyon Auto Court even after they put in real air-conditioning.

The FOR SALE signs went up, but there were no takers for a dead-end community on a dead-end road. And so, after a while, the people of Peerless just drifted away to places where they could stay alive. They abandoned their town to the desert wind and to the one man who chose to stay behind.

That was the story of Peerless as we'd picked it up that morning, heading west out of Gallup. Passing under the Route 66 arch at the state line, we'd left the wind-carved ramparts of New Mexico behind and started out across the mirage-haunted wastes of northern Arizona.

There's a lot of strange stuff out there. The highway led us past the Painted Desert, where the land is made of flame turned to stone, and then on through Petrified Forest National Monument, where the towering trees of an ancient woodland had toppled and become trapped in eternity, maybe as punishment for some prehistoric sin. Meteor Crater is out there, too, that huge cosmic shell hole that proves we are receiving visitors from outer space, only straight down and at twelve miles per second.

It's beautiful country, but it's an eerie kind of beauty, unearthly, almost as if you might look out across it and see somebody with three eyes and a couple of antennae looking back.

It's lonely country, too. There aren't a lot people living out here, and those who do know each other or at least of each other. Inquiring at some of the isolated gas stations and trading posts along the way, we soon started hearing about "that guy in Peerless." We didn't hit the real jackpot until we talked to the counterman at the Meteor Crater Café.

"Jubal Claster?" he said. "Sure I know him. He comes in here for breakfast pretty regular. I guess even he needs some-body to talk to every now and again."

"So is he still over in Peerless?" I asked, taking a sip of Coke I didn't particularly want.

"Mister, he *is* Peerless. He's the last guy hanging on in that dump, and frankly, I don't know how he keeps from starving to death. Nobody goes out that way anymore."

"It's funny, a man living alone like that," Lisette said, stir-ring the ice in her drink in a carefully unconcerned fashion. "What kind of person is he?"

The counterman shrugged. "Quiet, keeps to himself. There's not much to say about him, really. He's been running the gas station in Peerless ever since a couple of years after the war. I just figured him to be a returned vet who wanted to be his own boss. Say, what's up with old Jubal anyway?"

"What do you mean?" I asked.

"Well, for years nobody's said a word about him. Now you folks are the second batch of people in less than a day to come through asking about him."

Lisette and I glanced at each other. "Somebody else has been asking about Jubal Claster?"

"Yeah. Three guys were in here last night. What's going on?"

"He's just won the Irish Sweepstakes." I tossed a quarter on the counter, and Lisette and I started for the door.

The turnoff for Peerless was only a couple of miles farther west, marked by a faded and collapsing cluster of billboards adver-tising tourist services, the town's frantic last-ditch effort to draw in enough road dollars to survive. Leaving the highway, we bumped over the twin sets of Santa Fe tracks that paralleled 66 along this stretch and followed the cracked pavement out into the desert.

Peerless itself was as dusty and disintegrating a little ghost town as you could have wanted. Only about twenty or so small buildings strung out along either side of the access road, just short of the barricaded approaches and abandoned piers of the demolished bridge. It looked lifeless, but no way was I taking that for granted. I pulled over on a small rise just east of town and dug my binoculars out from under the seat. For the next fifteen minutes I systematically glassed every inch of the place, looking for unpleasant surprises.

Nothing moved except for the heat shimmer.

As I ran my recon, Lisette sat cross-legged on the '57's trunk lid, her pencil whispering. When I lowered my binoculars, she held up her drawing pad. "What do you think?"

It was a sketch of Peerless, silhouetted against the backdrop of the San Francisco range. Simple, stark, and elemental, yet she'd grabbed up a chunk of the loneliness and despair of the place and tacked it down on paper. I nodded. "Yeah, you got it."

"Are things any better closer up?" she asked.

"Have a look." I passed the field glasses to her.

Figuring out the focus, she studied Peerless for herself. "Do you remember me saying how I hid out in a movie theater that first night I was on the run?" she asked after a couple of minutes.

"Yeah."

"Well, one of the movies I sat through six times had a town in it just like this one. Giant radioactive grasshoppers had come out of the desert and had eaten everybody."

"I saw that one, too. *The Beginning of the End.* Peter Graves and Peggie Castle. Cool flick!"

Lisette made a sour face and handed the glasses back to me. "I wonder if Claster really is still living down there."

"Somebody is. The gas station hasn't been abandoned yet."

I lifted the binoculars to my eyes again. The station in question was the last building on the north side of the highway. A single-story white clapboard structure, it was an old-fashioned rural live-in station. What they used to call a double-ender. The end that faced the road contained the station office. The other end had a "front" porch in back that opened into the owner's living quarters. On the near side of the building there was what looked like a grease pit under a rickety shed roof, while over on the far side there were two big aboveground gasoline storage tanks. The setup would have had an LA County fire marshal screaming in anguish, but I guess nobody gave a damn out here.

A swaybacked wooden pump shelter big enough to accept a Model A extended in front of the station. The pumps themselves were a pair of genuine old hand-cranked Tokheim gas dispensers with ten-gallon glass reservoirs mounted atop their graceful columns. They must have been installed back in the 1930s. Hell, the whole station must have been, and not updated a day since.

But someone was keeping the place going. The building wasn't boarded, the glass was intact, and a loaded oil rack and a STATION OPEN sign had been set out. A Dodge power wagon mounting a wrecker's A-frame also sat parked next to the building.

As I watched, a man stepped out of the station office into the shade of the pump shelter. He was alone, and he sank down into an old kitchen chair parked beside the door. Tilting the chair back, he leaned comfortably against the wall, his arms crossed on his chest.

I had the strangest feeling that this guy was waiting for us.

I tossed the field glasses onto the car seat. "Let's go, Princess. He's down there all right."

Peerless's disintegration was even more apparent as we rolled slowly down the main street. Paint was stripping in the desert wind, stucco crumbled, and bristly masses of tumbleweed built up against the buildings and drifted in the alleys between them.

I didn't take the '57 into the gas station. Instead, I parked in front of the abandoned café across the street, backing us in so we were nose out to the road and set for a fast takeoff. I gave the Commander a hitch into place under my windcheater, and we were ready to go visiting. With Lisette at my side, we crossed the sun-baked concrete to where the sole citizen of Peerless awaited us.

I knew we'd found Jubal Claster before we'd even spoken a word. Clad in Levi's and a worn checked shirt, he had the same rangy frame, the same dark hair, and the same dark eyes as his brother, Ira. Jubal carried a little more weight, though, as well as a little gray in his hair. His eyes were also milder and shrewder than his younger brother's. He gave us a welcoming nod as we stepped into his patch of shade. "Afternoon. It looks like a hot one out there."

"It does come with the country," I replied, nodding back.

He gave a short chuckle. "It surely does. Now, can I help you folks with something?"

"You can if you're Jubal Claster."

He nodded again. "I am, and I guess you're the folks who've been out looking for me."

"I guess we are. Did Ira tell you about us?"

"He did." Claster lost his grin and let his chair come back on all four legs. "He called me the other night from Amarillo. Look, mister, I can't excuse what my brother did back there, but I sure hope that you can. He was worried some about me, and he was just trying to scare you off. Ira's a hothead sometimes, but I swear to God he didn't really mean to hurt you or the little lady here."

In an extremely large rat's ass he didn't, but diplomacy required I agree. "I guess I can see that," I replied, leaning against one of the pumps.

"I apologize for him," Jubal went on. "And since no harm was done, I hope you folks can see your way clear not to make too much over this. I'd sure appreciate it."

"Like you said, no harm done. Forget it."

It was my turn to smile and lie through my teeth. Little brother Ira was going to spend the next twenty years as some lifer's girlfriend if I had anything to say about it. There are certain things I take personally, and buckshot is one of them.

Claster seemed to relax at that and tilted back again. "I guess that brings us back around to what I can do for you folks. Mind if I ask how come you came all this way looking for me?"

"Didn't Ira tell you when you talked with him?" Lisette asked.

"He wasn't too clear on the subject. I suspect he didn't give you folks much of a chance to lay your cards out. Like I said, Ira's kinda a hothead. Best you explain it to me yourselves."

"It's because of my father," she went on, taking over the conversation. "Ten years ago, you agreed to help him with a certain job. I need to know about that job."

"Well, little lady, I'd say that all depends on who your father is and what this job was."

"My father's name was John Kingman, from Chicago."

Claster went still for a second; then he smiled again and shook his head. "I'm sorry, but I've got no idea who you're talking about."

"Your brother seemed to think you do," Lisette responded quietly. "And Calvin Reece said you should. He gave my father your name, just like he gave it to us."

Claster lost a little of his country *bon homme* at that. "You talked to Reece?"

"We did. He told us everything. How my dad needed a good man down in Kansas and about how you were the man he came up with."

"And what was this good man supposed to do?" Claster asked softly.

"He was to help my father steal a quarter of a million dollars from my father's gang." Lisette sank down on her heels, bringing her eyes level with the garageman's. "Did you, Mr. Claster?"

Nothing moved except for a sun-parched leaf skittering across the pavement in a puff of wind.

"If a man did do something like that," Claster said finally, "he'd have to be a fool to own up to it. Especially to someone who just turned in off the road." His voice was neutral now, no friendship, no enmity, just neutral.

"It would depend on who it was who came in off the road, wouldn't it, Mr. Claster? I'm Lisette Kingman, John Kingman's daughter. You can see that we aren't the police. [I studied the cans in the oil rack really hard at this point in the conversation.] I've got no grudge with you, and I just want a couple of questions answered. A little truth and then we'll disappear. You'll never see us again. I swear it."

Claster tilted his head down for a couple of seconds, thinking. "Little lady," he said finally, "I'm not saying that I'm the Jubal Claster you're looking for, but maybe we could go inside and talk about it some."

He got to his feet and led us in through the screen door of the station office. "It's not any cooler inside," he called back over his shoulder, "but at least we can all sit down and I can offer you something to drink."

A narrow hallway led back from the office and into the living quarters half of the station. Its walls were covered with a nondescript and faded wallpaper, and there were doors on either side that must have opened into bedrooms. I walked behind Claster as we moved down the hall, my hand close to the pistol on my belt. I didn't trust this guy yet, not by a long shot. I stayed focused on him, waiting for him to make some kind of move.

I guess I stayed too focused. As I brushed past one of the bedroom doors, it was yanked open. Something struck me on the back of the head, and white light exploded behind my eyes.

I wish Lisette wouldn't scream. It was too late to warn me, and it made things hurt a whole lot worse on the way to the floor.

* * *

The first thing I saw when my eyes started working again was a gun, one of the old hand-ejector .44 Specials Smith & Wesson had come out with about forty years ago. The model they call the Triple-Lock. Some of the old-timers in the sheriff's department swear that the Triple-Lock Smith was the best-made revolver ever produced in the United States, and they still rate it as one of the top combat pieces around. A really, really cool gun.

Too bad it was aimed at me.

I'd been dragged back into the living room of the house half of the station. Like the rest of the place, it was a room frozen in the thirties. Overstuffed chairs and a davenport done in dusty, sun-paled chintz, stuffing pushing out through failing seams. A cheap overcarved desk and coffee table, each carrying a complex pattern of cigarette burns and cup rings. An Oriental rug, its pattern gone muddy under decades of tracked dirt.

I'd been dumped on the davenport, and I had a little trouble pulling myself upright. My wrists had been tied in front of me. No, correction on that: my hands had been wired together in front of me. Lisette faced me across the room, sitting, stiff-spined and angry, in the desk chair. A grinning Jubal Claster stood beside her. He was the man holding the nice gun. There was somebody else there as well.

"Hello, Ira, you son of a bitch." The sound of my own voice rang off-key in my head like a cracked bell.

"Not such a wiseass now, are you?" the younger Claster sneered. He had a strip of surgical tape across the bridge of his nose and a few other new dings here and there as well. At the moment, though, he looked fairly pleased with himself. Leaning against the wall, he gestured at me with the barrel of my own automatic. "I put a lot of work into that truck, man. You owe me!"

"Sorry about your wheels, Ira, but I have this problem with letting people blow my head off. My fault; I should have mentioned it." I shifted my attention, bleary though it might be, to Jubal. "What's the deal here?"

"The deal is that he's already sold us out," Lisette blurted.

"Mace got to him first. He put a bounty on us."

"The little lady pretty much sums it up, son," Jubal added, sinking down to sit on the arm of one of the overstuffed chairs. "It seems that somebody wants his little girl back pretty bad. Oh, he wants you, too, but I don't think for the same reason."

"I'm not his 'little girl'!" Lisette gritted.

Jubal shrugged. "For ten thousand dollars cash, I don't much give a damn who you are."

"Is that a going rate with you, Claster?" I asked. "Did you hit Johnny Kingman up for ten grand to help knock off his partners?" What the hell, this was what we'd come for. And just at the moment, Jubal Claster sure didn't have any call not to talk.

Jubal nodded. "As a matter of fact, it was. And it sounded like a pretty good deal at the time." He gave a short grunting laugh. "I didn't find out till later that there was a quarter-million dollars involved. If I'd have known that, I might have held out for a little more. Thing is, I know about it now."

Claster reached over and gently brushed back a lock of Lisette's hair with the muzzle of the .44. "In fact, the little lady and I were about to have a talk about all that money when you started to groan and come around. I figured it was only polite to wait till you could join in, too."

"Thanks." God, but my head was exploding! "How the hell did you ever find out about the war chest anyway? Johnny 32 couldn't have been dumb enough to say anything about that amount of dough in front of you."

The older Claster brother frowned. "He didn't, but a lot of other folks did later. The state police and the G-men were all over around home after those bodies were found, asking questions, watching for anybody spending a dollar that they shouldn't have. And that Spanno man, he came around, too, asking his own questions."

"You should have buried Kingman's partners deeper. Your relations on your mother's side have a nose for blood and a knack for digging things up."

Ira came off the wall spitting an obscenity. He took a fast step across the room with the Commander upraised in his fist.

"Ira!" Jubal reined his brother in. "Leave it be! When the man's right, the man's right."

The younger Claster subsided, returning to his lean. Jubal gave that grunting laugh again, this time tinged with bitterness. "I did indeed make a mess out of that. But I was like Ira here back then, always impatient, always trying to do it the fast and easy way."

Jubal slid fully down into the battered armchair. "I made all sorts of mistakes, and I pulled all sorts of trouble down on myself. The law was bad enough, but that Spanno, now he can make you real nervous."

"So I've noticed," I said. "So that's how come you're out here. It got too hot around the old homestead. You lit out and hid."

"Pretty much. I always wanted my own garage, so I came out here where nobody knew me and I sunk my whole roll into this place. Things were real good at the time; this place was making money hand over fist." Claster shook his shaggy head. "Then I barely get settled in and the whole town goes belly-up. Ain't that just the shits?"

"My heart bleeds for you, man."

Jubal grinned without humor. "And you know what was worse, son? It was sitting out here in this forsaken pit all this time and thinking about all that money that just passed me by. I never imagined in a million years that I'd ever get another shot at a piece of it."

"Keep imagining," Lisette said in a low voice. "You don't have any of it yet."

"Maybe not, little lady. But let's say it's in reach again."

Claster sank back into his chair. "Here's how it sets. Last night, I just get back from picking up Ira over in Texas when a man I didn't particularly want to ever see again shows up here at my station. But then Mr. Spanno explains how he's not looking for trouble, just his stepdaughter. He tells me that you two are out here looking into how this girl's blood daddy was killed and such, and he figures that you might be passing by to talk to me. He offers me this deal. He'll pay me ten thousand dollars if I let him know when you show up and if I hold you here till he can come collect you."

Claster kept that cold grin on his face. "Ten thousand sure sounds like a ticket out to me. I could get me another start someplace where there's more people than there are coyotes."

"So, have you made that phone call yet?" I asked, pulling myself up straighter. I was really interested in this answer.

"No, I haven't. Not yet, anyway. You see, I've been thinking about things." Claster leaned forward again, shifting a sly look between Lisette and me. "This is about a whole lot more than some questions about a couple of hoods getting killed. Am I right?"

Lisette didn't respond, so I didn't, either.

"Look," Claster went on. "I know that the money this girl's daddy stole was never found. And it occurs to me that maybe somebody's figured out where it's hid. And since Spanno is real anxious to lay hands on you two, I figure that maybe you're the ones. Now if somebody might want to bid against Spanno's ten-thousand-dollar deal, say by offering Ira and me a half-share of that loot, then maybe that telephone call wouldn't have to be made."

Yeah, uh-huh, and if I leave the henhouse door unlocked, you'll make sure I'm the chicken that doesn't gets eaten. I shrugged my shoulders. "Don't look at me, man. I don't know what you're talking about."

Lisette just stared at the wall. "I told you why I was here."

"And that's all you have to say, little lady?"

The girl turned and looked defiantly into Jubal's face. "I suppose I could add, 'Go to hell.' "

Ira Claster reached out and grabbed a handful of Lisette's hair, yanking it back and tearing a cry of pain out of her. "You watch your mouth, girl," he hissed, "or you're the one ending up in hell. I ain't forgot about you and that radiator fan. You better believe I ain't forgot."

"Lay off her!" Tied hands or no, I was coming off that couch in about two seconds.

Jubal's Triple-Lock came in line with my chest. "Ira, you listen to this fella. Let the girl be!"

"Shit, Jubal, if she knows where all this money is, then let's get it out of her! I can make her talk, you bet—"

"Ira, I said leave off! There are ways to do things and there are ways to do things. Now shut up and let me show you how we're doing this!"

Ira released Lisette and fell back, glaring at the two of us. Jubal lifted the sights of his revolver until its muzzle was a cold eye looking into mine. "And as for you, son, don't get funny. Nobody can be for certain-sure about how much more time they have left in this world, so don't go throwing away any of what you know you got."

He lowered the gun. "Now, is this the last word you folks have on the subject? With you two, I've got ten thousand dollars cash money in my pocket. I wouldn't mind having some more, but that'll be your choice. I think you folks'll be a lot happier dealing with me than with Mace Spanno."

From where I sat, Claster's offer was like a choice between the gallows and the gas chamber. Lisette apparently felt the same. We answered him with two minutes of profound silence.

"Okay, folks, have it your way. Ira, you watch 'em. I have to go make a phone call."

Jubal levered himself out of his chair and started for the station office. As he did, Lisette spoke up suddenly. "Since it doesn't really matter now, will you please tell me about what my father paid you to do that night?"

Claster hesitated a second, then shrugged. "Why not? Wasn't all that big of a show, little lady. Your daddy set it all up with me over the phone. His kike boss had an extra bodyguard along on this trip, and he wanted a spare gun on his side to make sure of things. He also wanted a local boy to help hide the bodies. He was going to be moving fast, and he didn't want to be slowed down by having to get rid of the dead meat.

"Your daddy had it all planned out, the place where he was going to fake the car trouble and everything. He turned them off on a little dead-end side road north of Quapaw, and I came driving up a few minutes later, just a good old country boy anxious to help.

"Your daddy pretended to get out and help me under the hood while the kike just sat in the car. The other bodyguard, though, the little wop, he paced around on the road like being out there in the night made him itchy. Your daddy whispered to me that he'd kill the wop.

"After a while, the wop goes off into the bushes to take a leak, and your daddy goes after him real quiet, pulling that little pocket gun of his out from under his coat. Me, I'm still pretending to work on the engine, and I call to the kike to come out and get me a tool out of my toolbox. He does, and when he bends over the toolbox I pull my gun, put the muzzle behind his ear, and pull the trigger."

Claster smiled and flashed the worn Triple-Lock. "It was this same old revolver, in fact. A second later, there's another shot back in the bushes and your daddy comes out grinning. He still had that little gun in his hand, and he keeps it there even while he passes me the roll for doing my part of the job. He just says that he's dissolving a partnership, and then he drives off in that big car.

"I buried the bodies in the side of a chat heap, and that was just about all there was to it," Claster concluded, turning back for the hallway. "If that's what you came here for, little lady, I hope it was worth it."

It might have been what Lisette had come here for, but it wasn't what she'd wanted to hear. I watched the bleakness pass over her face as she listened to Jubal's casual story of cold-blooded murder. Beyond a shadow of a doubt, or a glimmer of hope, she knew what her father was now.

For me, I was busy taking inventory of our chances of getting out of this mess. We were far from Fatsville here. On the other hand, we still had a couple of things going for us. The Clasters had made an elementary mistake when they'd tied me up: they'd bound my wrists in front of me instead of behind my back. They'd made an even bigger mistake in not tying Lisette up at all. They must have rated her as no threat, and she was still free, kept in her chair only by the negligently held automatic in Ira's hand.

And finally, while they'd taken my gun, they'd missed something else. When I pressed my ankles together I could still feel that narrow strip of steel under the leather of my boot. I still had the paratrooper's knife.

"Not such a Miss Wiseass now, are you, girl?" Ira verbally prodded at Lisette. "Your boyfriend over there with all the fancy moves isn't so shit-hot either, now is he?"

I cut him off tiredly. "Yeah, we admit it. We're quivering piles of dog crap, and you're God third class. Just get past it, man. It's getting old."

Ira waved the Commander's muzzle in my direction and grinned. "Not like you, man. You ain't going to be getting old at all."

I bet he was really proud of that line.

Jubal wasn't gone long. Returning, he dropped into his chair again. "Well, I just talked to your stepdaddy, little lady. He's right up the road in Flagstaff, and he's real anxious to see you. He's on his way here right now. So, I guess we can start the negotiating again."

"About what?" Lisette asked dully.

Claster's grin came back. "Why, about whether or not you escape before he gets here of course. You see, Ira, there's no sense in us working up a sweat slapping these good folks around. You can bet that if they do know where that quarter-million dollars is, they're bound to come to Jesus before this gal's daddy shows up. We just have to sit here and wait. Only now, of course, I'm going to be asking for a full third share for each of us."

I lifted my head, "Jubal, can I ask you one question?"

"Why, sure, son."

"Why in *thee* hell should Spanno pay you ten thousand dollars when a bullet only costs a nickel?"

Jubal's brows lowered. "What are you talking about?"

"I'm talking about all of us being coyote meat when Spanno gets here! That's what I'm talking about! Don't you get it? Sure, he's using you to get us. But he's also using us to get you. He's using the girl and me to hold you here so he can take us all out in one shot."

Both Clasters scowled. "Why would he be wanting to do something like that?" Jubal demanded.

"Because ten years ago you killed one of his partners and helped to steal a quarter of a million bucks from him, you moron!" I roared.

"But we have a deal!"

"Yeah, so? What makes you think Spanno is such a pillar of virtue that he's going to keep his word? Hell, two minutes ago you were sitting here with us trying to stab him in the back!"

"We can take care of ourselves if he tries anything," Ira said belligerently.

"Yeah, sure. You two hillbillies are going to take on three pro Chicago hit men and come out of it alive." It was stretching a point to call Spanno's driver a hit man, but hell, when you're stacking it, stack it high. "That is a panic and a half, Ira. In fact, that is so damn funny you ought to wear a dress and go on TV with Uncle Miltie."

The Clasters were looking a little uneasy. Why not? It sounded good the way I was laying it out. I had no idea exactly what Spanno had in mind, but any distrust I could stir up in the enemy ranks had to work in our favor. Undercover cops have a saying: "When they've got you backed into a corner, spray the bullshit and pray."

"We're talking about Mace Spanno here, Jubal," I pushed. "Remember how he came around after the killings ten years ago? Remember how just having him in the neighborhood scared you across three state lines? If you were sweating about him then, you should be shitting your pants about him now."

"He wasn't sure," the older brother murmured. "He didn't know."

"He does now. Remember Calvin Reece? Remember us telling you how Reece gave us your name?"

"Yeah. What about him?"

"He's dead." Lisette's head even came up on that one. "Four days ago he was shot to death in East Saint Louis. Spanno got to him right after we did. If you don't believe me, call the newspapers or somebody back there and find out. All Reece did was give Lisette's father your name. What do you think Spanno's going to do when he gets you in his sights, kiss you on the cheek? He's cleaning up old debts, man!"

"What do you think, Jubal? Is he bullshitting us?" Ira asked, uneasily fingering the Commander's grips.

The older man swiped a handful of sweat off his brow. "I don't know."

"Just hang around, guys. You're going to find out real soon," I said, tossing in my last two cents.

Jubal stood up abruptly. "This kid might just be trying to set us up," he commented, frowning. "But we're not going to take any chances. I'll gas up the truck in case we have to get out of here in a hurry. Then I'm going to get my rifle. Watch 'em, Ira."

Jubal went on his way, leaving us alone with Little Brother. Ira eyed me and I could tell that he was making up whatever he used for a mind about something.

"You know what?" he said.

"No, what?" I replied laconically.

"I think you're right."

"You're getting smarter all the time, Ira."

"And you know what else?"

"Illuminate me, man."

Ira gave me a nasty grin and stepped up behind Lisette's chair. "When Jubal gets back, I'm going to tell him that I think you're right. I'm gonna say that we ought to get out of here before that Spanno outfit shows up. I'm also gonna say that I think we should take you two smart-asses with us."

Ira's free hand, the one not holding the gun, came down on Lisette's shoulder, and I saw her stiffen.

"You see, I think you do know where all that money is. And I think that Jubal and me can make you tell us where, the good old-fashioned way." He leaned forward a little more, and his hand slid off Lisette's shoulder and across her chest.

I didn't pay too much attention to what he was doing, though. I was looking more at Lisette, watching the fury building behind her eyes. I was getting myself ready to move, too.

Claster didn't notice. He was too busy gloating. "Hey," he said, "maybe if you tell us where the money is right away, my brother and me will even let you watch us screw this gal of yours awhile before we kill you." His hand slipped beneath Lisette's shirt to her breast.

Oh, he shouldn't have done that. Lisette might be afraid of Mace Spanno, but she was a lady not inclined to take a great deal of bullshit off of anyone else. She kept her fingernails trimmed fairly close, but well shaped and manicured. And now, with her lips curling into a snarl, she reached up and back to Ira Claster's face and sank those two handfuls of short, sharp-bladed knives bone deep into his cheeks. Then she ripped downward with all her strength.

Wasn't no kitten scratch, man. Claster couldn't have been shredded any worse if he'd tried to kiss a cranky bobcat.

He screamed and fell back against the wall, clutching at the bloody tracks raked across his features. Then we were all over him. Lisette grabbed the automatic's barrel with both hands, twisting it back and out of Claster's grip while I used my interlocked hands like a sledgehammer, pounding him down to the floor. There the steel toe caps of my boots finished the job.

It wasn't pretty. But then sometimes that's the way it is when you're trying to stay alive.

"Ira?" Jubal Claster's questioning yell came from the front of the station. "Ira!"

I reclaimed the gun from Lisette. I use a two-handed FBI grip with the Commander a lot of the time anyway, so my wired wrists weren't that much of a problem. Plastering myself against the wall next to the hallway entry, I motioned the girl aside and undercover with a jerk of my head.

Jubal didn't oblige me by rushing back into the living room. There was silence out toward the station office. Very gingerly I eased forward to take a look around the corner. I caught the silhouette of the older Claster brother doing the exact same thing down at the other end of the hall.

Both sides made a statement about where they stood in the situation. Revolver and automatic bellowed, .44 and .45 slugs passing in midflight. Neither round did much except spray wood splinters and plaster.

"Out!" I snapped back over my shoulder, throwing another bullet down the hall to keep Claster back. Lisette obeyed, flinging the back door open and ducking out onto the porch. I followed her a second later, only I went out low and fast, rolling in a parachute landing fall. A smart move, as another couple of rounds from Claster tore up the door frame.

Lisette and I got around to the right side of the house, pressing back against the gritty clapboards. There was not one damn bit of cover anywhere except for the two black-painted fuel tanks about fifty feet west of the station. Hiding behind a gasoline storage tank is not one of the most brilliant moves you can make in a gunfight. On the other hand, neither is shooting at one at close range. I nodded the direction and whispered, "Let's go."

No slugs chased us as we made the dash away from the house. We dived behind the sun-heated steel plating of the tanks onto the dry cheat grass and prickly brush stubble. With Lisette huddled against me, we took a second to gulp some air.

"You okay?"

She gave me quick, reassuring nod. "Okay."

"I've got a knife in my right boot. Get it."

Obediently she dug the weapon out.

"Good. Open the shroud line cutter, the button on the bottom of the grip. Get this damn wire off me."

It didn't take her long to get a strand into the notch of the little hook-shaped blade. She gave a yank, the wire popped, and in a few seconds I was loose. Lisette massaged my scored wrists, trying to help get some feeling back. "What do we do now?" she asked lowly.

"We get the hell out of here before Spanno shows up."

"How?"

"That is the sixty-four-thousand-dollar question, isn't it?"

We were literally in the middle of nowhere. We were cut off from the forested hills to our west by a mean-looking ravine, and everything else in all directions was nothing but desert. The nearest people were out on the highway a good five miles off. If we were going to make it out, we needed the car. And we didn't have time to be fancy.

"Okay, Princess. Here's how we work it. When I give the word, we run straight across the road to the corner of the café opposite us. If we're lucky, ol' Jubal will be too busy patching up his little brother to pay much attention."

Lisette nodded again, gathering her long legs under her, ready to move.

"Okay. Go!"

We weren't lucky. I lagged behind a little, looking back over my shoulder for enemy action. About halfway across the broad street, I spotted movement inside the door of the gas station office. I lengthened my stride and dived for Lisette. Catching her around the waist, I took her down, trying to take the worst of the impact as we hit the gravel. The first of what seemed to be an impossibly long string of shots snapped over our heads. With near-misses spraying pebbles around us, we scrambled around the corner and behind shelter.

Give him credit, Jubal Claster knew his guns. He was using an M-1 carbine on us now, a great weapon for this kind of work. Light, fast to handle, and using a thirty-round banana clip you could load it on Sunday and shoot it all week. The carbine had been my favorite carry back in the army, and I'd picked one up war surplus myself.

Too bad that mine was in the back of my bedroom closet at the moment.

I sidled up to the edge of the building and risked a look around the corner. The '57 was parked only about fifty feet away, but it might as well have been back in Chicago for all the good it did us. Jubal was directly across the road from it. He'd pulled his Power Wagon around in front of the station's gas pumps, and he was forted up solidly behind the vehicle. I could see him keeping low, cautiously peering over the truck bed in our direction.

He had all the approaches to the '57 covered. And any second now that little light was going to come on, telling him that if he just put a few bullets through my tires and radiator, nobody was going anywhere.

I drew back from the corner, trying to think. Lisette stood pressed against the wall beside me. She'd gotten us out and now she was waiting for me to do my share and get us away. I closed my eyes and did like they'd trained us to do back when I was earning my Ranger tab. I tried to build an image of the battlefield in my mind, hunting for a point of tactical advantage.

I opened my eyes again. Wait a second. What had changed about the front of that gas station?

I took another quick look around the corner. That was it! When we'd made our move on brother Ira, Jubal had been out front gassing up his truck. He'd pumped the reservoir of one of the Tokheim dispensers full, but we'd interrupted him before he could trip the release valve and empty the fuel into the truck's tank. That reservoir was still full. There was ten gallons of gasoline in a big glass cylinder right above Jubal Claster's head.

A guy with his eyes full of gas couldn't see to shoot very well. Come to think of it, a guy soaked to the skin in high-test probably wouldn't be all that anxious to fire a firearm at all.

I flexed my fingers and settled the grip of the Commander carefully into the palm of my right hand. Then I whipped around the corner, taking aim at the loaded pump reservoir and taking my shot.

I connected. The heavy glass tank popped like a balloon under the impact of my bullet, the hydraulic shock of the big hardball slug spraying gas all over the place.

That was all according to plan. What happened next, though, was bad timing, just plain-ass, doo-dah bad timing.

Jubal had seen me come around the corner of the café, and he tried to take a shot at me. He was not able to stop his trigger pull as the cloud of gasoline mist engulfed him. The crack of the carbine was lost in the roar of the explosion.

The *WHOOM* of the blast shoved me back around the corner of the café. It took me a second to get my feet under me again and look out to see what the hell had happened.

Hell had happened. Both Claster's truck and the entire front of the service station were a solid mass of flame. There was even a damned soul in there, a vaguely man-shaped blob of flame that danced in the heart of the holocaust, making sounds that no human being should be able to make. Then the spare gas cans on the back of the truck cut loose, blowing the figure back through the front wall of the office. Hopefully it also killed him.

"What happened?" Lisette gasped at my side.

"Something I sure didn't figure on."

It was about then that I noticed the flames racing around the building toward the station's main storage tanks. "Let's get out of here!"

We went for the car. I suppose that according to the professional hero's manual, I should have dashed across to the station to see if brother Ira needed rescuing or not. However, during the past few days he'd tried to assault me with a wrench, he'd attempted to blow my head off with a shotgun, and he'd succeeded in knocking me cold. He'd also gleefully been making plans to rape my girl and torture me to death. Excuse me, Sir Baden-Powell, but I just didn't like the son of a bitch all that much!

I swept a smoldering piece of board off the '57's hood, and we piled in. Car must have see the fire licking hungrily at the base of those tanks, too, because she caught the first turn of the starter. Tires scrabbling, we copped a breeze out of there, and I treated the main street like a drag strip.

It didn't take long for those several thousand gallons of gasoline to protest their mistreatment. We were only about a quarter-mile beyond town when premium and regular both cut loose with a double-barreled blast. It was like the pictures of the A-bomb tests out in Navada, a blazing mushroom cloud and the sky raining fire.

Thus endeth Peerless. Lisette knelt on the seat, looking back. "That," she whispered, "was bad."

We didn't realize it yet, but we didn't know what "bad" was. Maybe Mace Spanno really had been planning to screw the Clasters over. He'd told Jubal that he was forted up in Flagstaff. In reality, he and his boys must have been staying somewhere a lot closer.

Atop the little rise east of the town, sunlight flared on a windshield and a car materialized out of the road mirage. I got off the gas and let the '57 roll to a halt. The black Chrysler came to a stop about fifty yards away, straddling the center line.

"Oh, shit!" was an inadequate phrase for the moment, but it was all I could come up with.

The '57 growled deep in the twin throats of her headers. The only other sound was Lisette's ragged breathing as she pressed herself back into the seat. I twisted around behind the wheel and looked back. Heavy pale smoke engulfed Peerless, little fingers of fire dancing in the base of the cloud.

An ebony-and-chrome devil blocked the one road out of hell, and the only way to go was back.

I socked the gearshift into reverse and floored it. The '57 shot backward like a startled crawdad.

When I had the speed, I whipped us into an inverted bootlegger, aiming Car's nose toward Peerless. Up the road, smoke boiled out of the Chrysler's rear wheel wells as they came after us.

We fled toward the town, driving headlong into the holocaust. Grass, brush, and wood, all baked kiln-dry under the desert sun, had practically exploded alight, and little flame sprites of burning thumbleweed skittered out into the desert, spreading the conflagration.

We howled down Main Street again, thick ash-laden smoke streaming around us, heading for the dead end at the abandoned bridge abutments. Jubal Claster's gas station was my cutoff mark. Both the station and the café across from it were blazing now like cardboard boxes in an incinerator, the flames arcing across the road. I felt the radiating heat before I could even make out the buildings through the murk.

Weaving around a chunk of burning fuel tank that lay in the road, I cranked the wheel hard over and took us around into the alley behind the burning café. The Chrysler arrived a couple of seconds later.

I'd hoped that in the smoke they'd overshoot and go through the end-of-the road barricades and into the ravine. No such luck. Bannerman, Spanno's kid wheelman, was good. He threw that big coupe around in a bootlegger turn of his own and bounced away from the barricades without even scratching his paint. Running even, we thundered up the back of Peerless, he on the main street, me on the back alley, visible to each other only in flashes between the buildings.

He beat me. He got a lead and hooked in between two houses. Suddenly the long black nose of the Chrysler slid across the alley in front of us, cutting us off. The '57 sobbed to a shuddering halt, her front bumper a meager foot from the 300-C's dark, rakish fender.

Hemmed in between burning sagebrush and a back wall, I reversed away again. A gunshot from beneath the Chrysler's low roof chased after us, the pistol slug creasing my door handle and screaming away in a wild ricochet. I got the '57 into a forward gear and cut blindly into a driveway between another pair of buildings. Lisette cried out as we found ourselves confronted with a solid wall of fire.

I kept my foot to the floor. Either it was a drift of burning tumbleweed or it wasn't.

It was thumbleweed. We blasted through the brush in an explosion of sparks and embers, searing little dots of flame swirling in through the windows, stinging us as we tore out onto Main Street. A couple of buildings down, the Chrysler backed onto the highway as well, blocking us in, keeping the only escape route sealed.

Both cars came to halt, idling broadside to broadside and about seventy feet apart. For a few seconds we all just sat there, watching each other grill like racks of ribs as the fires spread around us. My throat was raw with the smoke, and Lisette choked beside me. I kept my fingers curled around the knob of the floor shift, waiting for Spanno and company to make the next move.

Maybe they mistook our passivity for surrender. At any rate, the passenger-side door of the 300-C opened and Nate Temple emerged. Gun in hand and leveled at us, he started over to take possession.

I let him get about halfway across the gap between the cars, and then I floored it again. I charged the '57 forward between two old stores across the street, as if I were going for the alley on the other side. Reacting, the Chrysler shot backward into another diagonal cross-alley to cut us off once more.

Fake out! The hole I'd been aiming for didn't even go through to the far-side frontage road. I started my move, then hit the binders and reversed hard for the third time, sweeping back out into the highway in a wild rubber-sobbing arc. In this automotive game of Tossing the Broad the bad guys had just picked the wrong card.

There was still the infantry to get past, though. Nate Temple materialized out of the smoke, sidling in across the front of the car, trying to lay the snub sights of his Detective's Special on me.

The '57 almost seemed to go after him on her own, snarling and hurling herself at the Chi-town gunman. By all accounts, Nathan Temple was bad news, a real tough guy. However, he'd never taken on a psychotic Chevrolet before. He took one look at the '57's glaring headlights and the chromed pushbars gleaming like fangs in her grillwork and gave up on his target practice and got the hell out of the way. He hurled himself up onto the smoldering porch of the old trading post as we hooked at him with a fender.

By that time, Spanno and his wheelman must have figured out that we'd screwed them over. The black Chrysler came lunging back out onto Main Street. Too late. We swerved past and we were clear, tear-assing out of Peerless for good this time.

Clean, smokeless air boiled in through the '57's windows. It wasn't as good as a cold drink of water would have been, but it was close. Twisting herself around in the seat, Lisette looked back. "They're coming," she croaked.

It hadn't taken them long to get Temple back aboard and to start chasing. That big black road shark that had started to haunt my dreams was streaming up the highway behind us. And I thought that nemesis was only meant for the bad guys.

I leaned into the gas pedal and sent the tach needle arcing up toward the red line.

"Okay, Car," I murmured. "Now we get serious."

It was a matter of numbers. The way I had it souped up, the '57's mill could produce a solid 283 horsepower and maybe a scooch more, 1 horsepower per cubic inch of engine displacement. The Chevrolet 283 Turbofire was one of the first two automotive power plants mass-produced in the United States that could be taken up to "one to one." Unfortunately, the other "one-to-one" mill was the Chrysler Hemi, the same kind of engine that lived under the hood of the 300-C chasing us. And it had a displacement of 392 cubic inches.

On a winding road where cornering and acceleration would have counted for more, I could have taken him. Spanno's wheelman was dragging an extra thousand pounds of car around. But as it was, there was just the single wide bend that aimed us back toward 66. We were like a quarter horse racing an English Thoroughbred—you got him beat off the line, but once he gets stretched out and in the high end, your ass is his.

There was nothing to do about it, though, nothing except keep my foot to the metal and see how it played.

We came smoking out of the bend with the Chrysler on our hip and nothing in front of us but the straightaway south to the main road. I didn't have to check the mirrors to know he was back there. I could hear him. The scream of the high-revving 283 was heterodyning with the baritone bellow of the Hemi, blending and phasing in an anarchistic chorus of steel straining toward disintegration.

I could feel him as well. We were shredding the air with our passage, shoving aside bow waves of turbulence. Wounded wind that patted and pressed against the sides of the cars, lightly, so lightly, but just enough to push you off that narrow band of concrete unless you fought the wheel with a constant series of sharp correcting jerks.

A small, suicidal bird flew across the road ahead of us. It touched the '57's hood and exploded, spraying the windshield with droplets of blood that flash-dried instantly.

I didn't know our speed; the speedometer had given it up as a bad job a long time ago. Anyway, beyond a certain point, miles per hour become irrelevant. All there is, is fast. The blur and the vibration make the whole world around you soft and hazy, and the only thing that's sharp and real is the ringing howl of your mill and the outline of that other car out there beside you.

Lisette huddled on the seat beside me, silent and scared. It was a good time to be scared.

The Chrysler had an overlap on us, a jet shadow creeping up our flank, its front hubcap a shimmering disk of mercury. Bannerman was a silhouette leaning forward behind the wheel, a blue-steel jockey urging his mount into the lead.

Temple, the gunner, gripped the frame of the passenger-side window and snarled into the air blast. He could have put a slug into a tire or into me easily enough at this range. But then his body would have been one of the five dug out of the bloody pileup that would have followed. The gun clenched in his fist was a pathetic toy when compared to the mass and energy locked up inside the metal of the two racing cars.

And Spanno? Spanno just sat in the back and stared, seeking Lisette's eyes.

Ahead, across the desert, light glinted on the traffic moving along on the highway. Too far ahead.

Suddenly Lisette grabbed my shoulder. She couldn't be heard over the hammering chorus of the engine and the slipstream, so she just pointed off to the right.

A third contestant had entered the race. An eastbound Santa Fe fast freight was thundering along the rail line that paralleled Route 66, converging on the uncontrolled crossing ahead of us. All involved parties looked like they were going to arrive at about the same place at about the same time.

It made things a lot simpler in a way. Either we'd make it across the tracks ahead of the train or we wouldn't.

Flip a nickel, God.

It wasn't like we were driving down a road anymore; it was more as if we were falling down it, like we'd had a streamer in a parachute jump and we were burning in with no reserve chute. Destiny was hurling straight up into our faces, and there was no way around.

The Chrysler was wheel to wheel with us now, trying to

inch ahead. Bannerman didn't dare ram at this speed, and I didn't bother with trying to block him. All the jazzy driving in the world wouldn't save us if we were cut off on the wrong side of the tracks. Out of the corner of my eye I could see the pale flash of the kid wheelman's face. He kept looking across at me, waiting for me to get off the gas and go shallow, praying for me to give it up so he wouldn't have to make the call. It wasn't Spanno or Temple now; this was our piece of the fight, Bannerman and me and the cars and that freight train out there.

Who are you anyway, Randolph Bannerman? Are you some guy like me who'd dreamed speed and who'd yearned for the transcendence you feel when you share your spirit with a piece of hot iron? Is that why you sold your soul to Mace Spanno? Okay then, let's see what you're willing to sell your life for.

Over our engines, I could barely hear the frantic honking of the train's air horn as the crew in the lead power unit spotted the two incipient suicides trying to cut across in front of them. The honking became a continuous baritone bawl, and chain lightning suddenly danced in the shadowy spaces beneath the rail cars. The engineer had hit his dynamiters, sparks flaying off the rails as the brakes on a thousand steel wheels locked up. Even with the Big Hold thrown on, there was no chance of shutting down that mile's worth of train in anything less than three times it own length. The train driver was just trying not to take a flying engine block in through his cab window.

The track crossing exploded toward us. I looked over and met the wheelman's wild-eyed stare for one last time.

I told Bannerman no.

The nose of the Chrysler dipped, and the big coupe shrieked in agony as its tires tore on the concrete. An instant later and the '57 hurled into space like a Navy Pantherjet launched off a carrier catapult.

The rail crossing was almost flush with the tracks. But at the speed we were traveling, even a couple of inches of ramp put three feet of empty air under our tires. We went weightless, seemingly frozen at the high point of our arc, caught in one of those eternal seconds when the universe locks up and you can look around and remember everything.

Behind us, the black Chrysler was sliding to a halt broadside on at the foot of the crossing, wreathed in rubber smoke and burning brake shoe. Beside me, Lisette twisted away from the passenger window, throwing her arms across her face in a futile instinctive gesture of survival. And outside of that window there was nothing but the orange-striped bumper plate of a railroad locomotive, close enough so that a tall man could have reached out and brushed it with a fingertip.

Then the '57 crashed through the time barrier. Clearing both sets of tracks, we touched down on the far side with the shock-straining WHUMP of a lion at the end of a long leap.

The freight blasted past behind us, chattering and squealing angrily, sealing Mace Spanno away on the far side of a wall of slow-moving steel. Given all the speed it had lost by braking, it would be a good ten minutes before the train would clear that crossing. And in ten minutes, man, we weren't even going to be in the same county.

Lisette and I tore away toward our junction with 66, laughing and crying in turn with survival hysteria, and I beat my fist against the steering wheel and screamed my triumph to the gods.

"CHICKEN! YOU FRIGGIN' HAD ME! YOU HAD ME AND YOU FRIGGIN' BLEW IT! YOU . . . FRIGGIN' . . . CHICKEN!"

Although a couple of people had pulled over to gawk at the smoke rising from the funeral pyre of Peerless, nobody paid much attention to us as we swung back onto the highway. It had been a long afternoon, and I knew that Lisette and I were going to conk out as soon as we ran out of adrenaline.

We had to find a place to lay low again. Up to this point, we'd always headed west. That's why I turned east now, doubling back over our tracks. Maybe that would throw the hound off for a while.

Bypassing Winslow and the isolated desert-side tourist traps, we retreated fifty miles to the little town of Holbrook. There the first motel vacancy we found was at one of the Wigwam Village chain.

These outfits have got to be one of the most god-awful pieces of tourist ticky-tacky on the entire length of Route 66. Riding on the Hollywood western craze, the Wigwam auto courts have been set up to resemble mock Indian villages, the half-circles of garishly painted little tourist cabins having being tortured by their builders into the conical shape of tepees.

The place did have certain advantages, though. I'd had a look at the Wigwam franchise out in Rialto one time and discovered that the phony wigwams were actually junior-grade blockhouse, formed out of heavy stucco over a steel frame. With one narrow door and one small diamond-shaped window not full of air conditioner, nobody was going get at you in a hurry unless he happened to be packing a bazooka.

The clerk at the office wondered a little about our appearance when we pulled up, and I was too shot to think of a good story. I just slammed an extra five spot on the desk to make him quit wondering and took the key.

Leaving the '57 parked in a slot behind the office and out of sight of the road, I helped Lisette over to our unit. She was sprawled across the bed and asleep before she could even get her shoes off. As for me, I had just enough left to lock the door and turn on the air conditioner. Then I dropped beside her and died for a little while.

It was dark when we awoke in the little odd-shaped room. We climbed out of our smoky, reeking clothes and took a shower together. No sex; it just felt good to touch and be clean and cool.

I donned a fresh shirt and Levi's while Lisette touched up her face and hair and put on the wine red sweater and skirt she hadn't worn since Saint Louis. Then we walked over to a road-house near the motel.

Good thing we weren't all that hungry, because the food

wasn't all that inspiring. You'd think that they could at least get a steak right in Arizona. Lisette ate even less than I did, and I was a little surprised when she asked if we could go into the bar afterward.

It was warm and dark in there, the low lights blue and hazy through the cigarette smoke. Other than the slow-moving barmaid, nobody paid us much mind as we slipped into a back booth. The few patrons of the joint hadn't come here for conviviality. It wasn't that kind of place. They'd come to get drunk in a quiet, businesslike fashion, and I suspected Lisette had that in mind, too.

I ordered a beer and Lisette asked for a vodka and tonic. She was all gathered up inside of herself again, and I could only get an occasional glimpse of the emptiness behind her eyes.

I let her put her first round away for anesthetic purposes before I started working on her.

"So, now you know."

"No," she replied softly, giving her head a shake. "I've known for a long time. It's just that now I believe."

Lisette took a hard bite at her second drink, coughing a little as the fiery liquor caught at the back of her throat. She wasn't adept at drinking the hard stuff, but she was taking it on fast tonight, courting the hope that the heavy-caliber shots would kill the despair and the pain building within her. It wouldn't, but that's something you have to learn for yourself.

"It was like Santa Claus," she went on after a little while, "When I was a little girl, there came a time when I knew in my mind that he wasn't real. I knew that my mother and father were really the ones who bought me all my presents and put them under the Christmas tree. But in my heart, I still believed in Santa Claus. And at least for a Christmas or two more, what I believed was still stronger than what I knew."

I could only nod and listen as it began to tear loose inside her.

"I knew . . . I knew that to be what he was, my father had to be as dirty and as ruthless as Mace or Temple or any of the others. I knew that Johnny 32 had to be that way, Kev. But I didn't believe that my father . . . my daddy . . . could be. That's stupid, I know. It doesn't make any sense, even to me."

"Makes a whole lot of sense to me, Princess. There's so much dumped on us in this life we don't want that sometimes we fight like hell to hold onto the things we do."

"But there is nothing to hold onto anymore! Today, listening to Jubal Claster tell how my father casually set up the cold-blooded murder of his partners, two men that he'd worked with for years, all the belief ended. All that I have left is what I know; that my father was a killer. There's just Johnny 32 now." Lisette's voice sank to a broken whisper. "There's no Daddy left at all."

Losing a father is a bad deal. Nobody should have to go through it twice, but it was happening to the Princess this night. I reached over and rested my hand on hers.

"You're wrong. There *is* something left."

She looked up, the first tears of many gathering in the corners of her eyes.

"Yeah, your dad ran with the dirty pack. And yeah, he could have been a hell of a lot better man than he was. But there's one thing left about him that you can still remember,"

"What?" So faint and soft a word that it was hardly there.

"That at the end, he was tired of being what he was. He wanted out. He wanted to become something different, maybe for the sake of his little girl. That's what's left for you to hang onto."

The tears came for real then. Lisette had learned to weep quietly in her life. Her face dropped down to rest across her arm, and her shoulders trembled so you'd hardly notice. I stroked her hair and glanced over at the Select-o-Matic glowing at the back of the booth. Dropping in a quarter, I carefully chose a couple of records.

The big, neon-lit Crosley jukebox over on the other side of the bar clicked and flipped a forty-five under its transparent dome. They had the volume set low, so that when Elvis Presley's "Lovin' You" issued from the speakers it didn't really break the quiet of the place.

I stood up and slipped my hand under Lisette's arm, lifting her to her feet. She looked up into my face, bewildered for a moment. Then she understood and buried her face in my shoulder. Hesitantly she began to move with me, her skirt swishing lightly against my knees. I could hold her now and no one would pay any attention. She could cry out her hurt and loneliness and nobody had to know. As we slow-danced, I could feel the dampness of her tears spreading down my shirt.

Back in that ridiculous cement tepee of ours, Lisette finally slept. The strain and fear of the day, the emotional release, and the vodka eventually had united to put her under. I wanted to join her in about the worst way, but I couldn't. Hell or high water, I had to talk to Jack tonight.

I managed to keep my eyes open until the even rate of Lisette's breathing beside me told me she was out. Easing out of bed, I pulled on my jacket and jeans again. Slipping out the door, I crossed to the office building and to the outside phone booth. The Bear answered at his home on the third ring.

"Could you try calling before I get to sleep sometime? Just for the novelty."

"Cut me some slack, Jack. I've had a nervous day."

"How'd the meet with Claster go?"

"FUBAR, man. Totally and completely Fucked Up Beyond All Recall. But I did get some stuff out of it. Look, can you remember the ballistics kickback on the Leopold and Vallessio killings?"

"Yeah, sort of." We were half a dozen states closer than when we'd started, and Jack's voice was clearer and stronger over the shortened phone link. "What do you need?"

"I need to know if Leopold was killed with a single .44 Special round behind the ear at close range?"

"He was."

"And was Vallessio taken out with a single .32 slug?"

"Yeah. Ballistics matched the bullet to the '03 Model Colt recovered from Kingman's body."

"Okay." I slid down onto the stool inside the booth and stretched my legs out through the open door. "That confirms what I got today. You can inform the authorities back in Kansas and Oklahoma and whoever else might be interested that the Leopold and Vallessio killings did happen on the Oklahoma side of the line. Jubal Claster was hired by John Kingman to back him up in the murders and to conceal the bodies afterward. Kingman hit Vallessio while Leopold was put down by Claster. I got this in a verbal statement from Claster, made in front of at least one other solid witness."

"Solid enough to go for a murder warrant?"

"There's nobody left to arrest. Jubal Claster's dead."

"Dead!" I yanked the handset back from my ear. "How?"

"It was kind of an accident, Jack. He still had the murder weapon in his possession, though. If the Oklahoma people want to recover it, they can probably dig around in the ashes and find it without too much trouble."

"Ashes?"

"Yeah. His gas station sort of got burned down, too."

"Was that also an accident?" The Bear was being very forbearing now.

"Well, I didn't plan on it. Anyhow, I've got some additional charges we can tack onto Ira Claster's tab if you want them. Assaulting a police officer, kidnapping, and criminal conspiracy."

"And is he alive?"

"I'm not sure."

"What do you mean, you're not sure?"

"I mean that after the rest of the town caught fire, I started losing track of the details!"

"*Aw Jesus'n'MarymotheraGod! Shiela, get up and fix me a pot of coffee!*"

It took awhile to get the whole story out, and by the time I was finished the Bear was the one on fire. "That," he said in a deadly monotone, "is totally crazy. You are totally crazy. This whole situation is totally, fucking crazy! *Are you hearing me, Pulaski?*"

I let the air trickle out of my lungs in a protracted sigh. "Yeah, Jack, I hear you."

"Then hear this! This thing is over! Now! Grab the girl! Get to the nearest highway patrol or sheriff's station and stay put until Captain Faraday and I can get out there!"

That got me back on my feet again. "Wait a minute, Jack! We can't cut this op off yet. It's just starting to produce! I'm almost there, man! I've zeroed the money! I know where it is, and I'm almost there!"

"Great. You and half a dozen state cops can go out and pick it up."

"No, dammit! I don't have enough on Spanno yet! For Lisette's sake, I've got to bury this guy for good!"

"We've got enough to put some kind of package together on him, especially if you can get the girl to testify for us. We can take it to the feds. Hell, we'll get something on the son of a bitch."

"Not enough, Jack! Not enough!"

"Then what is enough?" Le Baer roared. "What are you trying to do out there, kid? Will you answer me that? Just what in the hell are you trying to accomplish? Are you seeing yourself walking out to meet this Spanno character in front of the OK Corral at high noon? Are you trying to hand his head to this girl on a silver platter? Kevin, use your brains instead of your balls! It ain't going to happen! Next time you cross this guy he's going to kill you!"

"Maybe, Jack. But I've played this out for too long. I can't turn chicken now."

Jack's voice quieted as he pulled himself back under control. I think my partner was about as close to pleading as he could get. "Give it up, kid. Break it off and get yourself out of there."

"I can't do it, Jack. I admit it; I don't know exactly what

I'm going to do. But I have to finish this thing my way. I need a little more time, man.''

"Kid, tell me where you are?''

"I'll be in touch when it's over.''

"Kevin, tell me where you are!"

I hung up the phone. I felt like a deep-sea diver who'd just cut his own air hose.

I walked back to our motel unit, but I couldn't stand to go inside just then. I left the door ajar so I could hear Lisette if she woke up, and I started to pace a slow sentry go in front of the little cone-shaped structure. Earlier I could barely keep my eyes open. Now sleep didn't exist.

After a while, I put my back to the cool, stony surface of the tepee and let myself slide down the sloping face to a sitting position on the ground, looking up at the steel-splinter stars in the sky.

I'd bought a fresh pack of Luckys back at the roadhouse. I snubbed out the last one as the first peach shading came into the sky to the east.

CALIFORNIA

It is a region of memorable desolation and shimmering heat, yet after its occasional rains the floor of the desert is dotted with flowers.

Give my friend Don Blair credit; when he puts a car together, he puts it together bulletproof. As soon as I had daylight enough to work by, I brought the '57 over in front of our unit and went over her from bumper to bumper. I found that barring some loose fittings and a burst shock absorber, she'd come through yesterday's thrill show intact and healthy. She'd need a brake job and some new tires before long, but I could let that ride until we got home to LA.

Granted, of course, we made it that far. My last exchange with Jack kept hanging in the back of my mind.

"Good morning." Lisette stood in the doorway of our unit, wearing my commandeered shirt again. I figure I might as well just surrender possession of it to her permanently. Her hair flowed loose around her shoulders, and she was brushing out a backlog of tangles.

"Morning, Princess. How you doing?"

She still had her wry smile. "Lousy. But if I can feel this bad, it must mean that I'm still alive."

"Let's make that our beautiful thought for the day." I tucked a screwdriver back into its loops in my tool roll and leaned across the hood "Now, for real, how you doing?"

The stroking of her brush faltered, and she reflected for a moment. "I think the crying is over," she said finally. "But I hope I get the chance to go off somewhere someday and really sort out what I feel about my father. Even knowing what I do now, I'd still like to be able to love him. That's funny, isn't it?"

It was my turn to think for a second. "No, not particularly. Any man, anyone, isn't just one thing. We're all a lot of different pieces put together in a lot of different ways. I guess you could love some of the pieces of someone, even when you might hate the rest of him. Like you said, it's something you'll have to sort out."

"Thank you for the piece of him you gave back to me last night."

There wasn't any answer I could give beyond a shrug of my shoulders. "There wasn't anything to give back. It was just something you forgot you had for a minute."

"Then thank you for reminding me about it."

Lisette tossed her brush back onto the bed in the unit and removed the polished copper barrette from her shirt pocket. Gathering back her thick brown mane, she deftly clipped the barrette in place, settling her fall of hair with an unconsciously graceful toss of her head. Glancing around to make sure there wasn't anyone else up to notice her rather casual state of dress, she padded barefoot over to the car.

"How's your baby today?" she inquired, hopping up to sit on the fender next to me.

"Everything looks good except for a busted shock. We'll have to find an open gas station and put her up on the rack to get it replaced. That shouldn't take too long, and then we're set to go."

"That's good," she replied, looking down and idly swinging her bare legs. "Kev, there's something else I need to ask about."

"Sure. Shoot."

"Yesterday, when we were with the Clasters, you said that Calvin Reece had been killed. That wasn't something you made up, was it?"

I fumbled for a minute with the ties on my tool roll before answering. "No, it wasn't, Princess. They got him."

"How did you find out?"

"An old army buddy of mine who works on a newspaper in Saint Louis." The lie didn't taste good in my throat. "I was worried about what might have happened back there after we left, so I gave him a call. The police say they don't have any leads on who Reece's killers are, but it's easy enough to figure."

"It is. Why didn't you tell me?"

"I only found out yesterday morning. I was waiting for the right time when . . . things sort of got busy."

She didn't lift her eyes. "I'm sorry," she whispered to someone who wasn't there. "I didn't mean for that to happen."

I rested my hand on her thigh for a second. "It's not your fault, Princess."

He head jerked up angrily. "Oh, yes, it is! If I hadn't started this thing, Calvin Reece would still be alive."

"Yeah, and you'd be back in Gary, chained to Spanno's bed and dying by inches! Is that some kind of a goddamn solution?

I don't even think Reece would have gone for that. You have the right to live, too."

"Not if other people have to pay the price for it! That would make me no better than Mace!"

Abruptly she slipped down off the car and went back into the unit.

It's a good thing the '57 is built out of tough stuff. The punch I landed on her fender might have left a dent otherwise.

For the third time in two days, we traversed the stretch of 66 between Holbrook and Flagstaff. Out at the Peerless junction we saw a couple of Arizona Highway Patrol cars and a State Forestry deuce and a half pulled off to the side of the highway, the latter loaded with grimy fire fighters. Beyond them we could see a big patch of burn-off where the flames of the dying ghost town had spread into the desert.

My stomach cinched up at the sight of the patrol cruisers. Jack could really screw me over if he wanted by putting out a false APB on me. Heck, he didn't have to even do that. He could blow me out of the water with Lisette just by having them pull me over and politely ask that I contact my superiors at the LA County Hall of Justice.

He'd be doing it entirely in my best interests, too. Jack would never admit it, but he sweats blood when I'm working a deep-cover job. That's what a good contact man for an undercover cop does. He's the guy who has to sense if things are going screwy for the operative he's covering. He's the guy who has to call in the cavalry if he thinks his man is in trouble. And he's the guy who's supposed to maintain a sense of perspective about the job in case the hot dog out in the field starts thinking he's Superman.

In pushing this run the way I was, I was asking the Bear to violate every one of those principles of good police work. It was a shitty thing to do to a good partner and a friend. When I saw him again, he'd have every right in the world to kick me in the ass and tell me to go to hell.

The Arizona Staters paid me no mind. Jack was still keeping the faith with me.

Beyond the Peerless turnoff, we started to encounter trees again. At first they were just the usual scrubby desert cedar. But soon, as we started our steeper climb toward Flagstaff, they segued into real trees, yellow pine, tall, straight, and slender.

We passed new villages and ancient ones. Toonerville, Winona, and Walnut Canyon State Park, where prehistoric cliff dwellings cling to the sides of a rocky gorge. Then came Flagstaff, the city that might have become Hollywood if a blizzard hadn't been blowing when Cecil B. DeMille had passed through looking for a place to build a motion picture studio.

After such a long stretch in the dry country, it was nice to drive through a corridor of ranked green with a cooler blue sky overhead. There was even the faintest skiff of fresh snow up on the crests of the San Franciscos, the coming winter's notice of intent to occupy.

It couldn't last, though. We crested the Arizona Divide at 7,300 feet and started down again. Down and out of the pines. Down through the juniper and scrub cedar. Down through the sagebrush and shortgrass. Down toward the cholla and Joshua trees.

Let's do some semantics here. Up to this point on our journey, we'd crossed several large, flat, and arid areas that, for convenience sake, were referred to as "desert." Now, however, we were heading into the real thing. The genuine, sand-burning, buzzard-flapping, prospector-frying article.

Out here, we call it the Mojave.

It was a quiet drive. Lisette spoke in monosyllables when she spoke at all. She sat close at my side, almost as if she were afraid to get beyond touch. She seemed most content on the long straight stretches when I could slip my arm around her shoulders and gather her in. Even then, I occasionally felt her shiver despite the warmth of my body and the heat of the day.

We stopped for our afternoon break in Seligman. It's a little town that hasn't changed all that much since the days of the Arizona rangers, right down to the hitching rails and board sidewalks on Main Street. The intrusion of the twentieth century was limited to the paving on 66 and one weird little drive-in with the out-of-place name of the Snow Cap. The exuberant young Latino guy running the place managed to comment on the weather, compliment me on my car and my girl, and tell a pretty good joke all in the time it took to pop for a couple of Cokes.

Lisette had taken a seat at an outdoor table on the shady side of the building. Her sketchbook was in her lap, and she was idly flipping through the pages. During all of the previous days of our journey, her drawing pad had constantly been ready at her side. Today, this was first the first time she'd had it out.

Dropping down on the bench on the other side of the table, I parked her cup beside her. "Princess, we need to talk about something."

"About what?" she replied noncommittally, not looking up. No way was she in a mood to talk, but I was running out of time and options.

"Like about where we're going?"

"What do you mean, Kev?"

"I mean we've paid our visit to Peerless. We're back to hunting for the money again. And we still don't have a clue to where your dad hid it."

We were back to playing games about the lost war chest. It was the last pressure point I had to bring this case together, and I had to start pushing on it. I couldn't admit that I knew where the hiding place was, and Lisette wouldn't. One of us had to give.

"I know. That has me worried, too." Lisette looked up, her voice perfectly controlled, perfectly casual, just the right touch of puzzled concern on her face. It was her eyes that gave her away. She wasn't looking at me. She was looking past me, keeping her point of vision diverted just a little bit, refusing to meet my gaze.

I went on doggedly. "I was hoping we might find out something from Claster, but if you pardon the expression, that's a dead end. What are we going to do now?"

She looked back to her drawings. "I don't know. I guess we keep going west and hope we pick up on something."

"Why west? Hell, girl, we could have already run past the place by half a thousand miles."

"I don't think we have."

"Why not?"

"Because I just don't!"

I let it lay. There was a brittle edge to Lisette's voice, and pushing her any further now would only trigger an explosion that we didn't need. She huddled into herself and flipped another page of the pad.

"Could I have a look?" I asked.

She looked up at me, really at me, this time. She gave me her first real Princess smile of the day for letting her off the hook. Relaxing a little, she passed the pad across the white-washed tabletop.

"Why not?"

I'd stolen my looks at her sketches before. It felt better entering her world with her permission. It was all there, our run down 66 caught in her bold, quirky artistic style. From the first sketch of the Dixie dining room to the last picture of Peerless here in Arizona, all the people, places, and things that we'd seen and that had marked us on our journey together.

"Aw, Jesus! What's this?" I slammed the notebook shut.

She laughed her first real Princess laugh of the day then, too. "What's the matter? Nude studies are a mainstay of classic art."

"You did peek back there on the Canadian River."

"Well, of course, silly. Didn't you?"

"Never trust the female of the species. Why did you have to pick on me?"

"Because you're beautiful," she replied matter-of-factly, cupping her chin in her palm.

"Oh, jeez! I hope you don't go around saying that in public."

She arched an eyebrow. "Don't worry; it's solely in the eye of the beholder."

"Yeah, well, I think you need to take another look at me in a strong light." I pushed the sketch pad back across the table to her. "Barring that one exception, this is all really good stuff. You know what you're doing."

For some reason, that phrase hurt. I saw the pain cross Lisette's face, and she lost the lightness that she'd held for a moment. "No," she said, pushing the pad back to me. "I'm done with this now. You keep it. Please?"

"If you want me to." I hesitated a second before picking up the sketchbook. "What's the matter, Princess? What's wrong?"

"Nothing." She was looking past me again. "I guess I'm still a little tired is all. Could we stop early today?"

"Sure. Wherever you'd like."

"Needles," she replied, looking into nowhere. "I'd like to stop in Needles."

Lisette was quieter than ever once we were back in the car. All that long day she'd been studying on something, thinking hard on some problem. But the thinking was over now. She'd come to some kind of a decision. Crawling over into the far corner of the seat like a wounded animal, she hugged a private misery to herself.

As for me, I began to get that falling sensation again, like I'd had yesterday when we were doing that chickie run to the railroad crossing. That feeling that destiny was rearing back and getting ready to smash us in the face. The odometer kept ticking off the miles like the seconds on a bomb detonator.

We passed through Kingman, Arizona, also passing on any lame jokes about any possible relationship between Lisette's last name and the town. West of Kingman, as we headed out across the frying pan flats to the border, the terrain gave up its last pretense of habitability.

What little that grew bristled with spines and spikes to fanatically defend its few precious drops of hoarded moisture. What crawled in the sand carried a horny armor and spat poison. What hunted out in the wastes never tasted water from birth to death but quenched its thirst solely on the salt blood of what it killed. Lifting above it all were the lava ranges, rust red, glassily jagged, and naked in the heat shimmer and glaring sun. Skeleton mountains tearing at the sky.

The Mojave is many things: humbling in its immensity, amazing in its alien uniqueness, awe-inspiring in its stark beauty.

But it is not nice.

Even with a new water pump and a freshly flushed radiator I normally wouldn't have crossed this stretch during the day. However, it was getting on in September and we'd picked up some mare's tail overcast, so it was merely as hot as hell instead of totally impossible.

Even so, it was a relief to come down into the little belt of green that flanked the Colorado, that muddy and stubborn little river that insists on churning its way through places where all other more sensible bodies of water have long since given up the ghost and evaporated.

We crossed the steel arch bridge at Topock and were in California. There was the inspection station to clear of course, that snobbish little feature unique to the Golden Bear State. At one time, back in the bad old days of the depression, there might have been a cadre of LA Police officers on duty here. Their orders were to turn back anyone not bringing living money with them into the state. Now there were only a couple of casual questions about agricultural products and a wave on our way.

Needles was just a couple of miles farther upriver. Everybody knows about Needles. Every newspaper in the country that lists the hottest place in the United States mentions the little community with ominous regularity. It's the first town you hit on Route 66 coming in across the Arizona line and the last before you start across the heart of the desert. It's the jump-ing off point, the place you're nervous about leaving and the place you're relieved to reach. It's the last spot where the water doesn't have to be shipped in by railroad tank car.

Needles was also the last real town before we reached the site of Johnny 32's hidden horde.

I drove a security circuit around the place, checking for po-tential trouble before we shut down. There had been no sign of Spanno since our confrontation the day before. The black Chrysler seemed to have an eerie knack of being able to dis-appear and reappear at will, like the spook lights back in Oklahoma. It was out there, though, somewhere close by. It had to be. I could feel its presence.

We checked in at the appropriately named Trail's End Tourist Court at the southern tip of town, a tight little cluster of old-fashioned clapboard cabins at the Y intersection where 66 fed into the town's two main avenues. That night, I used the honeymooning couple line for the first time and got their big unit, complete with desert coolers, a separate bedroom, and a kitchenette.

Things were still quiet after we settled in. Lisette sat at the little kitchen table for a long time, her face buried in her crossed arms. Finally I cracked. "Okay," I said, dropping into the chair across from her. "Come on! Talk to me! What's going on here?"

"I've been holding out on you, Kev," she replied in a sad little muffled whisper. "I think I do know where my father's money is. I figured it out days ago. It's only a couple of hours' drive west of here. We'll be there tomorrow morning."

She straightened in her chair and met my eyes. "And then, tomorrow night, we'll be in Los Angeles and it will be over."

"What do you mean 'over,' Princess?"

"Just that. This trip, us, everything, it all ends tomorrow. Whether we find the money or not, I go on alone from there. You can't help me anymore."

"Don't I have anything to say about that?"

"No!" She shook her head emphatically, her glossy fall of hair swirling. "No, you don't!"

"Why?" I slammed my palm down on the tabletop. "Dammit, after everything we've been through, do I at least get to ask why?"

"Can't you see? If we find the money, then I have to go back to Chicago to set up the hit on Mace. If you come with me, you become an accessory to first-degree murder. I can't let that happen. And if the money isn't there, then I have to lead Mace away from you. If we stay together, sooner or later he'll get at you and kill you. I can't let that happen, either."

"Princess—"

"No!" It was a short, shrill scream of denial. I noticed the tears starting to glint in the corners of her eyes. "Please understand, Kev," she keened softly. "You are the best thing that has happened to me in a long, long time. I will not destroy you, and I will not let you destroy yourself for me."

She caught up my hand. Lifting it to her face, she gently nuzzled it. Now I could feel the cool wetness on her cheeks. "Please don't argue with me," she went on quietly. "I'd like to go put my good dress on now. I'd like you to take me into town and buy me a drink and some dinner. Then I'd like to go dancing for a little while until it gets cooler, and then I'd like to come back to this nice little house so we can make love again and again and again. Like my first time. Please?"

This was a situation not generally covered in your basic "guy" manual. Hey, we're supposed to be rescuing the damsels in distress, right? What do you do when the damsel looks you in the eye and says that it's her turn to throw herself on the hand grenade for you? Other than feel very, very humbled, that is.

I caught her hands up in mine. "Okay, we won't argue. But in between all that making love we're going to talk some, too. All right? Just talk."

I felt her nod. Thing was, I wasn't exactly sure what we'd be talking about. Maybe about an alternative way of dealing

with Mace Spanno? Maybe about how two people with
$200,000 could disappear beyond the reach of Spanno and the
Los Angeles Sheriff's Department both? I didn't know myself.

As Lisette had requested, we went uptown. Or at least as
up as Needles could get. We had that drink and that dinner
and that dance, and we took a few minutes more to drive up
on the little ridge beyond town to watch a scattering of flying
saucer clouds glow in a vivid Mojave sunset.

Coming down off the hill, I bought a tank of gas for tomorrow and cruised around the streets a little more, just to
make sure. No sign of trouble, no sign of Spanno, only a scattering of the townies coming out. Like all smart desert dwellers,
they wait for the cool after sunset before taking care of their
business.

Driving back to the tourist court, we parked the '57 beside
our cabin. There was no hurry and no one around, so we kissed
a little in the shadows before going inside to fill out the last
event on Lisette's agenda for the evening. She had me laughing
at some damn thing as I unlocked the door.

The cabin lights flashed on, and Mace Spanno was sitting at
the kitchenette table.

There was no chance to try for the Commander. Nate Temple was standing just inside the doorway with his Detective's
Special leveled at my head. "There's no odds in being stupid,
pal," he said with the first words I'd ever heard him speak.
"The show's over."

There wouldn't be any mistakes this time. These guys weren't
small-time country rubes like the Claster clan. They didn't
miss my knife, and they used sash cord to tie my arms to the
frame of a straight-backed kitchen chair, yanking the knots
tight with brutal, casual efficiency.

Temple sat straddling a second kitchen chair across the room
from me, his arms crossed on the back and his .38 snub-nose
fixed in his fist like it had grown there. His dark wolf's stare
never shifted for a second.

"Sorry if I make you nervous," I said just to be making the noise.

"Not nervous," he replied conversationally. "Just bein' careful. You've been giving us fits ever since Chicago. No sense in giving you the chance to ass us around anymore."

Not likely. I'd tested my bonds and they were pulled as tight as the cables on a suspension bridge. I'd have to tear the chair apart to get loose. And that would leave the distance across the room and the gun in Temple's hand. With desert coolers rumbling in every open window hereabouts he could probably get away with one shot. And one shot would be all he would need.

Temple angled the two-inch barrel of his revolver in my direction. "You know, pal, you know your shit."

"Thanks."

"You ever work the gangs?"

I shook my head. "I can't say I ever had the chance."

"That's a waste. That's a real waste. There's a lot of guys I know who could use a really good wheelman." Temple's eyes cut toward the third person in the room. "You know, the kind with brains and balls."

After we had been nailed, Spanno's wheelman had brought the 300-C up from wherever it had been hidden. Now he sat on the edge of the cabin's worn couch. In spite of the heat, he still had on the old army field jacket he'd worn in the rain outside of the Dixie Trucker's Home. He even looked cold. Likewise, he looked younger, sicker, and more unsure of himself. Somehow I doubted that Mr. Randy Bannerman had been having a very easy time of it lately.

"What the hell did you and Mr. Spanno want me to do?" he replied, a strained edge on his voice. "Did you want me to put us under that goddamn train! I thought that was where this crazy son of a bitch was taking us yesterday!"

"What we wanted you to do was *catch* this guy!" Temple let the disgust leak into his voice. "We give you the fastest, the goddamn most expensive car in the country, and you can't catch some kid from California in a goddamn Chevy!"

"He's crazy," Bannerman trailed off weakly.

"Crazy my ass!" Temple's voice was as cold and smooth as chilled oil. "You know, I think that maybe when we get back to Gary, you're going back to boosting cars again, pal."

There was a silent implication that a demotion was the least Bannerman had to worry about.

"Hey, man. You weren't the one driving out there. He was."

I was as surprised at my words as the two hoods were. I don't know why I said it. I sure as hell didn't owe Bannerman anything. I guess it must have come under the heading of professional courtesy. Bannerman aimed the briefest of shaky smile in my direction. Then he turned away as if he didn't like looking at the ropes.

The cabin went quiet again, quiet except for the murmur of a voice from behind the closed door of the bedroom. That was where Spanno had taken her. That murmur had been going on for a long time now, heavy, deliberate, and too low for the words to be made out. Just Spanno. I hadn't heard Lisette speak since our capture.

Then there came another sound, a single soft, agonized whine, like the muffled cry of a wounded animal. Explosively I threw my strength against my ropes, and I swore as nothing yielded.

"Easy!" Temple snapped, the muzzle of his pistol coming up on me again. "Believe me, pal. You don't want to get loose." Behind him, I could see Bannerman staring at the bedroom door in horrified fascination. He knew what was going on inside, too.

"You know, that's some kind of boss you work for," I said lowly.

"It's his family, pal."

"Yeah, that's supposed to be his stepdaughter in there!"

"So?"

I looked into the gunman's mud-colored eyes, and I found that he meant it. There was no hate there, no remorse, no pride, no guilt, no justification, no revulsion, just "so."

"So you like somebody getting away with shit like that? You think it's cool, somebody treating some poor damn girl that way?"

I was probing for a weakness in the enemy line. All I had to work with was my mouth, and the only angle I could think of was to try for an ally in the enemy camp.

I might as well have tried sticking a needle into a corpse.

"What the hell is it for me to like or not to like?" Temple replied.

"Just part of the job, huh, man?"

"Just part of the job," he agreed. "Hey, you and the girl, you got into it with Mr. Spanno. That's his affair, you know? Me and the punk-ass over there on the couch, we just work for Mr. Spanno. This is nothing personal. It's just business."

"How about you?" I aimed my words at Bannerman. "Is this the kind of shit you signed up for?" I tried to hold the wheelman's eyes, trying to make him remember that I'd spoken up for him a minute ago.

His gaze slithered away and focused on a worn place on the carpeting. "Like Temple said, it's no skin off my nose."

There was another muffled cry from the bedroom, more drawn out, more pain-wracked. Temple glanced toward the sound. "Like I said, pal. It's just business. That's why you should hope that it's me taking you out when the time comes. Like it'll just be a job so I can promise you it'll be neat, fast, and sweet. Professional."

. There was a final faint protesting whimper, and even the Aceman frowned a little. "Mr. Spanno, though, sometimes he's not so professional. He can take things personal."

Bannerman's face had gone gray. "I . . . I got to check the car," he mumbled, getting to his feet.

"Fine." Temple motioned toward the cabin door. "Take a walk around and make sure we're not collecting any nosy neighbors out there."

The gunner shook his head in disgust as the wheelman escaped from the reality of the cabin. I guess the kid just wasn't a real pro.

The bedroom door opened a few moments later, and Lisette emerged, stumbling across the room. Clutching at the edge of the little kitchen table, she fought to stay on her feet. I couldn't see any injuries, her dress wasn't even mussed, but she was ghost pale and panting for breath and her eyes were staring and unfocused.

"Princess," I whispered.

She looked at me. I hope I never see that kind of bleak, total despair in a human face again.

Spanno followed Lisette out of the bedroom, and we swapped stares for a long second. What was he feeling now? He had all the chips. He'd won. Was he feeling satisfaction? Pleasure? Was he waiting for me to beg? You'd like to think that your death at least means something to the man who's going to kill you.

I couldn't read him. There was nothing I could see.

"Where's Bannerman?" the big man asked flatly.

"He's out checking on the car, Mr. Spanno," Temple replied like the respectful employee he was.

"Good. There's no sense in hanging around this hole any longer. Have him bring it around and we'll get out of here."

"How about . . . ?" Temple gestured in my direction.

Spanno stared at me coldly for a long second. "We'll dump him in the desert," he said finally. "Use a garrote. I don't want to get blood in the trunk."

At least I knew my place in the world now. The big man wasn't going to make it personal after all. He had what he wanted, and I was beneath his contempt. His last concern about me was my not making a mess on his carpeting.

"No!" It was Lisette's voice, or a dry, cracked whisper of it. She pulled herself upright at the table and turned to face the big man. "You don't know where the money is yet. I'm the only one who does. If you kill him, I'll never tell you."

Spanno took two fast steps forward and grabbed Lisette's arm. Almost casually he tossed her across the room, piling her up with a crash against the kitchenette cabinets. This time I thought I felt the chair frame give a little as I threw myself against it. Nate Temple was behind me in an instant, though, his gun barrel grinding into the base of my neck.

Spanno towered over Lisette's crumpled form. "You will tell me what I want to know, when I want to know it," he said softly, aiming a finger at her. "And we both know that you will."

"It won't do you any good, Mace," the girl replied, looking up at him with a ghost of her old defiance. "Even with the money, you won't have it all. You still won't have me."

"I have you already, Lisette." This time there was a trace of emotion in his voice. God, but it was so out of place, that whisper of a lover.

"But not the way you want me to be. Not yet."

She let the words hang in the air. I watched Lisette move, gathering herself in from her awkward sprawl. So carefully she drew her legs under her, letting her skirt ride up her thighs as if it were unintentional, so carefully interweaving sensuality into her pain. She was still fighting, using the only weapons available to her.

"If you kill Kevin, I'll leave you again, Mace. I swear it. I'll keep trying to run. And if I have to, I'll run to where you can never get me back, just like my mother did."

She lay curled at the floor at the big man's feet, looking up at him, defiant yet supplicating. "You know I mean it, Mace. You won't be able to keep me away from every high window, or every bottle of sleeping pills, or every piece of broken glass. But if you let him go, I'll make you a promise."

"What?" You could barely hear the big man's single word over the rumble of the desert coolers.

All the male ego in me tried to squeeze up into my throat and scream a "No!" across the room. I choked it back down. She was trying to buy us an out with the only currency she had. If I broke the spell she was trying to weave, we'd both be lost.

"I promise I'll stay with you, Mace," she said, drawing herself up onto her knees. "No more running away. No leaving. I'll stay with you and I'll be whatever you want me to be for as long as you want."

There is something so incredibly appalling about watching someone you love bargain her soul away for you. And yeah, now that it was too late for me to say it to her, I was willing to apply that word to Lisette.

She was drawing him in. Holding him with the dark velvet of her eyes, the pale length of her body. Holding a dream out to the alligator with her bare hand.

"God, you think I'm crazy?" he said heavily, turning away from her. "He'd have the cops on us two minutes after we turned him loose."

"He wouldn't!" Lisette scrambled to her feet, catching at Spanno's arm. "I'd make him promise not to! He knows that you'd have me. He knows what you'd do to me if he tried to make trouble. Please, Mace! *Father, please!*"

The room, the universe, went silent and still. Lisette clung to the big man's arm, the streak of a single fresh tear down her face marking her new level of debasement. And for Mace Spanno somehow I sensed that this was a victory he'd waited a long time for.

"Father, please," Lisette repeated. "This is something I could love you for."

He smiled, and that was something horrible to see.

"And what about the money?"

"I'll tell you. I'll take you right to where I think it is. No lies. I swear."

He brushed Lisette's hand from his arm. "I'll have to think about it."

Spanno started for the cabin door. "Watch 'em both, Nate," he said without looking back over his shoulder. "I'll be back in a minute." He disappeared out into the night.

Temple fell back across the room, moving into a position to cover us both, still just doing his job.

Lisette took a deep, shuddering breath. Brushing her sweat-soaked bangs out of her eyes, she looked over at me. "Nate, is it all right if I talk to him while Mace is gone?"

Temple shrugged. "Nobody told me you couldn't. Just don't get too close to the guy; I don't know if Mr. Spanno would like it if I had to lay you out with a gun butt."

Lisette knelt a couple of feet away on the cabin's threadbare carpet. She studied me for a long time, as if she was trying to imprint me in her memory. "I am so sorry, Kevin," she whispered finally.

"I'm the one who's sorry. I let you down, Princess."

She smiled sadly. "It wasn't your fault, Sir Galahad. There were just too many dragons. It's my fault for pulling you into this. It wasn't fair. I used you to try and get out of the mess I was in. And now it's only fair that I get you out of the mess you're in. You heard what I told Mace. If he lets you go, you mustn't come after me. You have to let it go, too."

"How am I supposed to do that?" I demanded.

"By being realistic. Coming after me or going to the police won't help. Not with him. You'll just make things worse for us both. Let it go. Go back to your own life and let me go back to mine. Treat this whole thing like it's been a nightmare. And the only thing you can do with a nightmare is wake up the next morning and forget about it. Forget about me."

"The problem is that you're no nightmare, Princess. You were born a sweet dream."

Her smile strengthened and she even managed to preen just a little. "It wasn't bad for a first time, was it?"

"The best first time I'll ever have."

Her smile faded "You've given me so many good things to remember these past few days. That's important now because I'm going someplace where it's going to be very hard for me to remember what 'good' is."

"Ah, Jesus, Princess!"

"Remember what I told you, Kev. I will not destroy you, and I will not let you destroy yourself for me."

Outside we heard the rumble of a big-bore engine. The dim glow of a car's running lights played across the window curtains. It was the Chrysler moving up. Something was going on out there.

Lisette looked over at Temple. "Please, Nate. Only for a second. I won't try anything."

Across the room, Temple had been studying us with amused cynicism. He shrugged now. "Go ahead, but you better be done before the man gets in here."

Lisette's lips pressed against mine for one urgent second, and then she was across the room. She was leaning back stoically against the kitchenette counter when Spanno came through the door. She met his gaze levelly.

The big man nodded slowly and smiled again. "All right. We have a deal."

I saw Lisette shudder uncontrollably for an instant, but then she drew herself up. "I've talked to him already. He won't make any trouble. I won't either as long as you leave him alone."

"Good." Spanno nodded again. He reached out with that big paw of his, lightly running his hand over her bare shoulder. "That's good. I'm glad you're being sensible about this, Lisette. It will be better this time. I promise."

She nodded. I don't think she trusted herself to speak.

"Now, where is the money hidden?"

"Not yet. Not until we're away from here and I know that Kevin's safe. Then I'll tell you where it is. All you need to know now is that we'll be going farther west."

Spanno frowned and shot a hard look in my direction. He didn't like being reminded about me. And I suspect he liked Lisette's display of concern even less. But then he smiled once more. "All right," he said. "I guess if a man can't trust his own daughter, who can he trust?"

Damn, how he enjoyed that grotesque little joke. With his

arm around Lisette's unwilling shoulder he steered her over in front of my chair, showing her off to me, rubbing my nose in the fact that he had the claim now.

"Remember what I told you, boy? I told you, you were interfering with my family." His arm tightened possessively around Lisette. "This is my family, and what's mine stays mine."

I saw it coming, but there wasn't a hell of a lot I could do about it. The punch lifted the chair off the floor and threw me down on my side. My ears rang and I could taste the blood in my mouth. The world started to crawl away down a long gray tube, and I clung to the pain like a drowning man to a lifeline. I couldn't let myself go unconscious, not now. Come on, God; give me a break here!

I saw events in the cabin as if I were looking in through the wrong end of the telescope. A distant Spanno herded Lisette toward the door. "Okay, Nate," I heard him say faintly. "I'll get her in the car. You follow us out."

"No!" Lisette struggled wildly in the big man's grip. "We all leave here together! And cut him loose before we go."

Spanno laughed and that was even worse than his smile. "Whatever my little girl wants. Cut the punk loose, Nate, and let's get out of here."

Temple holstered his gun and came to lean over me. I heard the snick of a knife opening, my own knife. "There you go, pal," Temple said under his breath, slashing through one of the loops of cord binding me. "When you get out of here, go find a church and light yourself about fifty candles."

The switchblade thunked into the floorboards a couple of feet away, upright and quivering. And then they were gone, Temple, Spanno, and Lisette, and I heard the black Chrysler pulling away into the night.

The world came back into scale, and I spat my own blood onto the floor. Spanno had just screwed up sooo royally. He'd left me alive and that mistake was going to cost him everything he had and everything he was. In a frenzy, I tore my left hand out of the tangle of cord. Dragging myself to the knife, I cut myself free.

They'd taken my gun and they'd probably disabled my car. But there were other guns and cars in this town, and there was sure as hell a telephone. Now was the time to have Jack call out the cavalry. I was going to sic every brother cop in Arizona and California both on Mr. Son of a Bitch Spanno, and I was going to lead the pack as we ran him down. And when we got hold of him I was going to rip the living, greasy guts out of his belly and use them to pack the '57's wheel bearings.

I folded the paratrooper's knife and stuffed it in my pocket. Then I hit the door and charged out into the darkness, starting for the court office and that telephone. However, I'd barely jumped down from the cabin steps when a harsh whisper came out of the shadows beside me.

"Freeze, wiseass."

Grinning, Ira Claster leveled the gun in his hand.

There is more than one Route 66. All along the current highway there are older alignments that have been bypassed. Some, like at Peerless, dead-end. Others live on as county and state roads and byways. One such bypass leads up onto a desolate plateau northwest of Needles. Once it was part of the big highway; now it was just a little feeder loop leading out to a quasi-ghost town called Goffs.

That was the road we followed, a slow, winding climb past shaggy clumps of palm and jagged lava outcroppings, our headlights the only ones piercing the night. I sat behind the wheel of the '57 with Ira beside me, a revolver shoved in my ribs.

Life hadn't been too kind lately to the younger Claster boy. Between our fight and his car crash, he'd looked pretty chewed up back in Peerless. Now, though, he resembled something out of an American International horror flick. He'd picked up some mean-looking burns in the fire, and his sweat was lifting the Band-Aids he'd used to hold his face together. The claw marks underneath were starting to fester. There was also a madness in his eyes beyond what had been there before.

"So," I inquired, "are you working for Spanno now or are you on your own time?"

"I guess you could say both." Claster grinned again. "When he come back to look around in Peerless, him an' me, we made an agreement. We figured that we both wanted you dead just about as bad, so we decided to help each other out. Hell, I told him I'd be happy to kill you for free. But he made me the offer of coming in on his payroll, so why not make a few bucks on the side?"

"Waste not, want not."

"That's it, wiseass!" He gave a short, shrill laugh. "That's it!"

Oh, yeah. Definitely this guy was no longer firing on all cylinders. Fan-damn-tastic!

"You mean he drug you clear out here to Needles just to ax me? God, that was a waste of effort."

Come on, man; get pissed and keep talking. Let me know what the game plan is.

"Shut your mouth, wiseass!" Claster snarled. "I'm the one who set you up today."

"What are you taking about?"

"Who do you think tracked you down to that motel? Last night, that Spanno man fixed me up with a car in Flagstaff while he went on ahead. When you come through, I just climbed on your tail and stayed there all day. Did you know he has a radiophone in that big old 300 Chrysler of his? Every time you'd stop, I'd hit a pay phone and give him a call about where you were."

Now I remembered the nondescript gray Ford that had kept popping up in my rearviews all afternoon. I hadn't worried about it too much at the time. It's not uncommon to pass the same car half a dozen times in the same day if you both happen to be going the same direction on the same highway.

I'd become so fixated on watching out for that damn black Chrysler that I'd totally missed the kindergarten move of having a different tail car slipped in on me. Damn! And I'd been sneering at Spanno for screwing up.

"Is that when Spanno set you up to kill me?"

"Naw. From the sound of it, I figured he was going to do it himself and I'd just get the chance to piss on the corpse. I didn't get the job until only a little while ago. He had me keeping a lookout outside of that cabin you and that bitch-kitty daughter of his were staying in. When he's getting set to leave he comes out and he offers me ten thousand dollars to kill you and lose your body in the desert."

In the dashboard glow I can see Claster patting his shirt pocket with his free hand. "The same price my brother got, and I only got to dig one grave. I get to keep your car as a bonus. I guess I can get to like Chevys."

I nodded to the night. I was starting to think a little like Spanno, and that concept alone spooked me. Now I understood about the big production number he'd put on back at the auto court for Lisette. The one about letting me live. The big man was going to have his cake and eat it, too.

Spanno had pretended to allow Lisette to buy my life in return for her promise of obedience. A promise that he'd use to keep her under his control, probably combined with the implied threat of having me hunted down if she attempted to escape again. He'd know that Lisette's own sense of honor would be the strongest leash he could keep on her.

What the Princess wouldn't know was that her stepfather had kept a spare killer in his hip pocket. The last time she'd seen me, I'd been alive and more or less well. She would have no idea that she was staying Spanno's slave for the sake of a dead man. And Spanno would still have his vengeance on me for daring to take her away.

And what was worse, should the day come when Spanno would ever want to destroy Lisette for some slight or transgression, all he'd need to do was tell her the truth. That all of her sacrifice had been for nothing.

I could see him smiling.

The bones in my hands ached with the grip I had on the steering wheel. Everything inside me went as empty and black as the Mojave night. I had to get out of this. I had to get out of this, and I had to kill Mace Spanno. Not for the law or for me or even for Lisette. I had to kill him because he was too evil to let live.

A half-moon was rising as we passed through the finger count of darkened houses that made up Goffs. The flats glowed dull silver, rimmed unevenly by the shadowy, broken-glass mountains. There were no lights at all except for the distant ones in the sky.

"Slow down." Ira lifted his gun to emphasize the order, and I eased up on the gas. He was looking for a place now.

Soon enough, he found one. There was a turnout ahead. Maybe an old maintenance turnoff or something. Just an open half-acre of packed gravel and hardpan by the side of the road.

Claster gestured with the pistol barrel. "Pull in there."

This was where I was going to die.

The turnoff was on the right side of the road. As I wheeled into it, my headlights played out across the low tufts of rabbitbrush and across a shallow ridge of sun-baked clay not quite a foot high along the edge of the clearing. I let the '57's front tires roll up onto this ridge as I brought us to a stop.

Killing the engine, I switched off the car lights. I put my hands back on the steering wheel, being careful not to touch the floor shift, making sure that Claster could see that I'd left the car in gear. It was quiet out there, so quiet you could hear God breathe.

"Okay, now what?" I said.

Hell, I knew what. I was just praying that he wouldn't want to get blood on the upholstery.

Out of the corner of my eye I looked on as Claster took the keys out of the ignition. "Now," he said in a low voice, "you make up for my brother dying. Now you make up for giving me a whole lot of grief."

"I don't suppose it would do any good to point out that

none of this was our idea. You and your brother brought it all down on yourselves."

Claster shook his head. "Nope, wouldn't do any good at all."

Watching me intently from behind the leveled revolver, he reached back and flipped the door handle. "Now you keep your hands on that steering wheel till I'm ready to tell you to move."

The passenger door swung open, and Claster started to ease backward out of the car, keeping me covered. He was so busy keeping an eye on my hands that he didn't notice that I had both the brake and the clutch pedals shoved to the floor. When he had his feet on the ground but was still leaning into the passenger compartment, I slipped my foot off the brake.

The '57 lurched backward off the mound of dirt, the passenger door sweeping over Claster, taking him down with a startled cry. At the same instant, I bailed out of the driver's side. I was ready for the movement, and I stayed upright. Taking one fast stride back, I got my left hand on the rear fender of the '57, and I vaulted and rolled across the trunk of the still-moving automobile.

The paratrooper's knife was in my right hand as I came off the far-side fender. As I hit the ground in a crouch, my thumb closed on the release stud and I felt the little knife jerk as the fighting blade extended and locked. The one advantage a gun has over a knife is range. And Claster didn't have any.

He was staggering to his feet in the gray and shadow of the moonlight. Wildly he tried to bring his gun up as I moved in on him. The outside of my left wrist impacted against the inside of his right, sweeping the weapon aside and sending his last-chance bullet crashing away wasted.

My right hand hooked upward, targeting on that critical point just beneath the joining of the breastbone that marks the shortest path to the heart. There was that indescribable *wudge* of steel driving through flesh and cartilage, and I gave the knife handle that twist they teach you that opens the blood channel. Life splashed out hot on my wrist.

The difference between a gun and a knife is that with a gun, you smash the living out of a man. With a knife, it slips away. For a few seconds you stand there eye to eye with the person you're in the process of killing. And even though you are his killer, he reaches out to you, because you are the only person there at that last and loneliest moment of his existence.

"I'm sorry about your truck, man," I whispered.

I cleaned my blade off by driving it into a patch of soft dirt, and I reclaimed my car keys and Claster's gun. It was an old .38-caliber Iver Johnson top-break revolver, its barrel sawn back to two and a half inches and its bluing worn through from a lot of carrying. It was a five-shot with four live rounds left in the chambers. Ira Claster was also one of those overconfident individuals who didn't bother to carry reloads.

Oh, well. I guess a whole beltload of ammo wouldn't have helped him this time. I left Claster lying out there beside the road. Maybe I'd be able to send somebody back for the body before the coyotes and ravens worked him over too bad. I had other things to worry about at the moment.

I took the '57 back out on the old alignment, following it as it curved south, never letting the needle of the speedometer drop below a hundred as we wailed through the night. Goading me on was the terrible wrongness of the empty seat beside me. The Princess was riding elsewhere tonight, staring out into a darkness that was eternal, feeling it as every minute and mile took her farther away from light and life. Or maybe her eyes were closed and she was praying for God to be a nice guy and just let her heart stop beating.

The lights of another one-horse-two-gas-pump wide spot called Essex marked the junction with the current Route 66. My foot wavered uncertainly on the gas for a second as I considered stopping and calling the situation in. Then I stood on the throttle once more. It would take time to make someone open up and let me use a phone, time to tell my story to the local law, and more time while my story was verified. And I didn't have the time to spare.

All I had left was the location of John Kingman's hidden

money. That was the sole hard link I had with Lisette and her captors. If they beat me to it, they'd be gone. With his gang's old war chest in his possession and both a border and a coast within reach, Mace Spanno could drop off the face of the earth, taking Lisette with him.

God, what a lonely old road it was out there. The occasional set of headlights flickered weakly out across the flats like a star blacklisted from heaven. Half a dozen times I saw the taillights of another car ahead of me. Half a dozen times I watched them grow as the '57 closed with them. Half a dozen times they didn't belong to the black Chrysler.

Chambless . . . Amboy . . . Bagdad . . . more towns that were nothing but an arc light by the side of the road. As I blasted past each one, I prayed that a set of red flashers would appear in my rearview mirrors and the howl of a siren would announce the presence of a CHP cruiser or a sheriff's patrol car. But of course you know what they say about cops.

"Mount Pisgah Volcanic Crater, whose lava flow comes to the very edge of Route 66 . . ." I'd memorized the entry out of the Rittenhouse guide along with the mileages. One hundred and twenty miles west of Needles. Seventy-six miles west of Essex. Twelve miles west of Ludlow. Even running flat out, it would take the better part of an hour to get there. And what would be there to find?

Ludlow! At long damn last the town sign blazed in my high beams. Twelve miles to go and still no sign of Spanno. Ten miles left. My eyes kept flicking down to the spinning disks of the odometer. Eight . . . four . . . two . . . I started backing off on the throttle.

And then the land changed. The desert to the south of the highway had been pale in the light of the rising moon, just hard-packed sand and a few clumps of spiny brush. Now, in the space of a few yards, everything went dark. I stood on the brakes, and the '57 shuddered to a stop.

The darkness was a lava flow, a vast flattened sheet of broken and boiled rock. The tip of it, like the guidebook had said, just reached the edge of Highway 66. And farther south, outlined against the stars, was its origin, Pisgah Crater, a looming lopsided scab on the face of the planet. We were there.

There was no sign of Spanno. We were alone, the '57's engine ticking over softly as we sat in the middle of the highway. Jesus! Could we have beaten him here somehow? My head ached dully and I had to force the thoughts out of it.

No way we could have passed him on the road. No way we could have gotten ahead of him unless he'd been delayed for some reason. Maybe car trouble. Maybe he'd had to stop back in Needles or at one of the two-bit turnout towns strung out along this stretch of 66. Damn, what if they had spotted me going by!

Or maybe Lisette was holding out on them. Refusing to tell them where the war chest was.

Or maybe they'd already come and gone.

I pulled the '57 over onto the narrow left shoulder of the road and shut her down. Grabbing the flashlight, I bailed out. Slamming the car door closed behind me, I ran out into the shadowed black rock.

I wildly panned the flashlight beam around me, looking for— hell, I didn't know what I was looking for. Some sign of anyone else having been here. Some indication that Lisette had been right and that this was the place. Some clue that I could grab and get a little hope out of.

There wasn't anything. Wind ripples of glistening white sand lapped against the coal-colored lava like ocean waves against a rocky seashore. No footprints. No marks. No sign that anyone had been here, ever. I might as well have been the first man on the moon. The place even looked like it. I forced a dry swallow down my throat, and I ran on, my boots ringing metallically on the ropy stone.

I was about twenty yards back from the highway, just coming over the crest of another lava spine, when I brought myself up short, almost falling on my face in the sand beyond. Beyond the main flow, my light had flashed over another small mount of lava rock. Half-covered by a shallow dune, it was identical in every way to the half a hundred other lava mounds I'd seen in the last two minutes.

Only instead of being dull black, this one was a dull, rusty red. And ten feet away, half-buried in the sand, was an old paint bucket. Right where Johnny 32 must have tossed it ten years before.

For a second I stood and marveled at the sheer, blank-faced audacity of the man. And yet when you thought about it for a minute, it made sense. It made perfect sense. Why fuss with some overcomplicated and sneaky hiding place? Over the past decade, how many people had followed through with Rittenhouse's suggestion? How many had braved the 120-degree temperatures of the Mojave and actually stopped and walked out into this literal hellhole? Five? Six? Ten? And of them, how many would be inclined to fool around with one particular pile of rocks amid an infinity of piled rock, just because it happened to be kind of a funny color?

John Kingman had been a smart man and a meticulous planner. He'd put his money down on human nature, and that's always a solid bet.

I jumped down off the flow and dropped to my knees beside the rock pile. I pushed the tube of the flashlight into the sand beside me, letting its beam illuminate my task as I feverishly tore the pile apart.

A couple of scorpions skittered wildly out of my way as I flung aside chunks of the dense, jagged stone. I paid no more attention to them than I did to the way the edges and spikes of the lava abraded my hands. I was on the right track! Another man had stacked these rocks here. They didn't fit together naturally. And now I was through the layer of rock and I was digging down through the quartz sand like a dog. And then I tore a fingernail on something else hard.

I swept aside the last of the sand. It was a piece of old red-painted drill pipe, a cap on either end, just about yay long.

Panting through my teeth, I hauled the end of the pipe up

and out of the hole and wrenched at the end cap. Trapped sand grated, but the thick layer of grease packed into the threads allowed it to turn. The cap spun off in my hand. There was a plug of something in the end of the pipe, and I had to shake it a couple of times to get it out.

It was a solid roll of paper money, three inches across and tightly bound with brittle and aging rubber bands. I snapped the bands and the currency fanned out in my hand. They were all fifties and hundreds. More rolls of bills, identical to this one, packed the pipe solidly from end to end.

This was it, the legacy of greed, death, and hope that Johnny 32 had left out here in the wastelands.

Okay, Lisette, you can tell them now. Tell them where it is.

Could I kill three men with only four bullets and a knife? Oh, yeah. Just let me get them out here in the night and the black rock and I could.

Tell 'em, Princess. Bring them to me.

I stuffed the opened wad of cash in my windcheater pocket and screwed the cap back on the pipe. Lugging it over my shoulder, I started for the car. As I scrambled over the lava, I kept shooting glances back down 66 to the east, watching for headlights out on the road.

I'd have to get the car out of sight, and I'd have to set my ambush up near the pullout. I'd have to be close in; this damn cut-down belly gun wouldn't have any range at all. Whatever happened, the guy watching Lisette would have to be the first man dropped. As smart and quick as the Princess was, she'd evaporate the second I opened up, leaving me a clean field of fire. Two rounds for Spanno and one each for Temple and the wheelman? Or should it be two and two and let Bannerman run? We'd have to see how it played.

Reaching the car, I unlocked the trunk and loaded the pipe, taking an extra instinctive minute to center its weight and wedge it into place so it wouldn't shift around. Finishing the job, I looked east again toward Needles. Still just a dark and empty road. Where was Spanno?

It was about then that I heard the growing rumble of a powerful engine. I slammed the trunk lid and looked right into a glaring set of dual headlights.

Jesus God! I was screwed! They'd come in from the west!

They spotted the '57 parked at the side of the road, and they must have realized what its presence meant. Lithely the 300-C whipped around in a tight U-turn, and tore back up the highway in a swirl of dust.

I don't know what kind of curse or denial I screamed as I threw myself behind the '57's wheel. We blasted off the shoulder, riding twin jets of sprayed gravel and burning rubber, belly to the ground and breaking traction twice again as we accelerated through the gears.

By all rights it was an act of futility. They had all the numbers: a small block against a big block, a 283 Turbofire against a 392 Hemi, a Chrysler 300-C against a Chevy 150. They had Lisette and the faster car, and they could just stroll away into the night and leave me behind. I had nothing going for me.

Except maybe for the secret.

Racing drivers know about the secret. So do fighter pilots and truck drivers and railroad engineers. And sailors have known about it for centuries. The secret is in the love and respect a man can have for a fine machine. It's in the sharing of the spirit with the steel and in the treating of it as a comrade instead of a slave. It's in the belief that there is something more there than just dead metal and a set of engineered specifications. And if this is something you can understand, then you can also understand that sometimes, just sometimes, when you are right up against it, you can reach out beyond the metal and the numbers and something more will be there.

"Now," I whispered my supplication. Then I put her to the wall, sending the tachometer needle sweeping past the red line and over to the peg at seven grand. Car's battle cry became a razor-edged banshee shriek that sliced open the night above Route 66. And she held together and we reached out toward those taillights glowing scarlet ahead of us and we grabbed that son of a bitch of a Chrysler by the ass and we reeled it in.

As we came up behind the 300-C, I kicked up my high beams, pouring them in through the rear window and striking white fire off their rearview mirrors. Two faces looked back in the glare of my headlights. Just two. Temple and Bannerman were in the Chrysler's front seat. The backseat was empty. Spanno and Lisette weren't with them.

That made it easier. I was beyond playing it safe tonight. Beyond playing it smart or even sane. The '57 and I rode up on them, and I drove the reinforced push bars on her front bumper into the back of the big black car.

Wham! The Chrysler bobbled, Bannerman wildly fighting the wheel. I felt something that might have been a smile twist my lips. Yeah!

Wham! You assholes have chased me for two thousand miles. How do you like it for a change?

Wham! Okay, Bannerman, if you like to drive so goddamn much, then *drive!*

Wham! And remember, Temple, *this is all just friggin' business!*

I wouldn't let them slow down. Out here, on the two-lane, we were playing in my ballpark. And here was where I was finishing the game. I climbed on their crumpled rear bumper, and I whipped them down the road ahead of me.

I saw Temple roll down the passenger-side window. Gun in hand, he leaned out into the night, aiming back into my lights with narrowed eyes, trying to shoot me off their tail. No way. I weaved the '57 to the left, dancing sideways out of his field of fire, letting him waste a couple of bullets on the night.

C'mon, man! I'm right over here. Do something else stupid for me.

I faintly heard the crack of another shot over the raving of the engines. A single small hole appeared in the Chrysler's rear window, the rest of the safety glass exploding into a glittering radial pattern of cracks.

Yeah! That's why you don't shoot through a car window, you moron! I tapped the side of my bumper against the Chrysler's rear fender.

Wham! Hey, man! I'm still back here. What else you got?

I dropped back into the six o'clock slot behind the Chrysler just in time to see an arm hook over the car roof from the passenger side. With his hair whipping wildly in the slipstream and his face distorted in a snarl, Temple was pulling himself up and out of his window. He was going for a ride, Chicago sidesaddle. Sitting in the window with his legs in the passenger compartment and his torso outside would give him a clear field of fire over the car's roof in almost all directions. Or at least in any direction I could dodge.

Bracing an elbow against the slick black car top, Temple sighted back into my face. I think he was grinning.

Sorry, man. I know about that one, too.

I angled the '57 across the back end of the 300-C, hooking a push bar over the bumper bomb at the base of the coupe's left tail fin. Giving the steering wheel another sharp flick to the left, I yanked the Chrysler right out from under the Aceman.

As the big car swerved wildly, Temple's face distorted from snarl to scream. He dropped his revolver and scrabbled at the roof for a hold that wasn't there. Then he tipped backward out of the window and smashed into the concrete at a hundred miles per.

You bounce at that speed. In the sidelobe of my headlights I was aware for an instant of a flailing mass of arms and legs and shredding clothing. It seemed to chase the Chrysler down the road in a wild cartwheel that grew progressively wilder as bones shattered and tissue tore. Then Temple was gone, sprayed out over the pavement like a sack of trash thrown out by a litterbug.

Two down.

The loss of his tailgunner flipped Bannerman out completely. He didn't have Big Brother around to keep the bullies away anymore. Smoke jetted from the Chrysler's exhausts as the kid wheelman pushed his mill up into never-never land in a frenzied effort to pull away.

Let him run.

It was just the two of us out here now, thundering through the dark. I faded back a little, husbanding my engine and my fuel but still staying on his tail. I figured Bannerman had two alternatives. With one, he'd run straight home to Daddy, leading me right to the big man. With the other, he'd just run, pushing his wheels until he puked a Johnson rod or ran out of gas. Then I'd have him and we'd have a little chat about where Spanno had taken Lisette.

Remember that old saying about best-laid plans?

We'd been roaring along on a pool-cue straightaway across the desert for miles, and now, with no warning, a tight left-hand turn lashed at us out of the night. I'd been looking far ahead, driving by Bannerman's headlights, and I saw the line of reflectors materialize across the road. I barely had time to drop the flaps and throw out the anchor. The wheelman in the Chrysler must have been looking back over his shoulder at the wrong moment. He was into the curve before he knew it.

He might have been able to make it. He might have been able to save himself. He could have tried to drift the turn, using the awesome power of the 300-C's engine to hold him on the road. Or he could have played it safe and just aimed straight into the desert. He would have ended up about a hundred yards out in the cactus, but he probably would have been upright and alive.

Instead, as he howled into the curve and felt the back end of the Chrysler break loose in a wild skid, he made the worst possible choice. He went grandma and grabbed for his brakes.

The 300-C went off the road sideways, popping high in the air. Impacting, it went into a wild death roll, tumbling half a dozen times out across the lava pans, spraying shredded metal and wrapping itself in the blazing shroud of its own gasoline. A beautiful and deadly creature tearing itself apart.

Lacking the momentum to finish the seventh roll, it sank

back on its smashed roof with a final crunch of crumpling steel. I was already out of the '57 and running for the burning wreck. But after my first three strides I stopped. Flame curled out of what was left of the passenger compartment, and the night breeze was tainted with something more than burning oil and rubber.

Bannerman had found out that calling chicken doesn't necessarily mean you get to walk away.

I probably could have lived real well without Randy Bannerman, except for the fact that he was the only person who could have told me where Spanno had taken Lisette.

I stumbled back to the '57 and leaned against the warm hood, the vibration of the idling engine rippling up my braced arms. Okay, Mr. Hotshot Deputy, let's do some of this detective shit. Let's work it out. Spanno and company had to have headed west from Needles on Route 66. It's the only highway that goes from anywhere, past Pisgah Crater, to anywhere. But Temple and Bannerman had come in from the west. Spanno must have driven right past the burial site of the money, gotten himself and Lisette established someplace, and then sent his lieutenant and wheelman back to look for the loot.

Question: Why? Why not look for the money on the first pass? Why put temptation in the way of even a trusted subordinate?

Answer: Spanno must really be anxious for some time alone with his stepdaughter, planning a little family reunion no doubt.

Damn, it was getting cold out here all of a sudden.

Okay now, okay, so they're set up somewhere west of Johnny 32's hiding place and I don't think they had time to get all the way over to Barstow and back. It had to be somewhere fairly close. And they aren't that many somewheres out here. I straightened and looked around. Out across the flats, far beyond the burning wreck of the Chrysler, a single spark of light glimmered.

* * *

It was a place too small to have a name. The sand-scoured signs read: GAS and CABINS, and there was nothing else that you needed to know. I cut the '57's engine and lights well up the road and coasted in, a shadow slinking through the shadows.

There was a gas station with a short row of four small cabins behind it. Lights glowed in the back of the station building and behind the drawn blinds of the farthest cabin over. An arc lamp burned over the station pumps, and I stayed clear of it as I pulled into the turnoff. I didn't let the car door slam as I got out and ran light-footed across the gravel to the door of the station office.

There was a night service bell beside the door, and I leaned on it. A couple of years later, the lights went on behind the grimy windows of the office and a balding barefoot individual in a stained T-shirt and Levi's lumbered out and unlocked the door.

"What y'aunt? Gas or a cabin?" he mumbled.

"Neither. I need to know if you rented a cabin to some people tonight. A party of four, three men and a girl in a late-model black Chrysler coupe. Two of the men left in the car. One man and the girl would have stayed. How about it?"

The station owner got a little more awake and eyed me uneasily. I guess I was looking a little bit scary about then, between my battered face and the bloodstains on my jacket. "I don't want no trouble here," he said and tried to push the door shut in my face.

I kicked the door open and bulldozed the man back against the office counter. Grabbing a handful of his shirt collar, I took a reef in it and turned off his oxygen. *"Yes or no!"*

I think I was feeling just a little bit scary about then, too.

"Jeez God! Yes, sir! The man and the girl, they're in number four!"

"Okay." I turned him loose. "Now listen! I'm a Los Angeles County deputy sheriff. When I leave here, I want you to call the highway patrol and report an officer in need of assistance.

Got that? An officer in need of assistance! Do you have a spare key to number four?"

"B-behind the counter."

"Get it."

As he fumbled, I grabbed a pencil and some kind of waybill out of the junk stacked on the office counter and printed Mace Spanno's name and the license number of the '57. I'd retrieved the wallet hiding my badge and ID card from their hiding place in the car's trunk. I slapped it down on top of the paper as the station man came up with the cabin key.

"Right. If I'm dead when the patrol shows up, this is who I was, this is the man who killed me, and this is the car he'll probably be driving. Got it?"

"Oh, *jeez* God! Yes, sir!" The eyes goggling at me were about the size of tennis balls.

"Get on the phone. Then lock your doors and stay out of sight till the CHP gets here."

He had the receiver in his hand as I went back out into the night.

I hated every pebble of the gravel covering the parking area as I approached the shabby tourist cabin. It forced me to move slowly, easing every football to the ground, when I so urgently wanted to move quickly.

There wasn't much to it. A small box of a building made out of cemented desert stone with a small wooden porch in front. A dim porch light glowed over the door, luring in a flitting cadre of insects and forcing me to swing wide and come in from the flank. There were three small windows, one on either side of the cabin as a gesture toward cross-ventilation and a third in front beside the door. All three were open a crack.

I reached the corner of the cabin and pressed back against the wall. Inside, I heard the low, urgent murmur of a masculine voice. Spanno, just as he had sounded back in the motel in Needles. I eased up onto the porch, not daring to breathe, the .38 ready in my fist. The little Iver Johnson five-shooter had felt like a howitzer when it had been jammed in my ribs. Now that I was depending on it, it didn't seem nearly as impressive. There was a gap around the cracked roller blind on the front window, and I peered in.

They were there.

Lisette was on the bed. He'd stripped her naked, even tearing the clip from her hair, leaving her nothing. Her dress and underwear lay on the floor in a shredded tangle, along with the smashed and flattened barrette. Everything I had given her had been systematically destroyed.

I couldn't see if she had been physically injured, but the breaking process was already under way. The square-shouldered pride and regal bearing that had made her the Princess were gone. She was becoming someone else now as she stared into Mace Spanno's face, her eyes dull and empty as her soul drained out onto the grimy linoleum.

Spanno leaned over her with one knee on the bed, his tie pulled off and his shirt open. One massive hand pinned Lisette's wrist to the mattress. The other was closed around her face, his thumb hooking around her jaw, the fingertips sinking pain-deep into her flesh. Holding her immobile, he forced his gaze into hers in a visual rape.

And God, that gaze. The dam had broken and he was looking at Lisette now with all of the lust and warped desire of a hype staring at a loaded spike. And the words that slipped from his lips in a steady flow—words of love, words of hate, and words of need intermixed with the vilest epithets devised by the human tongue.

If it hadn't been for the fear of hitting Lisette, I'd have gunned him down there and then. Carefully, so carefully, I flowed past the window and over to the door, getting myself set to kick it in.

Suddenly Spanno's voice cut off inside the cabin. There was a second of total silence, and then the bed frame creaked and Lisette cried out. Ah, Jesus, now what? I risked another look through the crack of light around the front window.

I could have sworn that I hadn't made a sound, but somehow I'd blown it! Spanno had backed into the far corner of the room like an ambushed rat. His left arm circled Lisette, holding her in front of him as a shield. There was an automatic in the big man's right hand, the muzzle jammed hard against the side of Lisette's head. A Colt Commander .45, my gun. Those dead oyster eyes glinted, watching, waiting.

I took a fast step and got my back against the strip of wall between the window and door. Reaching up, I swiped the barrel of the .38 through the bulb of the porch light, extinguishing it. Then I dug the door key out of my pocket and slipped it into the lock left-handed, keeping most of me behind the shelter of the stonework.

The key turned easily. I twisted the knob and flicked the door open, pulling back a couple of inches from the frame. The door squealed on its hinges and came up with a bang against the inside wall. It took me a couple of swallows to get enough moisture in my throat to speak.

"They're dead, Spanno," I said. "All three of them: Temple, Bannerman, and Claster. I killed them. Your car's wrecked, too. You're alone out here and you've got no way out."

"You!" He turned the word into an obscenity.

"Yeah, it's me, man. And it gets worse. You've been set up. I'm a Los Angeles County deputy sheriff. We never forgot about Kingman, Spanno. We've been tracking you every inch of the way. I've already called it in, and every highway patrolman and county cop in a hundred miles is converging on this place."

"I should have left you dead back at the café." Cold, congealing venom dripped off Spanno's words.

"Better be glad you didn't," I said. "Because I'm the only guy out on this desert tonight who's going to offer you a deal. And you'd better listen close and fast, because neither of us have much time."

There was a second's hesitation. "What kind of deal?"

"It's real simple and all in your favor, Spanno. I found the money. I knew where that was, too. All two hundred grand of it. It's in the trunk of my car right now, and the keys are in the ignition. You get the money, a fast car, and a head start. In exchange, you let Lisette go."

No answer. No answer at all.

"Come on!" I prodded. "This is the only chance you've got! When the rest of the law shows, you're going to be looking down the barrels of about twenty shotguns out here! Hostage or no, you're not getting out!"

And then Spanno laughed. It didn't sound any better now then it did the first time I'd heard it.

"Okay, boy," he said. "Okay. I like your deal. I like it. I'll take you up on it. But there's just one thing first."

"What?"

"You walk through that door."

It was my turn to be silent.

"Did you hear me, boy! You want me to let this girl go, then you walk through that door, now!"

"What's that supposed to prove, Spanno?"

"Why, it's going to prove that you really give a damn for Johnny's little girl here," he replied. "I mean you took her away. You've been putting your hands on her and screwing her every night! I bet you've been all the time telling her you loved her. Now you get to prove it! You prove it by walking through that door before I blow this filthy little slut's head off!"

He meant it, too. He wasn't going to buy the package. Maybe he figured there was no percentage in trying to run. There was just Route 66 out there with a highway patrol station at both Needles and Barstow. With the word already out and the roadblocks going up, he'd be a rat in a drainpipe with a cat waiting at either end.

This was his dying night. He knew it. He'd known that from the moment he'd heard my voice. His only concern now was who-all was going with him to hell. My mind raced, trying to find some maneuvering room.

I tried to pull my voice back under control, keeping it cool, keeping it low. "You don't want to do that, Spanno. That's your stepdaughter in there. That's Lisette. You don't want to kill her. Remember, she's your family. You said so. Why not give her a break?"

"Because she spit in my face!" Spanno's voice edged toward hysterical rage. "Even after what her bastard father did to me, I took her in! I gave her everything she could have wanted, just like her mother! All I asked back was due me! But all I ever got back was shit! No respect . . . no thanks for what I tried to give. . . . Why shouldn't I kill the bitch?"

"Because you love her!" I found myself yelling it back. "Yeah, and I love her, too. Okay? Neither of us can help that! Neither of us wants her hurt! Neither of us wants her dead! You want to finish this between you and me? Fine! Let's get it done. But let's let her walk away. She can't help what we feel."

I thought I'd lost him. He went silent for almost a full minute. And when he spoke again, it wasn't to me. "I do love you. You never believed me all the times I said it, but I do love you."

The big man's voice was gentle in a way I didn't believe possible, and I risked another look into the crack around the window blind. They were still back in the corner, but the arm Spanno had around Lisette was a little less a restraint and a little more an embrace. The .45's barrel was angling away from her head, and very, very gently the big man was nuzzling the softness of her hair, just as I had done so often.

Up to this point, beyond that single small cry, Lisette had been silent. Now she spoke, her voice low and steady. "Mace . . . Father, if you want me to believe you, please let me go."

For a second I wondered if it could be that simple. Whether there might not be just enough human left inside of Mace Spanno to respond to that quiet plea. But then I saw the big man straighten, the iron coming back into the arm that circled beneath Lisette's breasts. "No," he said in a grating whisper. "You never understood that, either. What's mine stays mine."

Even unto death.

The automatic ground into the side of Lisette's head again. "Did you hear me, boy! Get in here! You've got thirty seconds more; then she's dead!"

This was it! He was pushing the button! I could hear it in his voice, see it in his face. It was all going to blow now, and I didn't have anything!

Peering in, I could tell that Lisette knew that the bite was coming, too. She must have been able to feel the coiling tension in the big man's body as he geared himself up to shoot. But even with a gun at her temple, I could see that she wasn't ready to yield.

The Princess had come back again. The sound of my voice had returned her to life. The defeated slackness had gone out of her body, and her eyes glittered beneath lowered lashes. Even pinioned by Spanno's arm, she was holding herself ready to make a move. That valiant and gutsy spirit that had carried her this far on her quest for deliverance wasn't willing to lay it down yet. Not while there was even a small chance.

What was it she had said to me that time? A little chance is better than no hope at all.

I pressed back against the wall, feeling the knobby stones dig into my back. I wasn't the one who could save us out here tonight. Like it had been from the beginning, it all boiled down to a matter of trust.

"All right, Spanno. You got it." I said his name, but he wasn't the person I was speaking to. "I'm coming in. I'm coming in . . . *now!*"

And then I turned and stepped into the cabin. Spanno reacted the way I knew he would. The moment I was outlined in the door, he whipped the Commander in line with my face and pulled the trigger.

But the instant she felt the gun come away from her temple and extend out past her head, Lisette exploded. Screaming, she clawed and bit at the big man's arm, shoving the gun aside, diverting his aim so that his bullet shattered the door frame instead of my skull.

He was strong. God, but he was strong. He threw Lisette off with a single convulsive sweep of his arm, flinging her across the room and onto the bed like a rag doll. And he was fast, the .45 coming up on me again in a blue-steel blur.

He was almost fast enough.

Almost.

Holding the Iver Johnson's sight picture in the center of the big man's chest, I burned through the four rounds remaining in the cylinder as rapidly as I could pull the trigger.

He stood there for a second, hating. Hating himself because he didn't have the strength to lift his gun again. Hating me because I was going to be walking out of here with Lisette and the money. Hating the universe because he was dying in a cheap motel room in the middle of Nowheresville, USA. Then he crumpled to the floor, his face turned to the wall as if he didn't want to look at us anymore.

I tossed the empty .38 onto the scarred top of the dresser. It was over. All ten years and two thousand miles of it.

Lisette got to her feet and came to me. She buried her face against my shoulder, and my arms closed around her in an embrace that I hoped would last for just about forever. We didn't bother with the ruined rags of her clothes. I wrapped her in a thin blanket stripped from the bed, and I carried her out to the '57. We waited there together for the first CHP cruiser to come howling in from the Mojave night.

At ten o'clock the next morning, I sat sprawled in the squad room of the Barstow Highway Patrol Station, a telephone to my ear. It had been a long, black-coffee night. Telling the story. Then telling the story again and again and again and guiding people out to pick up the bodies after they didn't believe me for the fourth time. Then came writing it all down in the duplicate and triplicate and I-don't-know-what-thehellicate required so that the bureaucracy could comprehend the concept of death.

"Yeah, Jack, I've finally got everything just about wrapped up on this end. We'll be heading into LA in a few minutes."

"You might want to stay out in the boondocks, kid," my partner replied. "If you think it's been bad there, wait till you get back to the office. It's going to take us to the end of the month just to sort out the involved jurisdictions on this thing. The coroner's inquests alone are going to keep you busy till Thanksgiving. Hell, we might have to send you back to Chicago and have you do it all over again."

"I think I'm going to need a little vacation first."

"*This* was your vacation, you knothead!"

"Ah, hell." I rubbed the back of my neck. "How's the captain taking it?"

"He's pissed off at you for the way you handled this, and he's pissed off at me for covering for you. But he's really pissed off because he can't get more pissed off because for the moment, you're the shining jewel in the crown of the department."

"What do you mean?"

"The crime reporters over in the pressroom got a hold of the story last night as it came off the Teletype from Barstow. They don't know what all they're talking about yet, but that's not slowing 'em down any. You ought to see the front page of the *Los Angeles Examiner* this morning."

I heard a newspaper rustle in the earphone. " 'Chicago Crimelord Dies in Desert Shootout with Undercover Deputy. Sheriff's Department Cracks Decade-old Killing and Recovers Lost Gangland Hoard.' "

"I never did get solid proof that Spanno killed Johnny 32," I mused. "And he operated out of Gary, not Chicago."

"Gary don't sell papers, kid," quoth the Bear, sticking as good an epitaph as any on Mason Spanno's life.

"I guess not. . . . Hey, Jack, thanks for sticking with me. And thanks for putting up with all the static I handed you."

"Ah, nuts! I've been dealing with a goddamn Polish Rebel

without a Cause for three years now. I should be used to the aggravation."

"I still owe you a big one."

"Skip it. The good guys won; the bad guys lost. Once you cut through of the bullshit, that's all that counts. But tell the truth, kid. You were in way over your head on this job."

"Hey, that's what I got gills for, man."

"Jesus!" Le Baer's laughter rumbled out of the phone. "You are a case! See you in the office tomorrow, kid." There was the click of the connection breaking.

"See you tomorrow, partner," I replied to the buzz of the dead line.

Lisette was waiting for me out in the front office. Our belongings had been recovered from the auto court in Needles, and she was back in her sweater and skirt. She looked just as she had that night back at the Dixie Trucker's Home, a little worn, a little tired, but again the Princess through to her soul. She gave me one of her patented wry looks as I held my hand out to her.

"A deputy sheriff, huh?"

"A stepdaughter, huh?"

She took my hand and I led her out to where the '57 waited.

There wasn't far to go now. Barstow to Victorville and Victorville to the pass at El Cajon. El Cajon isn't a true mountain pass, really. More it's the lip of the high desert. Route 66 tips over the edge here and snakes down through a gap in the San Gabriel range, running through fields of yucca to San Bernardino. And there, smeared across the sky at the base of the canyon, was the familiar brown smudge of LA's smog layer, welcoming me back.

From San Berdo, 66 turns west across the coastal plains, passing through that long row of small towns that aren't so small anymore. Rialto . . . Fontana . . . Rancho Cucamonga . . . the places where the orange groves and strawberry fields are losing out to the tract houses.

Glendora. . . . Azusa . . . the quiet residential streets of mellow little Monrovia and the palm-lined avenues of Pasadena.

Around Covina, a couple of my fellow LA deputies in a black-and-white car lifted their hands to me as they blew past, heading up-canyon. And on Colorado Boulevard, Skeetch Davis strafed me in his '32 three-window. The prodigal had returned and my integration back into the day-to-day had begun.

From Pasadena we took the Arroyo Seco Parkway downtown. Lately, Ike's had a real bug in his ear about building a whole lot more of these freeways, as they're calling them. They're planning on running them all over the country, and it's supposed to be quite a deal.

I wonder. I can't help thinking about Peerless and about all the other little towns strung out along old 66 and the other two-lanes. What happens to them when the superslabs cut them off and their mother roads die? If the Russians were to destroy a couple of hundred American communities, we'd call it an act of war. If we do it to ourselves, we call it progress.

Downtown, in LA proper, we passed City Hall, Parker Center, and the Hall of Justice. Jack was up there now, grumbling and growling through the mountain of paperwork his punk partner had generated for him. I lifted a couple of fingers in a silent salute to a helluva good cop and friend.

A hunk of the Sunset Strip. Then Santa Monica Boulevard and the big HOLLYWOOD sign up on the hill, looking down on so much that's put-on and cheap flash and phony glamour and that little, little bit that's still real magic.

Route 66 made its final big curve and started down that last long row of stoplights. I live out here, on the cheap side of Santa Monica, but I didn't turn off yet. I'd started this on the water, and it seemed right to finish it the same way.

And finally there was Ocean Avenue, a double-headed arrow marked 101 offering up a new journey and an eternity's worth of waves marching in from the horizon.

We parked the '57 where she could look out over the sea, both of us giving her a pat on the hood for being a good and faithful friend. Car had saved us more than once out there on the lonely road. She looked a little tired and battered now, and she'd picked up a nasty rattle in her valve train that I didn't like. However, I'd already promised her a touch-up job and an engine rebuild out at Uncle Don's. It was going to mean wintering on macaroni and cheese again, but so be it.

Lisette and I walked out onto the Santa Monica Pier, neither one of us wanting the journey to be over until we had paced off every last inch we had left. At last, the only thing left between us and Japan was a two-by-four railing and the Pacific Ocean.

We leaned against the rail for a while, sharing the last Fatima out of Lisette's purse and watching a couple of guys trying to drown themselves doing some of that Hawaiian surf-riding stuff.

"What now?" I asked.

"I don't know," she replied. "For so long, all I've lived with is hate. That's not a good way to live, but at least it gives you a purpose. Now, I truly don't know. I guess I start putting together a real life."

"Back in Gary?" I asked the question with a lot more casualness than I felt.

"No." Lisette shook her head decisively. "I'm never going back there. That would be returning to the hate." She gave me a sideways glance, the corner of her mouth crooking up. "I've heard that Los Angeles is a good place for a fresh start. What do you think?"

"It worked for me. But won't you have some affairs to settle back east?"

"Not all that many," she sighed. "People like Mace use things; they don't own them. We lived in a leased town house. And while Mace had plenty of money, the feds and the Indiana attorney general will probably have it all locked up. I'll have my clothes and some of my mother's jewelry and that will pretty much be it."

She shrugged her slim shoulders and let a little ironic humor creep into her voice. "I wonder what kind of money a carhop makes out here?"

"Oh, yeah, speaking of money, that reminds me."

I dug in the pocket of my windcheater, and Lisette's eyes widened as I pulled out a massive, musty wad of big bills.

"I think there's a little over ten thousand dollars here," I said, handing it to her. "I got it out of the pipe last night when I was checking things out. What with one thing and another, I kind of forgot I had it on me. Turning it in now would just screw up everybody's bookkeeping, so you might as well hang on to it."

Lisette studied the money in her hands for a long moment. Then she neatly divided the stack of bills in two and held out half to me. "Here," she said. "This is yours. That was our deal. A fifty-fifty split on all profits recovered."

I shook my head. "That contract is null and void. I came into it under false pretenses. Anyhow, with that ten grand you can get set in a place of your own. You can go back to college if you want and get a start on that new life of yours. I'd like to see that."

She drew her hand back doubtfully. "Are you sure, Kev?"

I reached up and gently stroked her cheek with my fingertips, trying to brush away the bruises Mace Spanno had left there. "I'm sure. I want you to have that life, Princess. And I hope I can be a part of it."

She bit her lip and she looked away quickly, taking a fumbling second to stow the money away in her shoulder bag. When she looked back, there weren't any tears in those lovely dark eyes, just something deep and elementally female.

"Did you really mean it?" she asked somberly. "Did you mean what you said back there when we were with Mace? Just before—"

"When I say something, I generally mean it."

She burrowed into my arms, tucking her head in under my chin in that right place so I could feel the cool softness of her hair, and there wasn't any sound except for the breaking hiss of the waves around the pier pilings.

"You're going to have to be patient," she whispered eventually. "It's going to be quite a while before I can let any man own a piece of me again. There are a lot of things I have to work out about myself and a lot of questions I have to get answers for."

"I know, Princess. Take your time. There are a whole lot of tomorrows out there."

And there are.

Like a lot of my generation, I've read some Jack Kerouac. I understand only about half of what the guy is saying, and I agree with only about half of what I understand. There was one phrase, though, that did stick in my mind, something about "a fast car and a coast to reach and a woman at the end of the road."

Well, I have a fast car and I've reached my coast. But my woman ran with me down every long mile of that road.

What happens now? Like Lisette, I truly don't know. Our relationship was conceived out there on the highway. Like the flight of the Okies down the Mother Road, it was something born out of fear and desperation, necessity and need. Whether it's also something we can make grow in a more or less normal world, that we'll have to learn. The Princess and I are the kind of people who understand that "happily ever afters" can be hard to come by sometimes. But we'll live it out, one day at a time, and see how it goes.

Life is like a run down Route 66. You never know what's waiting for you around the next curve.

AUTHOR'S NOTES

On October 13, 1984, near the town of Williams, Arizona, the last stretch of old Route 66 was decommissioned and bypassed by Interstate 40. On that day, the Mother Road ceased to be a highway and became a legend.

Route 66 is the last Great American Trail. It is one with the Natchez Trace and the Great Platte River Road—a pathway etched across the land, not by pork barrel politics or for the convenience of national policy, but born out of the needs and desires of the people who wished to travel it. It's a thin thread of concrete that stitches together the defining places and events of an era in the history of the United States. It was and still is a uniquely American adventure. In the author's opinion, a journey through the heartland along the remnants of Route 66 is one of the best ways conceivable to bring yourself in tune with what we were, with what we are, and with what we are becoming.

About 85 percent of the old two-lane can still be driven. The states and communities along the 66 corridor have done an excellent job of marking the old alignments as historic and scenic byways. Many businesses and even private homes along the route also proudly display the 66 shield. In addition, every corridor state has a Route 66 Association, eager to provide travelers with information on the old road.

Portions of this book were written "on location" during the author's own exploration of the Mother Road, and many of the story's events are set at actual sites along Route 66. Some of the concerns mentioned, such as the Coral Court motel, are gone now, victims of economic decay and urban development. Other's, such as the Dixie Trucker's Home, the El Rancho hotel, the Wigwam Village Motor Court, and Juan Delgadillo's Snow Cap Drive In, are alive and thriving. The only truly "made up" locale in *West on 66* is the town of Peerless, and even it is a composite of the numerous bypassed and abandoned road communities that can be found along the western interstates.

Likewise, Jack D. Rittenhouse's *A Guide Book to Highway 66* is also quite real. The epigraphs as well as the plot points used in *West on 66* come verbatim from this source. A facsimile edition of Mr. Rittenhouse's fascinating book, possibly the first complete travel guide for an international highway ever written, is available through the University of New Mexico Press. It is a must-have for anyone interested in the history of the Mother Road.

ACKNOWLEDGMENTS

The author would like to thank the members of the Federal Way Writers Group for their support, commentary, and assistance in the development of this book. Marv, Robin, Eric, Jean, Brandon, everybody, I'm not saying that it couldn't have been done without you, but it would have been a lot harder and the end product wouldn't have been as good. My thanks also to the many and varied friends, relatives, and other assorted hangers-on here at Otter Truth Enterprises. You're all part of the package.

I would also like to acknowledge the inspiration of Tom Snyder, the author of *The Route 66 Traveler's Guide and Roadside Companion*, Michael Karl Witzel, the author of *Route 66 Remembered*, and finally, especially, Michael Wallis, the author of *Route 66, the Mother Road* and the Commander and Chief of the Road Warriors. Thank you, gentlemen; you got me started.

The author of *West on 66* may be reached at DDG 79 @AOL.COM. All criticism and commentary gratefully accepted.